continued . . .

Prince of Charming

"Finally, a heroine who's a real woman. Finally, a hero who knows what a rare find she is. Finally, a book for us all to adore. Thank you, Karen Fox, for creating the most lovable hero romance has seen in a long, long time."
—Maggie Shayne, author of *Eternity*

"Highly engaging characters . . . A realistic, plausible fantasy . . . *Prince of Charming* has proved well worth the wait."
—*Romance Reviews Today*

"A fantastical journey into the faerytale realm of myth, magic, and happily-ever-after . . . Karen Fox's fantasy romance is sweet and charming, with plenty of Fae magic to burn up the pages."
—*The Romance Journal*

"What a fun read! I zipped through *Prince of Charming,* turning pages as fast as I could. . . . I urge readers of paranormal romance to pick up this book as quickly as they can."
—*Scribesworld.com*

"*Prince of Charming* is an amusing fantasy romance that will enchant subgenre fans . . . Enjoyable . . . humorous . . . Kathy Fox writes a novel that is fun to read."
—BookBrowser

"I breezed through this most enjoyable book and am eagerly waiting for more of the same from Karen Fox."
—*Romance and Friends*

"Fun and lively."
—*Old Book Barn Gazette*

"Highly enjoyable and well-written. I could almost believe the magic existed. . . . Here is an author that aims to please!"
—*Huntressreviews.com*

"Enchanting . . . Karen Fox has penned a warm, funny and quite delightful tale that is very special."
—*Romantic Times*

Impractical Magic

KAREN FOX

JOVE BOOKS, NEW YORK

MAGICAL LOVE is a registered trademark of Penguin Group (USA) Inc.

IMPRACTICAL MAGIC

A Jove Book / published by arrangement with the author

PRINTING HISTORY
Jove edition / May 2003

ISBN: 0-515-13536-4

A JOVE BOOK®
Jove Books are published by The Berkley Publishing Group,
a division of Penguin Group (USA) Inc.,
375 Hudson Street, New York, New York 10014.
JOVE and the "J" design
are trademarks belonging to Penguin Group (USA) Inc.

PRINTED IN THE UNITED STATES OF AMERICA

10 9 8 7 6 5 4 3 2 1

One

Brandon Goodfellow noticed her the moment she stepped into the back of the empty theater, sensing her presence even before registering her movement. Though his heart skipped a beat, he kept his hands steady as he completed rehearsing his illusion.

The flames rose higher from the palm of his hand and he casually set a piece of paper on fire to prove the flames were real. Then, with a majestic gesture and clap, he made the fire disappear. With a practiced smile, he displayed his unmarred palms to the vacant seats.

The sound of a single person clapping echoed in the massive theater, and Brand finally allowed himself to focus on her. "Hello, Rose."

She moved out of the darkness of the wings into the stage lights. "Impressive. A small illusion, but done with barely a flourish. No wonder they call you the best magician in the world."

She looked much as he remembered her—slender, her deep blue eyes filled with mischief and secrets, and her full lips curved in a teasing smile. Her dark hair was dif-

ferent—short now in a tousled cut that made her appear
as if she'd just rolled out of bed.

Brand's gut knotted. *Don't go there.*

She wore a short, simple dress that hugged her curves
and revealed miles of her to-die-for legs. A brief memory
surfaced of those legs swinging before him on a hot summer evening as Rose sat on a porch railing while he stood
before her. They'd both been almost thirteen then, and
he'd been hopelessly enamored of her.

He shook away that traitorous vision to concentrate on
the here and now. "Long time, no see."

Her brilliant smile held the power of shooting stars.
"I'm surprised you recognized me. It's been over ten
years."

"You haven't changed." If anything, the years since
graduation had added a maturity to her features that made
her even more appealing.

"I cut my hair." She ran her hand carelessly through it.
"Do you like it?"

Brand examined the sassy, sexy cut with grudging acceptance. "I liked it long better." Her hair had once fallen
halfway down her back, shimmering like a silken water-
fall when she moved.

Rose shook her head. "It's easier to take care of this
way."

"I didn't know that was a problem for you." He didn't
bother to keep the dryness from his voice. Nothing had
been a problem for Rose—not since she'd hit puberty and
blossomed . . . in so many ways.

A brief glitter in her eyes indicated he'd hit his target,
but she didn't respond to his barb. Instead, she walked to
the middle of the stage and surveyed the empty seats. "I
understand you have a special illusion coming up in a few
weeks."

"I do." Sudden suspicion crept in and he stalked over
to whirl her around. "What are you doing here, Rose?"

She didn't try to be coy or evade his question—something he'd always admired in her. But when she worried

her bottom lip in a familiar gesture, he knew.

He *knew*.

Disgusted, he folded his arms across his chest. "I wondered when you'd get to me."

"I—"

"You've done exposés on all the other illusionists. I figured it was only a matter of time."

He hadn't seen her over the past decade, but that hadn't stopped him from keeping track of her.

Graduating from college with a journalism degree, she'd started small, but rose to prominence with her in-depth features on the top magicians and how they performed their most intricate illusions. Heresy.

Had she chosen this line of work because he'd become an illusionist? Another way to torment him?

"I don't want to write about you," she said. "You're my friend."

When he didn't respond, she grimaced. "Or you used to be."

"Then don't do it," he snapped. She could ruin everything he'd worked so hard to obtain.

"I have to." She held out her hands in a supplicating gesture. "You're the only one left and you're the greatest, the best, eclipsing even David Copperfield."

"You don't *have* to." Nobody made Rose do anything she didn't want to do. "You just want the glory of revealing all my secrets."

"No, I don't." Her anguish sounded real. "But it's my job. I don't want to lose it."

"Right." Brand dropped his arms as he paced away from her, then stalked back to face her, his fists clenched, his nerves pulled tight. "Why now, Rose? When I'm about to perform the biggest illusion of my career?"

"Bad timing?" She gave him a tentative smile.

"Bullshit!" She'd waited until he'd achieved some success, until he was on the brink of performing an illusion he'd spent years preparing for. Good publicity for her. The possible end of a career for him.

Fresh sparks flared to life in her eyes. "Look, I came to tell you I was doing this, which is more than I've done for anyone else."

"Doesn't matter. You're not welcome here. You're not about to do an exposé on me."

"I'm doing this—with or without your cooperation."

He recognized the stubborn tilt to her chin. Damn, she probably would. The other magicians hadn't even known she was there in their audiences, stealing their hard-won secrets until her story appeared in *Uncovered* magazine.

He squeezed his fist so tight that he inadvertently triggered the ignition switch for the fire from his last illusion, and flames shot out over his palms. Before he could even react to stop them, the flames disappeared, and he glared at Rose as she lowered her hand from over his.

"I could have taken care of it." He'd been practicing illusions for years. Did she think he hadn't dealt with mistakes before?

"I didn't want you to get burned." She offered him an apologetic smile, but he didn't return it.

"Or you just wanted to flaunt your power." To remind him he would never have what she had.

Rose released an exasperated sound. "That's what this is all about, isn't it? You still resent me for having real magic."

"Why shouldn't I? You have what I've always wanted, and you treat it like it's nothing."

Her gaze hardened. "I didn't ask for this. Is it my fault my mother was a faery?"

"My father was a faery." Something Brand hadn't learned until that fateful thirteenth summer that had changed everything. "And I sure didn't get any magic."

"The circumstances were different, Brand. You know that. I inherited my mother's magic when she gave birth to me. Your father gave up his long before you were even conceived."

Brand knew that, but he didn't have to like it. Even before he'd known of his father's heritage, he'd been obsessed with magic, starting with card tricks at age six. To survive around a man as charming as Robin Goodfellow, Brand had needed that extra edge to be noticed at all. That his father had given up everything—his magic, his immortality—to be with his mother irritated the hell out of him.

His father had been a fool—a fool in love—a curse Brand planned to avoid at all costs. What a waste of power, of a gift unlike any other.

"So you use your power to reveal all the secrets of those of us who have to work for our mortal magic." Since she'd begun her series of features, attendance had dropped significantly at shows. Why come and marvel if you knew how the trick was done?

She winced. "I only use my magic if I have to."

"Ha." He'd seen her use it throughout high school—missing assignments that suddenly appeared, delicious lunches replacing the cafeteria slop, changing outfits in the middle of the day. "You couldn't survive a day without your magic."

"That's not true." Her heated denial came quickly, but he caught the swift flicker of doubt on her face.

"Isn't it?" He hesitated only a moment before rushing ahead. She planned to do the exposé anyhow. Why not make it on his terms? After all, she'd never been able to refuse a dare. He moved closer, forcing her to look up to meet his gaze. "I'll make you a deal, Rose."

She narrowed her eyes. "What kind of deal?"

"I'll allow you into my theater, my tour, provided you don't use your powers on any occasion—personal or professional. If you can figure out my secrets like an ordinary mortal, you're welcome to them."

"No magic at all?" Her voice held a barely disguised tremor, and Brand bit back a smile.

"None. Not even if I'm on fire." He met her gaze, daring her to refuse. She wouldn't be able to, not if she was the Rose Thayer he once knew. She thought she lived like an ordinary person, but he knew differently. "If you use your magic, even once, you have to go away and give up writing your exposés."

"And why would I agree to that?" Her expression had hardened.

"Oh, you probably won't." She wouldn't be able to make it. Within a matter of days she'd slip and he'd be free of her and the magicians would be safe from further intrusion. Brand gave her a harsh smile. And now the dare. "You can't handle not using your magic, can you?"

"I can survive without it just fine." She extended her hand, her blue eyes gleaming. "Deal."

He took her slender fingers in his, unprepared for the unnerving awareness of her closeness. "Deal."

He dropped her hand abruptly. "I start work at eight A.M. and leave on a ten-city tour on Wednesday." Of course, by then she would have failed to keep her part of the deal, so it was a moot point. When she slipped up, she'd keep to their bargain. He trusted her to keep her word even if he couldn't trust her.

"I'll be here." She pivoted and left without even a backward glance.

But Brand watched her every step of the way until the door closed after her. Even then the tightness in his chest didn't ease.

He was asking for trouble by inviting her into his life where she could mentally and physically torment him. He still wanted her, had longed for her since he'd first realized what that ache in his groin meant.

And he'd never have her. Never.

That hot July day of seventeen years ago returned with startling clarity. He'd rushed home after stealing his first kiss from Rose and informed his parents that he intended to marry her when he grew up.

Now the significant glance his mom and dad had exchanged made sense. They shouldn't have been surprised. His family had been friends with the Thayers forever. His parents had sat him down and explained that Rose was different, that once she reached her mid-twenties, she'd quit aging, that soon she'd discover the power within her.

He'd refused to believe them at first. Especially his father's incredible story that he and Rose's mother had once been Fae. That Rose's mother had been the Queen of the Pillywiggins. Ridiculous!

So his father had insisted Brand talk to Ariel, Rose's mother. She'd verified the unbelievable, explaining that her magic had gone into Rose at her birth, that fun, wonderful Rose was a faery. His Rose? How could that be possible?

But soon after that, Rose's powers had erupted, resulting in broken windows, lightning bolts inside the house, and the sudden appearance of roses until she'd learned to control her magic.

Brand had never forgotten the betrayal of that summer. He'd lost both respect for his father and adoration for his best friend. Nothing had been the same from that moment on. He'd avoided Rose as much as possible and rebelled against his father, leaving home immediately after graduation from high school.

Only in his illusions had he found solace. Only in his illusions did people notice him. Only there did he emerge from his father's large shadow. That summer he'd vowed to become the best magician in the world. And he'd achieved that goal through dedication and hard work.

He would show Rose. He would show his father that he could be just as good as them.

Now Rose was a part of his life again—even if only for a short time. He shook his head, fighting a surge of unwanted anticipation.

He had the horrible feeling he'd made a big mistake.

The shrill ringing of the alarm clock jarred Rose from her romantic dream. With a moan of disappointment, she extended her hand to shut it off magically. Abruptly she jerked her hand back and bolted upright as she recalled her previous day's promise. No magic.

She could do that. Rose slapped the alarm into silence.

After all, she'd lived in the mortal world all her life as one of them. How hard could it be to not use her magic?

She hadn't even known she had magical powers until she was nearly thirteen. And she'd managed fine until then. If Brand thought he could stop her with this stupid deal, he had another think coming.

After a quick shower, she combed her hair with her fingers, grateful for the easy, short style. No fuss, no muss. Perfect for the journalist on the go.

Pulling open the closet door, Rose frowned. Okay, this was going to be a problem. She usually carried only a handful of clothes with her, preferring to use her magic to create whatever style she needed for the occasion. All she had with her was a slinky party dress and a one-piece blue jumpsuit.

Damn and blast. She'd have to buy some clothing. Brand's resentment of her magic was going to cost her some serious money.

Naturally the jumpsuit was wrinkled. Great. She hadn't ironed anything in ages. Well, it wasn't like she'd forgotten how. The hotel kept an ironing board and iron in the closet, and she set them up and went to work.

Ironing wasn't difficult—just time-consuming . . . and boring, which left her mind free to wander.

Her deal with Brand defied explanation. Why had she agreed? Probably to prove to Brand that she was as normal as he was. She didn't need magic to get her story. She didn't need magic to live. To admit otherwise meant accepting she was fully Fae—something too distasteful to consider.

After learning of how the Fae had treated Brand's father and her mother—forcing them out of the magical realm—she wanted nothing to do with that world, especially if it meant meeting Titania, the wicked Queen of the Fae.

The odor of something burning jerked her mind back to her task. "Dammit." She yanked the iron up, but it was too late. The leg of her jumpsuit now displayed an iron imprint.

She could fix it in a heartbeat. No. No, she'd made a deal. Rose sighed. With luck, the scorch wouldn't show after she put the jumpsuit on.

She dressed and examined her reflection critically. The scorch barely showed.

She met her gaze. What did Brand see when he looked at her? What did he feel? When he'd first looked at her, a brief flare of emotion had lit his eyes only to be quickly shuttered like usual.

Surprisingly, his resentment and withdrawal still hurt even after all these years, though this pain didn't begin to compare to the devastation she'd suffered at thirteen.

She had adored Brand. He'd been her best friend, the one person with whom she could talk for hours. In her naïveté, she'd been unable to imagine a future without him.

Then her magic had arrived along with her changing hormones, throwing her entire life into chaos. At first she'd been unable to control her powers, never knowing if a sneeze would produce a tiger, make a bouquet of flowers appear, or transport her across town.

Losing Brand's support, his friendship, had cut deeply. She hadn't asked for this. It wasn't her fault.

But he'd distanced himself, refusing to see her, to talk to her, not even acknowledging her tentative smile in the school hallways. And she'd been miserable.

Still, she'd tried to avoid doing this feature on him. She'd covered every other magician until only he was left and her editor at the magazine had insisted she get the goods on Brand Goodfellow or find another job. She'd stalled long enough.

Rose glanced at the clock and gasped. Where had the time gone? This actually getting dressed—and ironing— took up valuable minutes. Grabbing her notebook, she raced from the room.

No time for breakfast. She usually conjured up something in her room. Rose grimaced. Magic definitely made life easier.

At the front of the hotel she paused. Without being able to transport magically, she needed a ride.

"May I call you a cab, miss?" the porter asked.

"Yes, please." She waited several impatient minutes until he hailed a taxi. Before she could step forward, a man burst through the hotel doors and jumped inside.

"I'm late," he called, then slammed the door.

"Hey." Rose ran toward the vehicle. "So am I."

The cab sped away and she turned her angry gaze on the porter, who gave her an apologetic smile. "I'm sorry, miss." He raised his arm to stop another taxi, but several whizzed by before one paused before the hotel.

Rose leaped inside before the vehicle completely stopped and snapped out the theater's address. Great, she was going to be late for her first day with Brand. He'd love it. She knew he expected her to wimp out of their deal, but she wasn't about to give him the satisfaction.

Okay, so maybe she had used her magic more than she'd realized. She was also determined. Brand Goodfellow wasn't going to defeat her that easily. She'd uncover his secrets through regular investigation . . . without any magic.

When the taxi stopped before the theater, Rose tossed money at the driver, then rushed outside. As she crossed the threshold, her heel caught and she stumbled forward, nearly tumbling to the floor.

She caught herself, then examined the offending shoe. The heel had come off. Of course. What else could go wrong?

She grimaced. *Don't ask.*

With shoe in hand she lurched into the stage area. Brand stood beneath the lights, surrounded by several members of his crew.

Damn, why did he still have to be so handsome? She'd followed his rapidly rising career over the past ten years, but the photos hadn't done him justice. He wore his black wavy hair shorter than she remembered, but the style only added to his magnetism. He'd always been good-looking with his brilliant green eyes and slender build, but the years had added muscles to his frame and a sense of mystique to his persona.

He focused on her as she approached the stage. "You're late."

"So?" She hobbled forward. "I don't work for you." She glared at him. "I ran into some problems."

I-told-you-so amusement danced in Brand's eyes. The fiend. He knew it had been a horrible morning so far. "If you're not here when we leave tomorrow, you're on your own," he added.

Rose swallowed her retort. This not using her magic was going to be more difficult than she'd expected, but not impossible. She met Brand's steady gaze. Surely, not impossible.

A horrible suspicion crept into her mind and refused to leave. *This can't be . . . it isn't . . . surely I haven't made the biggest mistake of my life.*

Two

Turning his back on Rose, Brand faced his crew again. Rose grimaced as she pulled off her other shoe, resisting the urge to throw it at him. Just like him to make her feel like an idiot, then ignore her.

"As I was saying, Mike, you and Larry pack up the sets. Stan and Davy, handle the equipment. Terri, help out with the props." Brand motioned toward the rear of the building. "We'll be loading the buses this afternoon."

Rose dropped her jaw. They were packing? She'd killed herself to come in and watch them *pack*?

As the crew dispersed, she rushed to the stage and grabbed Brand's arm. "I had to be here at eight A.M. to watch you load a bus?"

Mischief danced in his eyes. "You wanted to be included, didn't you?"

"I want to watch you practice, watch your show." And he knew that, damn him. "Somehow, I don't think I'm going to learn much from observing your crew loading your set."

The corner of his lips twitched. "You never know."

"Oh, do you plan to let me help?"

His frown answered her. He would never let her near his equipment. She'd learn too many secrets that way.

She waved her broken shoe at him. "Do you have any idea what I went through to get here this morning?"

His grin broke free. "I have an idea. A little more magic-dependent than you thought, aren't you?"

"Maybe." She hated revealing that. "But I learn quickly and adjust just as fast."

"We'll see, won't we?"

She heard the triumph in his voice. He didn't expect her to last through his tour. Knowing Brand, he no doubt assumed she wouldn't even make it to his departure tomorrow. "Don't count me out, Brand. There's more to me than you think."

His gaze darkened. "There always has been."

Her pulse took an unexpected leap, but she forced herself to meet his gaze. "Since there's nothing for me to do here, I'll be back in the morning ready to leave." She whirled around and headed for the door. At least now she'd have time to shop for some clothes.

"No."

She stopped abruptly and pivoted to face him. "No?"

"No." The humor left his eyes. "You want to be a part of this? That means staying here while the crew works."

"Stay here? Bored out of my mind watching your crew pack? That's not fair." Her voice rose. "That's punishment."

"That's the way it is. Take it or leave it."

The coldness of his voice made her pause. He meant it. Of course, Brand would do about anything to get her to back out of this deal. Well, she wasn't one to give up.

Rose lifted her chin. "Fine." She jumped off the stage and stalked to the center of the theater. Plopping into a seat, she tossed her shoes to the floor, crossed her arms, and stared at him.

Brand didn't speak for several moments, but she could almost hear him grind his teeth. "Stay off the stage," he ordered, then disappeared behind the side curtains.

Could she be made any more ineffective? Rose scowled. Probably. He could have insisted she wear a blindfold and earplugs. Brand probably assumed she uncovered all the other magician's illusions through using her magic, but he'd be wrong. She knew how to watch, how to listen, how to pay attention to minute details.

Two men were dismantling the sets on the stage, revealing secret doors and traps. Rose allowed a slow smile. Perhaps the day wouldn't be a total waste after all.

She reached for her notepad, then frowned. Where was it? She'd grabbed it before she left the hotel. Trying to remember, Rose retraced her chaotic journey to the theater.

She'd had it in her hand when she finally got into the cab. But she'd been in such a rush when she'd arrived. Closing her eyes, she groaned. Damn. She'd left her notepad in the taxi. Why not? It was that kind of a day.

But there had to be paper here somewhere.

She stood and made her way onto the stage, pausing at the top of the stairs. "Hello?" A cacophony of voices and thuds answered her. She raised her voice. "Hello?"

A young woman poked her head out from backstage—a woman Rose recognized at once.

"Sequoia." Rose didn't hide her joy as she rushed forward to embrace her cousin. "I thought you left Brand's show." And the fact that she hadn't made it even more difficult for Rose to do the exposé.

"He talked me into staying through this tour." Sequoia grinned as they parted. "To be honest, I wasn't that hard to convince. I love doing this."

"Then why quit at all?" Rose had been surprised to hear Sequoia was leaving her job. The last time they'd talked, Sequoia had mentioned how much she enjoyed her position as Brand's on-stage assistant.

Her friend rolled her eyes. "The usual."

"Are Aunt Liz and Uncle Michael still insisting you go to college?" When her cousin nodded, Rose grimaced.

"You're an adult now. They can't tell you what to do."

"I know." Sequoia sighed. "But they want this for me."

"They want it for themselves." As much as Rose adored her many aunts and uncles, she also knew their faults. "Tell *them* to go to college."

Her cousin laughed. "I have so missed you, Rose. What are you doing here?"

Rose hesitated, catching her bottom lip between her teeth. "It's complicated."

Dismay crossed Sequoia's face. "Rose, you're not doing an exposé on Brand, are you?"

Rose forced a weak smile. "Got it in one."

"How could you? We've known Brand all our lives. He's practically family."

Her disapproval hurt, and Rose shifted uncomfortably. "It's my job."

"And you so enjoy ruining magicians' careers." Sequoia didn't hold back on her sarcastic tone.

They'd been through this before and neither had been satisfied at the end. "The first one deserved it. He was a jerk and a horrible illusionist."

"And after that?"

Rose grimaced. "It was the challenge—to find out how these illusions were done." Plus her editor had insisted she pursue these stories since their readership had increased significantly after Rose's first article.

But she had felt more and more guilty with each ensuing story—the main reason she'd asked for a transfer to meatier stories, to something different. But her editor demanded she expose Brand first.

"So now the challenge is Brand?"

"That's one way of putting it." Brand had always been a challenge in one way or another—especially after he'd stopped being her friend.

"I can't believe you'd do this."

"Come on, Tree." Rose reverted to Sequoia's childhood nickname. She had to make her friend understand. "It's not like Brand is making this easy for me. He's forbidden me to use my magic. At all."

Sequoia's eyes widened and a slow smile crossed her face. "Oooh, devious."

"You're telling me. In return I get to come along on the tour and attempt to get my story." Rose met her cousin's gaze. "Still hate me?"

"I don't hate you. I couldn't." Sequoia wrapped Rose in another hug. "You've been my best friend since we were toddlers. I don't always understand you, but I will always love you."

To Rose's surprise, her eyes watered, and she returned Sequoia's hug with enthusiasm. "That means a lot to me." She blinked away the tears before they could fall and turn into opals—another side effect of her Fae blood. "Believe me, I wouldn't be here if I didn't have to be."

Stepping back, Sequoia grinned. "I'm not so sure about that. You've always had a crush on Brand."

"And you haven't?" Rose had to smile as she remembered the hours they'd spent as teenagers discussing Brand Goodfellow—what he wore, what he said, how he looked, hoping he'd notice them as more than childhood friends. In Rose's case, she would have been happy if he'd noticed her at all after that thirteenth summer.

Pink stained Sequoia's cheeks. "That was a long time ago. I prefer him as a friend. Besides, he's my boss now."

"And the greatest illusionist who ever lived." Rose eyed her cousin. "I bet you know a lot about how his magic is created."

Mischief lit Sequoia's face. "I do and I'm not telling."

Not that Rose really expected her to reveal any secrets. Rose would figure out how the illusions were done on her own or not at all. "Good."

"What the hell are you doing up here?"

Both women jerked around at Brand's explosive tone. He advanced on them with long strides. Fire blazed in his eyes and Rose's throat went dry. "I . . . I was looking for paper and ran into Sequoia. Are you going to tell me I can't talk to my cousin?"

"Not if you're going to pump her for information."

Rose moved to face Brand, clenching her fists, the urge to punch him almost impossible to resist. "If you think for a moment that I would ask or she would tell, you don't know either of us very well."

His gaze met hers, something dark and undefined lingering in those depths. Rose refused to look away despite the trembling that threatened her limbs. When his gaze dropped to her lips, her breath caught.

He nodded his head slightly, speaking to Sequoia more than Rose. "My apologies." His gaze returned to Rose. "The deal was you stay off the stage."

"I just need some paper. I left my notebook in the cab."

Humor replaced the darkness in Brand's eyes. "There are probably some old flyers in the lobby. Check there."

Rose felt him watch her until she reached the floor level again. At the exit to the lobby, she glanced back to find him in conversation with Sequoia. They were both laughing.

Something bitter rose in Rose's throat, but she swallowed it. She was *not* going to be jealous of her own cousin. Especially not because of Brand.

Pushing through the doors, she paused in the large theater lobby to scan the area. So what if Brand was gorgeous and oozed male sex appeal? So what if he was intelligent, talented, and had sensuous eyes greener than any emerald? That didn't mean she was going to go all gaga over him again.

She hadn't been thirteen years old in a long, long time.

Ah, there. A stack of flyers advertising Brand's last performance were piled on a nearby shelf. That would work. She sighed. Normally she could have produced a tablet with magic and saved all this time and grief. But no . . . Brand wouldn't allow it.

Cursing the stupidity that had led her into making the deal with Brand, she grabbed several flyers and returned to her seat in the theater. The crew was still dismantling the sets, revealing secrets without intending to.

Good. Time to take notes.

Brand paused by the rear doors and lifted one hand in farewell to Gary as he drove the last bus away. That was it. They were done. Though weary, he found it a good tired. They'd accomplished a lot getting everything torn down in one day. He normally didn't push his crew that hard.

But Rose's appearance yesterday had thrown him completely off schedule.

Rose.

The last time he'd seen her, she'd been engrossed in scribbling notes from her seat in the theater. She'd stayed there all day, breaking only to share in the pizza he'd ordered at lunch, when he'd hoped she would have stalked off in disgust and boredom. The woman was even more tenacious now than she'd been as a child, and that was saying a lot.

Brand stepped onto the center of the stage and found her at once. She still sat in that same center seat, but was no longer writing. In fact, her hands were limp, her head lolled back. He grinned. She'd fallen asleep.

She'd survived the day and hadn't used her magic. Though Brand hated to admit it, she'd impressed him. Her appearance alone upon her arrival this morning had told him how much a change this was for her . . . and no doubt an awakening as well. Maybe now she'd agree she used her magic more than a little.

Brand paused beside her, intending to wake her. But not yet. While she was asleep, he could admire her loveliness. She'd been a knockout in school, but now she embodied what it meant to be a woman—soft curves, rounded breasts, full lips that begged to be kissed. Her long dark lashes lay against her fair skin, her sculpted cheekbones adding to that air of otherworldliness she'd inherited from her mother.

Rose Thayer was a faery. No matter how many times he told himself that, he still found it hard to believe. They'd ridden bikes together, climbed trees, shared Popsicles on hot summer afternoons, played on the same soccer teams. She'd been his first love. Hell, his only love.

Until everything had changed. He'd fought hard to stay away from her, to fulfill his dreams on his own.

And now she was back in his life whether he wanted her there or not . . . with the power to destroy his career. He gently ran his hand over her short hair. Even worse, he feared she had the power to destroy him as well.

Brushing the back of his fingers against her cheek, he bent closer, her lips beckoning him. What harm could one kiss do?

"Brand?"

He jerked back to find Rose staring at him, her expression still sleepy. Had she realized his intention? He produced a bright smile. "Time to wake up."

She blinked several times as she straightened, smothering a yawn with her hand. "Are you done?"

"The buses are loaded. Everyone else has gone home."

"Even Sequoia?"

"She has things to do to get ready." In fact, he'd insisted Sequoia leave. She and Rose had been friends for far too many years for him to be complacent about leaving them alone together.

Rose stretched as she stood, briefly thrusting her breasts into prominence. Brand took a step back, wiping his suddenly damp palms against his slacks. For crying out loud, why did he feel like he was thirteen again?

"I guess I'd better get home, too," Rose said.

"Want to share a cab?" He knew from past experience Rose rarely rode in vehicles. Why should she when she could teleport wherever she needed to be? In addition, the iron in the car's steel frames usually made her ache. But now she had to suffer public transportation like the rest of the real world.

"I can . . ." She stopped as her memory of their deal

apparently returned. Her dry smile confirmed it. "I guess I do."

"Don't forget your stuff." He motioned toward her purse and the pile of flyers covered with her notes. Even as he tried to decipher some of her words, she snatched up the papers and purse.

"Thanks."

"This way." He touched her arm, then jerked his hand away. Even that brief touch of her silky skin made him ache for more. He should be trying to entice her into using her magic, into losing the bet, not asking her to share a ride. He wanted her gone. At least, his brain did.

It was the other—less intelligent—parts of his body that worried him.

He managed to hail a cab right away, uncertain why that would cause Rose to give him a quick pissed look. Why would she want to wait?

"Where are you staying?" he asked as he climbed in after her.

"The Four Seasons."

"Me, too." Which he was willing to bet wasn't a coincidence.

She gave him a wicked smile that sent an arrow of heat firing to his groin. "I know."

Swallowing hard, he leaned forward and passed on their destination to the driver. By the time he leaned back against the seat again, he'd managed to regain some control. "All in the pursuit of your story, I assume," he said, trying to keep his voice cool.

Her smile faded and she glanced out the window. "Of course."

"You did well without your magic today." He frowned as the words emerged without thought. He hadn't meant to tell her that.

Looking back at him, she raised her eyebrows in disbelief. "You have to be kidding. Look at this."

She tilted her hip toward him, and he rolled his hand

into a fist to resist touching the smooth curve. "What?" he croaked.

She motioned toward a shiny spot on her pants. "I had to iron for the first time in who-knows-when and scorched one of my few outfits. It's ruined."

Now that he could focus, he did see the iron imprint against the material. "I didn't notice."

She rolled her eyes. "You wouldn't. You're a guy."

"What does that mean?" He often noticed what women wore, especially when it accentuated their natural assets.

"Remember the time I came over after bike riding and was nearly covered with mud? All you noticed was that I'd put new rims on my tires."

Brand grinned. He did remember that day. They'd been twelve. His mother had thrown them both outside and ended up rinsing Rose off with the hose. "I noticed more than the bike," he said.

Within her mud-splattered face, her even teeth had gleamed a bright white and her blue eyes had sparkled with delight. When her wet T-shirt had clung to her just developing curves, he'd experienced a strange twist in his gut that had frightened him, so he'd ignored it. A similar twist attacked him now at the memory, not nearly as easy to ignore.

"Your hair stuck straight up in the back," he said quickly. "You looked like you'd stuck your finger in a light socket."

"That wasn't as bad as the time you tried to dye your hair purple." Rose's laughter filled the cab, warming him. "You should've waited for me to help."

"Hey, the grape Kool-Aid worked." All too well.

"Sure, it did." Mischief danced in her eyes. "Dyed your hair, your ears, your face."

Brand joined in the laughter. "And Mom still made me go to school. Talk about humiliation."

"There are worse things than being known as The Grape."

"Not when you're in sixth grade." At least the effect had faded after a couple days.

"Sure there are." She leaned forward, her eyes sparkling. "What if it had been picture day?"

They both dissolved into laughter until Brand had to hold his side. Trust Rose to find the good point. Then again, she always had made him laugh.

"Ah, we're here."

The cabby clearing his throat made Brand realize they'd reached the hotel. "Sorry." He glanced at the meter, then handed the man the fee and tip. "Thanks."

Brand was still smiling as he held open the door for Rose to step out. He hadn't laughed like that in a long time. Years even. When Rose started toward the hotel doors, he caught her arm. "Wait." He didn't want to let her go just yet. He enjoyed this lighthearted feeling.

She raised one expressive eyebrow, a particular quirk of hers. Once, when many, many years younger, he'd painted Vulcan eyebrows on her in retaliation.

"Let me walk you to your room."

"Why?" She tilted her head as if studying him. "Want to know where the enemy's encamped?"

"No." But he wasn't about to tell her how much he was enjoying her company. "I want to hear how the rest of your first magicless day went."

She rolled her eyes and headed for the hotel, but didn't complain when Brand fell into step beside her. "Today was probably the worst," she said finally as they waited for the elevator. "I can do it, Brand."

"That's what scares me," he admitted. "You can ruin me, you know."

Her eyes darkened, but she didn't speak until they stepped onto the elevator and the doors closed. "I don't want to hurt you, Brand, but my job depends on this."

"You don't need a job." With her magic, she could produce anything she'd ever need.

She jabbed her finger against his chest. "How would you know, Mr. Big Star Magician? Just because I have magic doesn't mean I don't want to accomplish something on my own, to be a part of this world I live in. What do you expect from me? That I'll spend the rest of eternity lying on the beach, never working a day?"

"The thought had occurred to me." She didn't need to work, not like the rest of them who weren't so fortunate as to have magical powers.

"Then you don't know me at all." A single tear slid down her cheek, falling to the floor where it changed into a flawless opal.

Before he could respond, the doors opened and she dashed out of the elevator. He didn't follow, but bent to retrieve the opal. He'd been shocked the first time her tears had changed like this, but seeing it now only added to the ache in his chest. Wrapping his fingers around the gem, he could still feel the warmth of Rose's tear.

Maybe he didn't know her as well as he thought. Maybe he'd assumed a little more than he should have.

Maybe there was more to Rose Thayer than her magic.

Rose slammed the door to her room behind her and flung herself full length on her bed. Damn Brand. One moment he was laughing with her, the next condemning her for the magic that fate had given her.

Did he really think she was so shallow as to play through life? Her parents had raised her better than that. She wanted more than that. Making a life for herself was important. Her job was important. She wrote her stories after careful research, without using her magic. She'd worked hard to reach this pinnacle in her career. She'd earned this promotion to more hard-hitting investigative news stories.

And if she had to reveal some of Brand's precious secrets to do it, then she would. Whether she liked it or not.

With a sigh, she sat up. The buses were leaving in the morning and she intended to be on one, which meant she had to pack. She switched on the television for background noise, then went to grab her luggage.

To keep up appearances, she usually traveled with a suitcase and a few changes of clothes. But not enough to survive Brand's tour. She'd have to shop at their next stop since she couldn't magically produce something to wear. At least she always kept a pair of jeans around. Those would do for tomorrow.

She tossed the suitcase onto the bed and threw the few pieces of clothing into it. This wasn't going to take long. Going into the bathroom, she paused. She couldn't pack her few toiletries until morning.

Recalling this morning's ordeal in getting ready, she grimaced. Perhaps she should shower tonight and save some time.

And set her alarm an hour earlier.

After removing her jumpsuit and packing it, she stepped into the shower. The pulsating hot water helped to ease her anger. Brand didn't understand what it was like for her. In fact, he'd been so jealous of her magic he'd never bothered to try. She snapped off the water. Maybe it was time he learned.

She wrapped a large towel around herself, then stepped out into her room. Thank goodness she'd kept the nightgown she'd worn last night or she'd have nothing to wear to bed.

She'd only taken two steps when she froze, unable to believe her eyes. It couldn't be. She'd locked the door.

But there was a man in her room.

And he wasn't Brand.

Three

The bare-chested man sat on the end of her bed, watching the television, clad only in a skin-tight pair of breeches that clung to his well-toned muscles. Seeing her, he stood and gave her a charming smile, which only made her even more wary.

"Who the hell are you?" she demanded, grasping the ends of her towel tighter. Surely Brand would let her use magic to defend herself. Or would he?

"I am Ewan." He held out his hand as if he intended her to take it. "You are to come with me."

"I don't *think* so."

"Titania demands it."

Just hearing the Queen of the Fae's name made Rose's blood run cold.

"You are to come live in the magical realm." His gaze pinned her in place. "Forever."

Rose stared at the man, noticing his extreme handsomeness, his long straight hair so blond it was almost white and the brilliance of his blue eyes. She should have realized the aura around him wasn't normal. He was Fae.

"I'm not going to the magical realm," she said. She'd sworn years ago to have nothing to do with the Fae, especially not Titania. Rose had been raised among the mortals *as* a mortal and intended to remain here.

"Titania insists." Ewan answered in a tone that indicated no further discussion was expected.

"Titania can take a flying leap." Rose aimed her finger at him. "I am never—hear this—*never* going to live in the magical realm. No way. Nada. Not going to happen."

For the first time confusion showed in Ewan's eyes. "But you're the only fully Fae to be born to a mortal. Titania wants to examine you."

Rose knew she was unique. Her mother had explained that years ago. Before Rose, the only Fae born to mortals had been half-Fae, half-mortal, the result of a male Fae mating with a mortal woman. But in Rose's case, a Fae female had mated with a male, which led to Rose's mother losing her magic when she gave birth to her fully Fae daughter. Rose might be unique, but that didn't mean she was about to let Titania "examine" her.

"I'm not going." She edged toward the suitcase and snatched out her jeans and T-shirt. "So either you can leave or let me get dressed before we continue this conversation. I prefer you leave."

Ewan waved a hand. "Nudity does not offend me, but create yourself some clothing if you must."

"I can't." Damn Brand and his stupid bet. "I'll be right back."

She dressed quickly in the bathroom and returned to find Ewan again staring at the television, chuckling. "What is this show?" he asked. "I like it."

Glancing at the TV for the first time, she spotted James Cagney lowering a grapefruit he'd just smashed into a woman's face. "It's an old gangster movie," she said. "*The Public Enemy.*"

"I like the way he takes control."

Rose rolled her eyes. That sounded like a typical macho man. "You would." More confident now that she wore actual clothing, she went to face him, discovering she was actually an inch taller than he was. He didn't look pleased when he noticed it, either.

"Look, Ewan, I know Titania sent you, but you're just going to have to return and tell her you lucked out. I'm not going to the magical realm."

"You must." Ewan frowned. "Titania is Queen. She is obeyed."

"She's not *my* queen." From the tales Rose had heard of the Fae Queen, she considered the woman a first-rate bitch. "I was born here and I intend to stay here."

"But you are Fae. Why would you want to stay here?"

"Maybe because I like it. This is my home."

Ewan's expression indicated his disbelief. Rose didn't care if he believed her or not. She wanted him gone.

"Look, I'm not coming. Accept it and get out of my room." In an effort to avoid using magic, Rose raised an unopened bottle of wine threateningly. "I don't want to hurt you, but I will."

"A Fae cannot kill another Fae."

Rose rolled her eyes. She'd heard that since she first discovered her powers. "But it doesn't say I can't kick the stuffing out of you."

Ewan backed away, his gaze on the bottle. "Very well. I will leave for now, but we are not finished."

"Oh, yes, we are." Rose advanced on him and he disappeared at once.

Lowering the bottle, she sighed. Great. Like she needed a pesky faery after her. Wasn't giving up her magic enough?

She shook her head and resumed packing. Go live in the magical realm?

Not in this lifetime.

Rose ran toward the buses, her suitcase banging against her leg. Nothing like cutting it close. She'd allowed enough time to dress and finish packing, but had forgotten how unreliable getting a cab could be.

Spotting Sequoia outside the bus talking to Brand, she eased to a walk and struggled to control her breathing. They hadn't left yet. She grinned at the painting on the side of the bus—a life-size figure of Brand with flames burning on his palm, one of his specialties. Nothing like subtlety. But it was great promo.

By the time she reached Brand, Sequoia had left, but at least Rose could now speak without panting.

Brand glanced at his watch. "Five minutes later and we'd have gone, Rose."

"I got here as quickly as I could." She lifted her chin as she met his gaze, daring him to accuse her of using her magic.

Instead, he grinned, which was almost as bad. "Stow your bag under the bus. You'll ride on this one with me."

She raised her eyebrows. "With you? You mean the world-famous Brandon Goodfellow rides on the bus, too? I always assumed you flew to wherever you performed."

"Sometimes I do, but I wanted to ride along this trip."

The way he avoided her gaze gave him away. "You're riding along because you don't want me alone with your crew, aren't you? Afraid I'll discover too many secrets?"

"Let's just say I prefer to keep my eye on you."

She gave him a slow seductive smile, implying a meaning she knew he didn't intend. "Do that." Adding more swing to her hips, she approached the bus and climbed on board, aware of his gaze following her.

She paused in the doorway. "Wow." Now this was the way to travel. Instead of the bench seats she'd expected, the interior more resembled a luxurious living room with couches and easy chairs placed throughout. A table, chairs, and small kitchenette made up the rear.

Sequoia waved at her from a nearby couch and Rose slid beside her cousin, wincing at the too familiar ache the iron in vehicles always brought. Rose managed a grin. "I made it."

"Brand was actually fretting whether you would show or not."

"I'm sure he expected I would have given in to my magic by now." But she was tougher than that.

"Have you been tempted?" Humor danced in Sequoia's eyes now, but Rose only smiled in return.

"Many, many times, but I've managed to resist. The worst part is I'm afraid I'll just forget and do something I shouldn't."

Sequoia laughed. "I'll pinch you if you look like you're going magical on me."

"What? Do the magic sprinkles show?" Rose had to tease her cousin. Somehow Sequoia had always known when Rose intended to do something.

"No, it's that gleam you get in your eyes."

"Ready to go?" Brand stepped into the bus, his stage manager Carter Rhodes behind him.

"Ready," Sequoia answered.

Brand and Carter moved to the back, settling into plush chairs, and the driver climbed into the front seat. After closing the doors, he started the engine and let it idle for a short while before pulling away.

Rose glanced around the inside in surprise. This was it? Just the four of them? "Are we the only ones riding on this bus?"

Obviously discomfited, Sequoia nodded. "The rest of the crew are riding on the second bus."

Rose grimaced. "Because Brand doesn't want me talking to them." He really was doing all he could to place obstacles in her path. As it was, she couldn't hear him and Carter talking in the rear of the bus.

"You can't expect him to make it easy for you."

"I don't." He'd already been more cooperative than she deserved, even with this stupid deal. Not using her magic was difficult, but she'd existed the first thirteen years of her life without it. Surely she could do so again—at least for a short while.

However, her growling stomach reminded her how nice it would be to produce something to eat. Once again, she hadn't allowed enough time to purchase anything for breakfast. She was going to have to set her alarm two hours earlier at this rate.

On top of that, after Ewan's sudden appearance the previous night she'd forgotten to eat dinner as well. Rose turned to Sequoia, eager to discuss her unwelcome visitor. "You'll never guess what happened to me last night."

"You actually sat through an entire TV program."

Rose gave her cousin a wry smile. "I had a visit from one of the Fae. I came out of the shower and found this man in my room."

"My God, weren't you scared?"

"For a moment, but he immediately started telling me I had to go with him to the magical realm and live there. As if."

Sequoia hesitated. "So, he was Fae? From the magical realm? How exciting. It wouldn't hurt to see the place, Rose. You might like it."

"No way." Rose refused to budge on this issue. "I belong here, not there—magic or no magic."

"What did you tell him?"

"To get out and leave me alone."

"And he did?"

"After I threatened him." Rose frowned. "But he made it sound as if he might be back."

"What did he look like? Same as you?"

"Not at all like me." Rose paused, trying to think of a good comparison. "Remember the elf Legolas in the movie *Lord of the Rings*? A lot like him. Very Fae looking, in fact."

Sequoia's eyes lit up. "Yummy. I wouldn't mind if he did come back."

"You can handle him, then." Rose's stomach abruptly rumbled again, louder this time.

Her friend raised her eyebrows. "Hungry?"

"Starving."

"There's food in the back. Help yourself."

"Food?" Rose jerked her head around to eye the kitchenette. She'd have to pass Brand at the table to get there, but the thought of sustenance was worth it. "Thanks, Tree."

Pushing to her feet, Rose started toward the back, then jerked to a halt as her cell phone rang. She retrieved the phone from her purse and answered the call. "Hello?"

"Rose, it's Larry. How's it going?"

Her editor. Keeping her expression bland, Rose moved to a solitary chair on the opposite side of the bus, thankful the outside noise made it difficult for anyone to overhear her conversation. "I'm in."

"How long before you'll have the story?"

"That's hard to say. As long as it takes." In the past, she'd been able to discern an illusionist's secrets after watching only a few performances. But everything she'd discovered through her research indicated Brand was better than anyone else.

"Get it as soon as you can. I want this on the cover of our next issue."

That only gave her a couple of weeks to produce something. "I can't make any promises."

"Do this, Rose, and the promotion is yours."

Rose closed her eyes. Oh, how she wanted that promotion—to never have to do another exposé, to be involved in stories with real news impact. "I'll do my best." Larry disconnected without another word and Rose slowly closed her phone. Get this story and she'd get what she wanted, what she'd worked so hard to achieve.

And destroy any chance of rekindling the friendship she'd once shared with Brand.

Of course, he'd been the one to throw that away. Not her. Recalling her emotional pain of those teen years, Rose bolstered her defenses. She could do this. She had to.

Her stomach rumbled again and she grimaced. What she wanted right now was something to eat. She glanced toward the back of the bus. Carter had moved to the side of the bus and had papers spread out all over a coffee table. Only Brand remained at the circular table by the kitchenette.

With a grimace, Rose stood and made her way to the back. Brand was doing some simple card tricks, making the flipping and placing of cards look easy.

Spotting her, he fanned out a deck of cards with the faces toward her, an impish grin on his face. "Pick a card, any card."

Rose had to grin in response. He'd been asking her to do that since they'd been six years old. She plucked a card from the deck and hid it behind her back. "What is it?"

"Put it back in the deck and I'll tell you."

She shook her head. "Tell me without that." She had no doubt he could do it. He'd long surpassed the tricks he'd started with.

Brand folded the deck closed and set it on the table, then raised his gaze to meet hers. "Queen of hearts," he declared.

"Correct as always." Rose tossed the card on the table. Even though she knew how he performed the apparent mind reading, she still appreciated his skill. He made the simplest illusions appear sophisticated and real.

"Thanks for not changing it." Humor danced in his green eyes, and she produced a wry grin.

"Hey, I only did that once. Besides, I can't use my magic now, remember?" She glanced over at Carter, suddenly remembering his presence, but he was absorbed in his work, and the road noise apparently masked her conversation.

"How are you managing?" For once his tone held no mockery. "Really?"

She shrugged. "I've had better days, but I'll survive." Placing one hand over her protesting belly, she nodded toward the kitchenette. "If I ever remember to eat. Sequoia says you have food."

"Fully stocked. What would you like?"

What did fully stocked mean? "Do you have any muffins?" That would quiet the subversive rumblings within.

"Don't know." He swung around in his chair to peruse the small area, then shook his head. "Sorry. Guess we'll have to use magic."

She raised her eyebrow. She wasn't so hungry that she'd break this deal by using her power. As she opened to mouth to tell him that, he leaned forward and swept his hand behind her ear. Pulling his hand away, he displayed a huge blueberry muffin.

"Will this do?"

Rose burst into laughter. "That will be fine." Trust Brand to be melodramatic in everything—even muffins.

She took it, then found herself stumbling toward him as the bus came to an abrupt stop. Brand grabbed her waist and swung her onto his lap, holding her tight until the bus steadied.

As she clung to his shoulders, Rose found his face only inches away, his vivid eyes swirling with a mixture of jade that held her gaze captive. Her breath caught. Damn him. Why did he still have this affect on her? She'd left her childish infatuation with him behind years ago.

Yet her pulse leaped as his gaze dropped to her lips. She found herself leaning closer, her fingers touching the edges of his wavy hair.

"Rose." His voice sounded raspy and she shivered, the single word creating goose bumps over her skin. For a moment—a brief moment—he appeared ready to kiss her.

Then he blinked and the moment was gone. Brand swallowed before speaking again. "You okay?"

"Fine." More or less, considering her insides were quivering like her father's favorite green Jell-O. Too aware that she remained on his lap, Rose pushed away to stand on shaky legs. Forcing a smile, she reached behind his ear and produced the same muffin. "And I still have breakfast."

He grinned. "Enjoy it."

Rose nodded and nearly ran back to the seats by Sequoia. Even a bus length wasn't far enough for the moment. She dropped into a cushioned chair, struggling to calm her runaway heartbeat. Brand shouldn't be able to do this to her. Not now. Not after so many years.

"Are you all right?" Sequoia leaned forward with a frown. "You're flushed."

"I'm fine. It's nothing." Rose focused on unwrapping the muffin, picking a piece off, and pushing it into her dry mouth.

Sequoia glanced over her shoulder to where Brand sat, then looked back, her smile smug. "Right. Nothing."

Rose pointed a finger at her. "Don't go there, Tree."

Her cousin merely grinned. "Go where?"

Rose refused to answer and devoted her attention to eating the muffin. She already felt like an idiot letting a simple thing like Brand's touch unnerve her. After all, she'd been able to handle men since she'd first developed breasts. Yet a close encounter with Brand had her flustered.

Ridiculous.

If she let him rattle her, she'd never get her story.

Rose took another bite. And she couldn't allow anything to interfere with that.

Brand stared out the bus window as they entered St. Louis, the next stop on his tour, but he was only dimly aware of the passing surroundings. His gaze still saw the enticing fullness of Rose's lips, the brilliant blue of her wide eyes, the pink flush of her creamy cheeks. His hands still felt the softness of her body.

He'd never wanted to kiss anyone so badly in his entire life.

Smothering a groan, Brand closed his eyes. He was far removed from the naive thirteen-year-old who'd been head over heels in love with Rose, yet his body acted as if it had forgotten the ensuing seventeen years.

She was the last person he should want. She was trying to ruin him.

And he wouldn't put it past her to use her wiles to

weasel information from him. That had to be it. She'd been actively enticing him.

Opening his eyes, he glanced to where Rose and Sequoia laughed and talked together, just as they had years ago. A quick stab of envy pierced him. At one time he'd been a part of that.

He jerked his gaze away. Those days were long gone. No one could have expected him to sit idly by and watch Rose abuse a gift he would've died to receive. It had been agony enough to watch from a distance.

Especially when the boys had flocked around her like lost sheep. As much as he'd wanted to accuse her of using magic to ensnare them, he knew better. She'd always been lovely, especially after she'd gone from a flat-chested tomboy to a well-rounded female, but more than that she had a vivaciousness that drew people to her—men *and* women.

Another reason she'd been so successful in her exposés. People talked to her without even realizing they were doing so. Brand frowned. Was Sequoia at this moment giving away secrets he'd worked so hard to perfect?

No. He dismissed that thought as fast as it came. He trusted Sequoia. She might be Rose's cousin, but she was loyal. She wouldn't betray him.

And fool that he was, he'd believed Rose when she'd said she wouldn't pump Sequoia for information. Apparently even a career killer had ethics.

Which made it that much more difficult for him to hate her.

Returning his attention to the window, Brand spotted their hotel and the horde of women in front of it contained behind police barriers. He grimaced. Though he didn't advertise where he intended to stay, word always leaked out.

His publicist thought it wonderful that these sex-starved females laid in wait for him, and often promoted his so-called appeal to women. Brand just wanted to do magic.

But he'd learned to play the game that went along with
it.

Even if it meant smiling at screaming women and
avoiding lusty ladies who lurked in the elevators.

At least the police were on-site this time. He should be
able to get inside with no problem, and once inside his
suite, he'd work further logistics from there.

The screams began before the bus came to a complete
stop and Brand winced as he stood. He motioned Carter
to his side. "Flank me," he murmured.

Carter grinned. "Any time."

Passing Sequoia and Rose, he saw amusement in Sequoia's gaze and amazement in Rose's.

"Are all these women here for you?" Rose asked.

She didn't look as if she liked that idea, which pleased
him for some inane reason. Brand grinned and straightened his shirt. "Haven't you heard?" He winked at her.
"I'm supposed to be a great catch."

"Boy, are they misled."

He heard the teasing note in her voice and caught the
glimmer of mischief in her eyes. With a shrug, he headed
for the door. "Blame my publicist."

The bus doors opened and the screams escalated. Panic
hit Brand. No matter how many times he went through
this, he couldn't stop this feeling that he was going to end
up torn to pieces.

Forcing a smile, he stepped down into the wide path
created by the barriers. Thank God for those.

He paused to sign autographs along the route to the
front doors, struggling against the urge to run inside to
safety. Carter stayed by his side, easing Brand away when
a fan became too enthusiastic.

Brand glanced over his shoulder to see Sequoia and
Rose following. His entourage. That made him grin. Rose
would hate being called that.

As he reached for another pad of paper, he heard a
woman yelling to her friend, "I wish these barriers weren't
here!"

Immediately the blockades disappeared, stunning everyone. But the screaming fans recovered quickly, swarming around Brand until he could barely breathe. His panic escalated.

Spotting Rose through the crowd, he met her wide alarmed gaze. She'd picked a fine time to break their deal. He'd always known she wouldn't be able to keep it.

But he hadn't expected it would cost him his life.

Four

Fanglike fingers tore at his shirt as the women mobbed him. A long nail scraped his arm, drawing blood. He winced at sharp tugs on his hair. Brand's throat closed. He couldn't breathe. Did Rose intend to let him get mauled before she did anything to help?

Or would she help at all?

"That's enough. No more," he said, pushing away the prying hands. But no one listened. The women screamed and grabbed for him as if he were the last man on Earth.

Trying to pull free of the crowd, he caught a brief glimpse of Rose's horrified gaze. Was she just now realizing how dangerous this could be? No doubt she'd meant it as a joke. Well, he didn't find it funny.

His shirt ripped, the buttons flying, as two women tugged at it. Another woman grabbed his face in both hands and kissed him. Brand jerked back only to have someone else perform the same act. "Stop!" His chest ached from the loss of air, tight bands of tension closing around it.

He wanted to punch, shove his way to freedom, yet some inner code kept him from doing so.

"Step back. Keep away." The calm tones of two police officers penetrated the screaming women.

Thank God.

As the officers cleared a path for him, Brand noticed that Rose had drawn closer, her hands raised palm out as if to cast a spell. Had she finally decided to stop this assault? Too late now. The police had saved him. Not her.

It wasn't bad enough that she wanted to ruin his career. Now she was trying to destroy him physically as well. He should have known. Hadn't his father warned him of the perniciousness of the Fae?

Brand sucked in a deep breath as some officers formed a protective wall around him and led him toward the hotel door. Though he limped from where some women with their vicious heels had stabbed his foot, Brand hurried to get inside to relative safety.

In the lobby, order reigned. The screaming mob remained outside and the tension eased from Brand's chest. He ached from head to toe, had scratches on his chest, arms and neck, lipstick smeared across his face, and his shirt had been nearly torn in two. Enthusiastic fans were one thing. Crazies like that were another.

Carter approached with room keys and handed one to Brand. "I'll add extra security for the rest of the trip."

"Do that." Brand started for the elevator, eager to reach the quiet of his room. An officer fell into step with him and Brand grimaced. A grown man should be able to defend himself from a group of women without police interference. Damn Rose and her warped sense of humor.

"Brand."

He turned to see Sequoia and Rose approaching. They both looked concerned. Good. They should be. He glared at Rose, part of him wanting to shake her, another part wanting to get as far away from her as possible.

No, he needed to know why the hell she'd done this.

"You two come with me," he ordered.

Exchanging tentative glances, Rose and Sequoia joined him in the elevator. Tension filled the small space as the doors slid shut, so heavy Brand found it difficult to believe the elevator could rise to the penthouse level.

"I'm anxious to see your show," the officer said, breaking into the thick silence. "My wife and I have tickets."

"Thank you. Let Carter know where you're sitting and we'll get you onto the stage." Brand managed to keep his tone polite, but he couldn't lose the rigid formality of anger.

From the look of unease on the officer's face, Brand assumed the man wasn't sure if he actually wanted to get on the stage. Especially with Brand's current foul mood.

By the time they reached the suite doorway, the officer appeared anxious to get away and left as soon as Brand had the door open. Rose looked as if she wanted to flee with the officer. Well, she wasn't going anywhere. Not yet.

Brand caught her arm and pulled her inside, leaving Sequoia to follow. Once the door closed after them, he pushed Rose away from him, unable to endure the feel of her warm, soft skin beneath his fingers. Damn her.

He stalked to the bar on the opposite wall and poured himself a tumbler of bourbon. They stocked the good stuff here and he downed it in one shot. The burn eased the tightness of his throat and soothed the wrenching in his gut.

Hearing someone move behind him, he turned and impaled Rose with his gaze. Her eyes were wide and filled with trepidation, her face pale, her lips parted. Why did she have to look so damned enticing?

He swallowed in an attempt to control his anger, to resist the urge to yell. "Do you hate me so much that you'd get me killed?" Though he kept his voice calm, his inner violence vibrated beneath the words.

Rose straightened, defiance replacing the fear in her gaze. "I didn't do anything, Brand."

"Those barriers disappeared." He *saw* them vanish. "The only way that can happen is magic. *Your* magic."

"But I didn't do it. I swear it."

She sounded convincing, but he knew better. Barriers didn't just disappear on their own.

She held out her hands toward him. "Think, Brand. Why would I do something like that?"

"You tell me." Was she jealous of the attention he received? "Did you enjoy seeing me crushed by that mob? Did that fulfill some sick secret fantasy?"

He couldn't look at her anymore. Her expression of innocence was too good. He hadn't realized what a consummate liar she'd become over the years. But then it went with her job. His hands shook as he poured himself another drink.

"Are you all right?" Rose asked.

He whirled around to find her close behind him, and she froze, dropping her outstretched hand. "No, I'm not all right." Couldn't she see that for herself? "My watch was ripped right off my arm. I'm bruised and scratched and I think someone snipped some of my hair." It was ridiculous.

"I'm sorry. I wouldn't put you through that. Surely you know me that well."

Sincerity shone in her eyes, and for a moment he wavered. No, magic had been involved here. He didn't doubt that at all.

"I might have once, but I don't now." He downed another tumbler of bourbon. "You have no conscience. Hell, you write exposés on people merely doing their job. I don't know you at all."

She flinched, which didn't give him nearly the satisfaction he'd expected. Instead, he wanted to reassure her he hadn't meant it. God, what was she doing to him?

Rose sent a pleading look toward Sequoia, who finally stepped forward. "She was as surprised as I was when this happened, Brand. I don't think she did it."

"Then you explain it." What other answer could there be?

"I can't. It had to be magic. Perhaps someone else."

Someone else? Sure, he believed that. How many Fae

were likely to be hanging around? "Like who?" He directed the question at Rose. Had she acquired some magical buddies he didn't know about?

She shook her head. "I don't know. None of this makes
sense. I . . . I felt something, a pull. But I didn't do it.
You know I can't lie, Brand."

So he'd been told, but he'd always had trouble believ-
ing that.

"It's too late." All at once, weariness washed over him.
She'd never admit to using her magic. Once she did she'd
also have to acknowledge reneging on her end of their
deal. "It's over. You lost. Go back to your magazine and
find another victim."

"But—"

"Go." He snapped the word, needing her gone before
he weakened.

Her eyes watered and he clenched his fists to keep from
touching her. "You're making a mistake," she murmured.

"No." Magic had done this. The only possible answer
was Rose. "You already made it."

She didn't respond, but accusation shone in her gaze
before she turned to the door. Now he felt guilty. Dammit.
She was the one who'd nearly gotten him killed. What
did he have to feel guilty about?

Turning away, he poured another drink, then paused
upon hearing the door click shut after her.

Damn.

Thankful that Carter had given her a room key, Rose
rushed to the elevator and sagged against the wall once
the doors slid closed. *This can't be happening. I didn't
make those barriers disappear.*

But someone had used magic. She'd stake her life on
that.

She just had to find out who.

Reaching her room, she stomped to the window and
stared outside as if the answer would appear in the wispy
clouds. She clenched her fists, fighting the urge to hit

something. This was so unfair. "What the hell is going on here?"

"Your magic is leaking."

She whirled around to find Ewan leaning against the door, arms crossed, still wearing nothing more than tight pants and an insolent smile. "What are you doing here?"

"I have to bring you to Titania." He straightened. "I don't dare return home otherwise."

And no doubt he'd do anything to get her to go with him. Including risking Brand's life.

Rose rushed toward him and jabbed her finger against his bare chest, her anger hot. "Why did you make those barriers disappear? You almost got Brand killed."

"I didn't." Ewan met her gaze. "You did."

Dropping her hand, Rose shook her head. "I didn't."

"Not on purpose, but it was your magic that was used." He gave her a tentative smile. "Didn't you feel a tug on your power?"

"A little one, yes, but I didn't do a spell."

"You're right. You didn't. But a mortal made a wish."

Rose frowned. She remembered hearing a woman wish the barriers were gone, but it hadn't meant anything. Mortals had no magic. "I don't understand. How can someone else use my magic? It doesn't work that way."

"This is one of the reasons why Titania wants you in the realm. This foolish deal you made with Brand Goodfellow."

"How does she know about that?" The words emerged before Rose thought. Titania had spies everywhere.

"She's made it her business to keep tabs on you. You're unique among the Fae, Rose, and now you're becoming a liability."

"Why is that?" How could she possibly be a danger to the Fae?

"You've used your magic regularly since you first came into it."

She opened her mouth to protest, then stopped. This

deal with Brand had forced her to admit she did use her gift more than a little. "So?"

"Now that you have not used it for three days, the power is building up within you."

"Building up?" He made it sound as if she would explode. She hadn't felt anything different . . . other than frustration at doing things the manual way.

Ewan nodded. "So much so that it's emitting from you, surrounding you, leaking."

"Leaking?" Rose glanced around the room, half expecting to see magic sprinkles in the air.

"Thus, if a mortal makes a wish, this excess power allows the wish to come true."

Rose sank onto the bed. Her magic had made the barriers disappear. This was too unreal. "I don't believe it."

"I can't lie."

Fae couldn't lie, which had caused Rose no amount of grief as a teenager. Though she had become adept at circling the truth on occasion.

"How do I stop it?"

"Use your magic again."

Somehow she'd expected him to say that. "I can't. I'll lose the bet."

"This bet is a mortal custom. You are Fae." Ewan knelt down before her, his gaze intense. "You don't belong here. You belong with the Fae."

For a brief instant she considered it. To be where she wasn't a freak, where no one hated her for using her magic. "No. I belong here." Though Fae, she was more mortal in temperament. A large loving family had seen to that. She not only had two younger, very mortal brothers, but oodles of aunts and uncles and cousins—all of them warm and loving. "But nice try, Ewan."

He sighed. "You are more difficult than I expected."

Rose had to grin. "Chalk it up to my mortal nature. I'm a lost cause. Give up and go home." She had other problems right now.

"I cannot return until my mission is complete." Ewan stood, but didn't move away.

"Then you're going to be in the mortal world a long, long time." Ewan could wait forever. She wasn't going with him.

But what could she do about Brand? Rose covered her face with her hands. He had no right to cast her out. Okay, so she *had* caused the barriers to disappear, though totally without her knowledge. Surely he could understand that.

She jerked up. Especially if Ewan vouched for her.

Snatching his hand, she tugged him toward the door. "Come with me."

"You've changed your mind?"

"No. I need you to talk to someone for me." She pulled him along to the penthouse, returning wide-eyed stares from people they passed with a broad smile. What else could she expect, dragging a handsome half-naked faery?

Reaching the penthouse, she pounded on the door. Brand had to give her another chance. He had to believe Ewan.

As soon as Brand opened the door, she pushed inside, not giving him a chance to deny her entry. "I know what happened," she announced.

Sequoia stood by the patio window, her arms crossed, her expression obstinate. Rose didn't have to be a genius to know her cousin had been defending her.

Brand slammed the door shut. "I already know what happened. You and . . ." He caught sight of Ewan and his voice trailed off. ". . . your magic."

"As it turns out, you're half right." Rose faced him, daring him to say a word. "And half wrong."

"Who's that?" Sequoia asked, her gaze fixed on Rose's companion.

"This is Ewan, one of the Fae. He knows how the barriers disappeared."

"That's Ewan?" Sequoia came to Rose's side, a slight smile framing her lips. "Hmm, he *is* yummy."

"And stubborn." But for once Rose was glad he'd appeared. "Ewan, tell Brand what you told me about my magic, about what happened."

Brand had his arms crossed now. "Where did you get him?"

"He keeps appearing. Wants me to go to the magical realm, but that's another story. I want you to listen to him."

"Why should I?" Brand's gaze hadn't warmed at all while she'd been gone.

Forcing back the angry words that wanted to emerge, Rose stepped closer and touched his arm. "Because I didn't lie. I didn't do it. Not on purpose anyway."

Brand remained silent for several long seconds. Finally he nodded. "Fine. What happened, then?"

"Rose has made a foolish agreement in which she refuses to use her magic," Ewan said. Before he continued, Rose lifted one eyebrow at Brand. Basically, this was all his own fault for talking her into such a stupid deal to start with.

"Because of this, her unused magic is building into dangerous levels, spilling over into the mortal realm. All it takes is for someone to make a wish and this extra magic will grant it." Ewan motioned toward Rose. "Rose has no control over it. She leaks."

"So you're saying the woman who wished the barriers gone made it happen?" Brand asked.

"Yes."

"Why should I believe you? I don't know you. I've never seen you before. Rose could have plucked you from anywhere."

Ewan straightened, majestic and powerful but still appeared diminished beside Brand's fiery presence. "I am Fae. I cannot tell other than the truth."

"Yeah, I've heard that one." Brand darted a look at Rose. "Try again."

Rose sighed. Now he was simply being bullheaded. As usual. "What do you want? A display?"

"And what would that prove? If someone here made a wish, you or your Ewan could make it happen." Brand shook his head. "Just leave. Both of you. It's over, Rose."

"Dammit, Brand! You're just using this as an excuse to get rid of me."

He met her gaze, unblinking. "Perhaps." A dark light glimmered in the depths of his eyes—a glimmer that gave her a small sense of hope.

If only she could prove Ewan's theory.

Rose bit her lip, creating then discarding several wild ideas. Focusing on Sequoia, she grinned.

"I really don't like that look," Sequoia muttered.

"If what Ewan has said is true, which I believe it to be, if you make a wish, it will happen."

"*If* you believe him," Brand added.

Rose cast him a sharp look, then turned again to her cousin. "Whisper a wish, Sequoia. One that I can't hear, that Ewan can't hear. Whisper it to Brand if you like or just whisper to yourself. Ewan and I will move by the door so there's no chance we can overhear."

"Then what?" Brand asked, his tone even drier, if that were possible.

"We'll see if her wish is granted." And he would hate it if it was.

"This is a bunch of nonsense." Brand waved toward the exit. "When you reach the door, just keep on going."

Rose frowned. "Give me a chance, Brand."

Their gazes locked for several long moments. She could feel his anger, his frustration, and the hint of something else, something more elusive. Finally he turned his back on her.

Emitting a disgusted exhale, Rose dragged Ewan toward the door.

"You're being a jerk, Brand," Sequoia said. She gave a wicked laugh. "I know just what to wish for, too."

Maybe Sequoia would turn Brand into a frog or something. That would be nice. For a while anyway.

Rose glanced at Ewan, who returned a look filled with confusion. Before she could reassure him, she heard Sequoia gasp, then burst into laughter.

Whirling around, Rose inhaled sharply. "Oh, my God."

Five

As Sequoia clutched her middle, nearly doubled over with laughter, Rose struggled for breath. Brand stood in the middle of room clad only in his tiny bikini briefs, which did little to disguise his obvious assets. Her throat went dry. She'd always known he'd grown up, but she hadn't realized he was quite this fine beneath those jeans.

His chest was muscular, sculpted without being ridiculously so, his six-pack evident and dusted with dark hair that arrowed down to disappear into his briefs. His hips were taut and lean, his legs well muscled.

Heat rose into her cheeks, but she couldn't look away, didn't want to look away. He was all she could want and more. An uncomfortable itching began low in her belly, the heat spreading through her veins.

Instead of looking flustered, Brand jutted his chin out, his gaze daring Rose to say something. As if she could speak. "I assume you can also wish my clothing back on," he said to Sequoia.

She straightened, swiping at the tears in her eyes. "If I wanted to. You're no fun, Brand. You never lose your composure."

"For which you should be grateful."

"Do you believe Rose now?"

Brand hesitated, then met Rose's gaze. He had to know she'd been telling the truth. "Yes, I believe her." Instead of heading for his bedroom to put on pants, as Rose had expected, he remained, proud and too damned sexy, and turned away to stare out the windows at the famous St. Louis Arch.

"As you should," Ewan added. He touched Rose's shoulder. "Now you will come with me."

She jerked away. "I never agreed to that. How many different ways do I have to tell you I'm not going with you?"

"I can force you." His eyes were dark, power radiating about him.

"You could try." She met his gaze, daring him. She would use her magic before she'd let him drag her to the faery realm.

"I'll handle this." Sequoia wrapped her fingers around Ewan's arm. "Come with me, gorgeous. We have to talk."

"I—" He protested, but allowed her to lead him from the room.

Rose eased a sigh of relief. Ewan's continued persistence was already a pain. How could she convince him she meant to stay here? She darted a glance at Brand's bare back and tight buttocks. One problem at a time.

She approached him, then hesitated, her physical turmoil making her hesitant to touch him. "Brand?" He didn't respond and she managed a small smile. "I could conjure clothes for you, but then I'd lose the bet." Besides, she enjoyed the view far too much.

He whirled around so quickly, she almost lost her balance and placed her hand against his chest to steady herself—his rock-hard, too-warm chest. She jerked her hand away, vividly aware of his near nudity and her response to it.

"I wouldn't want you to lose the bet," he murmured, his gaze intense, a half-smile on his lips.

Struggling to control her erratic pulse, Rose kept her gaze on his face. "Is the deal back on, then? Can I stay?"

"That's all you care about, isn't it?" Sadness mixed with the resignation in his voice.

"No, that's not all I care about." Having seen him almost crushed by the swarm of women had brought home the unavoidable truth that she still cared about him—whether she wanted to or not. And seeing him like this stirred even deeper feelings, yearnings she didn't want to acknowledge.

Seeing the blue of Rose's eyes deepen, Brand's anger faded and something far more sensual took its place. He'd never been able to stay mad at her. But the episode with the barriers had provided an opportunity to send her away . . . before it was too late.

After their encounter on the bus, he knew he wasn't nearly as in control around her as he wanted to be. Putting distance between them was the only reasonable solution to protect his reputation as a magician . . . as well as his emotions.

Now, as she stared at him, her eyes wide and lips too damned provocative, he wondered if it wasn't already too late.

"I'd never hurt you, Brand." Her voice was quiet, sincere. "Not on purpose anyway," she said.

No, never on purpose, but she hurt him simply by existing, by having the magic he desperately wanted for himself, by reminding him of feelings he wanted to avoid. He should hate her, had convinced himself he did.

Until she reappeared in his life. "I know."

He curled his hands by his side to keep from touching her. Judging by her dark pupils and flushed cheeks, she wasn't as immune to his near nakedness as she pretended. Hell, neither was he, but he'd be damned before he'd let anyone know that.

Neither was he immune to her presence. How would she look in her underwear? If he didn't move away from her soon, they'd both know.

He grimaced, searching for another subject. "What are you going to do about your magic leak?"

"I don't know." Her confusion reflected in her expression. "I have to use my magic to stop it, and I'm not willing to give up that easily."

"Stubborn as always." He shook his head. She would never willingly break their deal, but he'd assumed she would have unthinkingly used her power by now. His mistake.

"I choose to think of it as determined." Rose gave him a hesitant smile. "Are we okay?"

He hesitated, staring at her. Okay? They'd never be okay. With Rose his world always tilted to one extreme or the other, and he felt much safer on the angry side of things. "You can stay, if that's what you're asking."

"Thanks." Her smile widened and he could almost feel her relief. Evidently, writing this exposé meant a lot to her. Of course it did. It would make her career while it ruined his.

"Just go on back to destroying me," he muttered. He had to remember that when he was around her.

She caught his arm when he would have turned away, her touch affecting his control far more than he liked. "Brand . . ."

Glancing back, he waited for her to speak, only to see her swallow several times. The rapid pulse in her throat caused his own heartbeat to accelerate. He searched for something to say, anything to break the rising tension. "Have you changed your mind?"

"No, I . . ." She drew in a deep breath. "I'm sorry. I don't want to hurt you."

He retorted with a derisive laugh and let himself touch her face. "But you will, Rose. One way or another, you will."

Sequoia dragged Ewan into her room, then paused in the center. Now what? A giggle rose in her throat, but she swallowed it down.

Not too many women would consider having a devastatingly handsome man in their bedroom a bad thing. And if he wasn't so good-looking, she'd be better able to think of what to say.

He was taller than she was, but then most folks were. Still, he didn't loom over her like Brand, which helped ease her nervousness. Rose's description had been very accurate. He did look like Legolas with long, glowing blond hair, brilliant blue eyes, and a lean, toned physique that drew her gaze constantly to his bare chest. She ached to touch that chest, to touch him, to see if he was real.

He gave off an aura of sensuality that brought her heart into her throat, yet he appeared more confused than threatening, more intriguing than dangerous.

"Are all these rooms alike?" Ewan turned in a circle in the middle of the room.

She jerked into semi-coherency. "Probably. It's a hotel."

"And mortals say they value their individuality." Ewan snorted as he scanned the surroundings, his ennui obvious.

"They do."

Come on, girl. Remember why you brought him here. Think of Rose.

Sequoia rested her fists on her hips. For the first time in her life she had the opportunity to do something for her magical cousin. She wasn't about to let Rose down. "You have to leave Rose alone."

That brought his brilliant gaze to focus on her. "Why?"

"She's told you she's not going to the magical realm and she means it. The best thing you can do now is go back where you came from."

"No."

Not much of a conversationalist, was he? What did she expect from such a hunk? "Why stay? I know her better than anybody. She won't change her mind."

"Won't she?"

Sequoia paced to the window and back. How could she make him understand?

Family, of course.

In the widespread Thayer clan, family was everything—its heart, its soul, its strength. "Rose's family is here. They love her. She loves them. She's not about to leave them."

"Love." Ewan nearly spat the word. "I've heard much of this mortal affliction but have seen nothing to merit its high esteem."

"Maybe you're not looking in the right places." All he had to do was watch her mother and father together and he'd know the meaning of the word.

"Mortals kill for it, fight for it, behave foolishly for it." He came toward her, his expression defiant, forcing her to look up to meet his gaze. "Why?"

"Love is difficult to explain." She spread her hands. "You have to feel it."

He stepped closer and Sequoia shifted as her skin tingled. What was he doing? "Feel it how? I've seen the way mortals touch each other. I know this brings pleasure, but pleasure is not love." As he spoke, he gently ran the back of his hand over her cheek, and she caught her breath in a gasp. He smelled of the forest—the musky scent of dirt, the brisk freshness of the wind, the raw bark of the trees.

Damn, talk about sex appeal.

"It . . . it's more than that." Her voice sounded strangled. No surprise given the sudden tightening in her throat.

"A kiss, then?" He brushed his soft lips over hers, and Sequoia's body reacted as if he'd lit a match. Every hormone she owned and a few she didn't burst into flame.

She pushed away and staggered back, her eyes wide, her breathing ragged. "Was that magic?" It had to be. She'd never experienced a kiss like that in her life, and he'd barely touched her.

"Only what comes naturally." He smiled, his eyes crinkling at the corners. "I liked it as well, but that is not love."

"No, it's not." Sequoia placed her hand over her chest

to even her breaths. "A kiss is part of the physical attraction that usually accompanies love."

"Then explain love to me."

"I can't."

A dancing flame burned in his eyes. "If you can show me what love is and why it is so important, I will let Rose go."

Oh, gee. Why not ask her to fly while he was at it? "It's not that easy."

He crossed his arms. "I have time."

Sequoia hesitated. Rose had done so much for her over the years, but now her cousin wasn't using her magic. That vulnerability gave Sequoia a chance to repay Rose for her unflagging support through broken hearts, lost dreams, and of course, the constant college battle with her parents.

She'd always enjoyed a challenge and this promised to be that, but could she make him understand? Fae didn't experience intense emotions like love and hate. Was he even capable of grasping the concept?

He had to be. Rose's mother, Ariel, had learned to love Rose's father.

"Let me think about it," she said finally. She needed a plan before she gave him an answer.

"Very well." Ewan nodded, an abrupt movement. "We will meet again."

His gaze bored into hers, adding to the warm tingle within her, then abruptly he disappeared.

"Oh, man." Sequoia sank onto the edge of her bed, glad growing up with Rose had exposed her to these sudden departures. Her already rapid heart rate couldn't stand any more.

Now, that was a faery—far more than she'd ever expected. Though she knew that Rose's mother and Brand's father had both once been Fae, she'd always seen them as regular people, and she'd grown up with Rose. Ewan was something completely differently. Could she teach him about love?

She grinned wryly. She was willing to try.
Especially if it involved more kisses.
But what if it didn't?

Early the next afternoon Rose dashed off the elevator, her
heart pounding, Sequoia close on her heels. Once the
doors slid shut behind them, they glanced at each other
and burst into laughter, which helped to ease Rose's tension. She was going to have to be more careful.

The danger past, she shifted the shopping bags in her
arms and started toward her room.

"I am never going near another child," she declared.
"At least not while my magic is operating on its own."

Sequoia darted a look over her shoulder toward the elevator. "It could have been worse. What if he'd wished
for a horse instead of a candy bar?"

Rose froze, her eyes wide. "A horse wouldn't have fit
on that elevator. Gads, his parents were freaked as it was."
When her cousin merely grinned, Rose shook her head.
"There has to be some way to control this."

"Go back to using your magic."

"I can't." Rose slid the card into the door, then pushed
the door open as it clicked.

"Not true." Sequoia followed her inside. "You can. You
won't."

True enough, but Rose wasn't going to be the one to
give up. "Brand started it."

Sequoia dumped her packages on the bed. "Now you
sound like you're ten years old again."

"Me?" Rose grinned. "What can I say? Brand brings
out only the best in me."

A mischievous gleam sparkled in Sequoia's eyes. "Was
that why your tongue was hanging out yesterday?"

Rose turned away to drop her bags on the bed as well,
not wanting her cousin to see her face. Tree knew her too
well. "I don't know what you're talking about."

"Oh, yes, you do." Sequoia sank into an overstuffed

chair. "Seeing Brand nearly naked definitely got your attention."

Drawing in a deep breath to steady her nerves, Rose glanced at her friend. "Any naked man would get my attention." Unwilling to pursue those feelings, she continued, "Was that why you wished him undressed?"

"Partly. I was hoping to shake his unflappable calm, too." Sequoia stretched out her feet. "With no luck, as usual."

"He's always been that way." Even as a child Brand had remained in control no matter what happened. A familiar ache filled her chest. He'd had enough control to break off a friendship that had endured for thirteen years, to break her heart when she'd needed his support more than ever before.

Sequoia must have sensed Rose's depression for she produced a bright smile. "Well, are you going to model some of this stuff for me?"

"Everything?" Glad to change the subject, Rose examined the pile of bags on the bed. Thank goodness, she rarely had to spend money. She couldn't afford sprees like this often, but she had to have clothing. Being unable to magically produce something to wear put a serious dent in her bank account.

"Sure. Why not?" Sequoia pushed to her feet and joined Rose beside the bed to rummage in the multitude of sacks. With a grin, she held up a slinky baby-doll nightgown in a pale green silk. "Think Brand will like this?"

Rose snatched the gown away. "Did you buy this? I told you not to."

Her cousin laughed. "You might need it."

The thought of Brand seeing her in the gown sent a ripple of trepidation along Rose's nerves. "Never going to happen." Brand wasn't even her friend any longer, let alone anything more than that.

"We'll see. Try this outfit, then." Sequoia tossed a pant suit at her.

This Rose could handle. She took it with her into the

bathroom and changed quickly. The black slacks and knee-length jacket could dress up or down, depending on the blouse she wore with it. Or perhaps no blouse at all.

Rose buttoned the jacket and stared at her reflection in the large mirror. The vee of the jacket dipped low, revealing her bra. If she ever did decide to go blouse-less she'd need to go braless and use double-sided tape for sure.

After removing the jacket, she added the rose-colored blouse. Better. She stepped into the main room and pirouetted for her cousin. "What do you think?"

"Nice. Of course, everything looks great on you with your figure and coloring."

Rose smiled wryly. "I could say the same about you."

"Ha. When you're as short as I am, nothing ever fits the first time. I'm always having to shorten things."

Whereas Rose was considered average height, a surprise considering how petite her mother was. "But the end result is what counts." She tilted her head toward the bags. "Try on that dress you bought."

"Only if you try on the red one." Sequoia waggled her eyebrows. "I'm dying to see how you look in it."

Rose held up the slinky dress, eyeing it with some trepidation. "I don't know how I let you talk me into this."

"It's made for you, Rose. Try it on." Sequoia pushed Rose toward the bathroom, then drew back. "Let me run to my room for a moment. I have a necklace that will go perfect with it. I'll be right back."

She darted out, leaving the door open just enough so it wouldn't latch, and Rose entered the bathroom again. Once undressed, she held the fire-engine-red gown against her. It had looked great on the model, but what would it be like on her? Her curves weren't quite as pronounced.

With a sigh, she shimmied into the silky material, tugging it into place over her hips. The full skirt dropped to her knees and swirled around her legs, flaring as she moved. The waist nipped in, making her appear even slimmer. The bodice, however, was another story.

She couldn't wear a bra. That was a given with the spaghetti straps. She removed her bra, then straightened the material again and turned to the mirror. Though not quite as daring a dip as the jacket had been, the dress dived in a vee, accenting the beginning swells of her breasts while the rest of the material clung to her slim curves, leaving little to the imagination.

Sequoia had called it a woo-hoo dress. Rose had to agree. She turned to glance at the back, which dipped even lower to highlight the long line of her spine. But did she have the courage to wear it in public?

She'd bought it hoping to wow Brand, to convince him to loosen up around her and perhaps share some of his magic secrets. At least, that's what she'd told herself.

But viewing her reflection now, she wondered about his reaction, her interest more emotional than logical. If he found her attractive, would he stop hating her? Would he see her as a woman? Hold her? Touch her?

Imagining Brand's strong hands against her bare back sent an arrow of fire through Rose, her gut clenching, her nipples pebbling. She caught her breath, watching her cheeks stain pink.

She shook her head to clear away such thoughts. The last thing she needed was to get any closer to Brand. She had an exposé to write and it was tough enough already. She'd bought the dress to get a story. Nothing more.

Hearing the outer door open, she blew out a puff of air. Sequoia would be waiting to see the woo-hoo dress. Rose yanked open the bathroom door and danced into the bedroom, her arms outstretched. "What do you think, Tree? Will Brand like it?"

She stopped, abruptly. Sequoia hadn't returned yet. Instead, Brand stood just inside the door, his hand still resting on the edge of it.

Rose's heart jumped into her throat as his gaze traveled the length of her, top to bottom, then back up to her face. A slow smile slid across his face.

"Can I make a wish?"

Six

Brand couldn't stop staring. A dress like that was designed to send a man's hormones into overdrive and his were revving right on cue. *Like* it? What he felt at this moment was far more than that.

He stepped toward Rose, unable to stop himself, the urge to touch her overpowering. "Oh, yeah, I like it," he added. All his memories of Rose had her in jeans and T-shirts. If he remembered correctly, she usually didn't like to dress up. "What's the occasion?"

Pink stained Rose's cheeks and she glanced away, her hands fluttering in a very un-Roselike gesture. Nervous? Rose? Well, her words had made it clear she hadn't expected him. He grinned.

"I . . . ah . . . bought it for your final show, for when you do your big act." She recovered quickly, the tilt of her chin reflecting her defiance. "What are you doing here? Do you always just walk into someone's room?"

"I knocked and the door opened." He stepped closer yet, his smile widening as her eyes grew large. "Not safe to leave your door unlatched, you know."

"Sequoia was coming right back."

Rose didn't retreat, but he sensed that she wanted to. How like her. Defiant no matter what the circumstances. "Actually, I was looking for Sequoia. I heard you two had been shopping."

He glanced at the bed laden with packages, articles of clothing strewn over them. Spotting a filmy negligee, he lifted it and glanced at Rose, his blood warming as he imagined her wearing it. "Is this for me, too?"

"Sequoia bought that for me." Rose snatched it from his hand. "It's not your size."

He had to laugh. That was his Rose.

His smile faded as quickly as it came. *His* Rose. No, never that.

Clenching his fists, he stepped away from her, his brain finally starting to overrule the heat in his veins. "I'll find Sequoia."

"I'm here." Sequoia stepped inside, a necklace dangling from her hand. She hesitated, her gaze darting from Rose to Brand. "What do you need, Brand?"

He wasn't sure if what he felt was relief or annoyance. "We're going to the theater now. I want to do a run-through before tonight."

"Sounds good." Sequoia turned to Rose and her face lit up. "Wow, you're gorgeous, Rose. I told you that dress was perfect." She jammed her elbow into Brand's side. "One sexy dress, eh?"

As if he needed her to tell him that. The evidence was standing before him, making it extremely difficult to remember to keep his distance. "Very," he admitted. He heard himself continue, his mouth working without any assistance from his brain. "Wear that dress tonight and I'll buy you dinner."

Odd what a fire-engine-red dress could make a man do.

Rose smiled for the first time. "I bought a different dress for tonight."

"Is it as nice as this one?" Brand wasn't sure his heart could take it.

"That'll be for you to decide." Mischief sparkled in her eyes and he suddenly wanted to see that dress as well.

"Then we'll see about dinner, too." Maybe he could undo the impetuousness of his mouth.

He eased out the door. "We'll leave in fifteen minutes, Sequoia."

She nodded. "I'll be ready."

"I'll be ready, too," Rose added.

Brand started to protest, then grimaced. She was keeping her part of the bargain. He had to do the same. "Fifteen minutes," he repeated.

And fled.

Rose stepped from the taxi that evening, then slid her hands over her dress, smoothing out the wrinkles with damp palms as she glanced at the signs outside the Fox Theater. *Brandon Goodfellow, Magician Extraordinaire— Two Nights Only.*

Magician Extraordinaire. Too true. He was doing something to her, that was certain. Why else would she be so nervous about seeing Brand after the show tonight? Or have spent so much extra time in dressing? Of course, part of that had been necessity. Damn, she missed using her magic.

People surged around her and she melted into the crowd, eager to find her seat. She'd never seen one of Brand's live performances before and couldn't deny the anticipation building within her. What she'd seen of the rehearsals promised an excellent show.

Once inside the lobby, she paused. The recently renovated theater was even more impressive at night, the interior lined with the massive columns and illuminated by dim lamps. The place shimmered with ambience and elegance—perfect for a Brandon Goodfellow performance.

Letting the crowd carry her along, she made her way to the enormous auditorium dominated by great Oriental arches and a massive stage. Gilded ornate plasterwork covered the walls, drawing Rose's gaze up to the magnificent chandelier dangling in the center of a concave ceiling. She hadn't noticed it earlier in the day, but it made a world of difference to the setting.

She could feel magic in the air.

With a smile, she found her seat—only a few rows from the stage and almost directly in the middle. Perfect for observation of mirrors and trapdoors.

Okay, the show can start any time.

She'd only been sitting for a few minutes when someone behind her kicked her seat. Looking around, she spotted a boy of about eight years old swinging his legs as he chattered to his mother beside him.

"Would you mind not kicking, please?" she asked.

The boy's mother immediately placed her hand on the boy's legs. "I'm sorry," she said. "Hold still, Niall."

The lights dimmed as Rose faced front again and her anticipation surged. Finally she would see Brandon's live performance.

She removed a pen and notepad from her purse to take notes, but from the moment Brand appeared on the stage, she forgot to write. Maybe it was the lighting or the way he dominated the stage or the tailored black tuxedo he wore, but he appeared taller, elegant, mysterious, and far too handsome for a mere mortal.

He bantered with the audience as he worked, drawing them into his world, directing their attention where he wanted it. Rose had always thought Brand's father, Robin, was the most charming man she'd ever met, but Brand easily had enough charm to seduce a small town.

His illusions appeared effortless, yet drew enthusiastic applause, especially when he pulled members of the audience on to the stage to assist him. At first she tried to watch for clues as to how he performed his magic, but he captured her interest, too, until all she could do was watch him.

Damn, he was good.

He made her believe in his magic. She, who knew better than anyone alive the difference between real magic and that of illusionists. No wonder he was the best. His mastery was far superior to that of the other magicians she'd exposed.

Which meant this exposé was going to take much longer than she'd expected—a thought that didn't entirely displease her. After all, that gave her more time to spend with her cousin.

As Sequoia pushed a water tank onto the stage, Rose tensed. No matter how many escapes she'd seen, she always found them unnerving, and watching Brand with his hands cuffed climb into the tank and the lid locked down brought her heart into her throat. Sequoia covered the tank with a curtain, then held up an oversized clock so everyone could watch the seconds tick by.

Rationally, Rose knew exactly what Brand had to be doing in there, but that didn't ease her racing pulse or tight throat. As the seconds passed, she gripped her armrest so tightly her knuckles turned white. Shouldn't he be out by now?

About the time she was ready to jump to her feet and take action, Brand appeared on the stage in a puff of smoke, damp but breathing. Thunderous applause echoed in the theater, but Rose didn't join in. She couldn't. Her bones felt like jelly, her muscles incapable of moving.

Brand caught her eye and his smile broadened. He gave her a quick wink, then bowed again to the continued applause.

Rose grimaced. He would notice her worry. No doubt, she'd hear about it after the show. After her stunned reaction to his appearance in her room, he was going to think she was interested in him for more than his illusions. And she wasn't. Well, not entirely.

Okay, so he was devastatingly handsome . . . and charming . . . and intelligent . . . and turned her insides to mush. That didn't mean she still harbored any feelings for him. She didn't dare. Getting this story was complicated enough already.

"Isn't he going to fly, Mom?" the boy behind her asked, his voice carrying easily.

"Shh, dear. He doesn't do that. That's David Copperfield."

Rose resisted turning around to tell them that Brand would solve that illusion someday soon. She knew he'd been working on it for years, and with his persistence he would figure it out. After all, it had taken David Copperfield years to develop his illusion of flight as well.

The boy kicked Rose's seat once. "I wish he could fly," he muttered, his tone sulky.

Rose realized what the boy had said at the same moment Brand's eyes widened and he rose slowly off the stage. He glanced at Rose, and she responded with a wry smile and a nod to the boy behind her. What could she do now?

"And now, ladies and gentlemen, you will be the first to see my newest illusion." Brand spread his arms wide and rose even higher until he floated at least ten feet off the stage. "That of flight."

"All *right*." The boy pumped his fist into the air over Rose's shoulder.

She watched Brand carefully. What kind of ability had her magic given him? How reliable was it?

Adapting quickly to this new talent, Brand leaned forward and soared through the air, reminiscent of Superman. All he needed was the cape as he flew to the ceiling and over the heads of the audience, pausing to perform somersaults or elaborate twists.

Rose had to smile. Leave it to Brand to make the most of the situation.

The crowd stood now, the applause deafening, as Brand made his way back to the stage and finally stood on the floor again. He bowed low, then straightened, his smile wide.

"That concludes tonight's show. Thank you for coming. And be sure to watch my television special on November fourteenth, live from Las Vegas, when I will make the moon itself disappear." He bowed again. "Thank you."

The audience refused to let him leave, calling him back for three curtain calls before the clapping finally ceased and people headed for the exits. Rose remained in her seat, waiting for the crush to ease.

After several minutes she found a side exit and headed down a dimly lit hallway toward the backstage area. Was Brand trying to explain his flying to his crew? She grinned. That would take some doing, as they'd know they hadn't done anything to assist him. Only Sequoia would be aware of the truth, and she'd be laughing in a corner somewhere.

Close to the stage door, Rose paused to examine her dress. Would Brand like this one, too? It wasn't nearly as sexy as the red dress, but it did flatter her figure, the soft turquoise material clinging to her curves. The neckline was scooped but stopped short of revealing any cleavage. The hip-hugging skirt made up for it, however, stopping several inches above the knee.

She shook her head. It shouldn't matter. Having Brand like her dress was taking on a more personal than professional feel. If she attracted him, all the better. Maybe he'd be more willing to talk to her.

After all, what did matter was getting her story, and she was doing a pretty poor job of that. She'd been so engrossed in his performance, she hadn't once searched for clues on how his illusions were accomplished.

Next performance. Then she'd know what to expect and wouldn't allow herself to be sidetracked.

"Stop right there."

Rose froze at the snarled words, then turned slowly to see a man emerge from the shadows. "Ewan?"

He looked like Ewan, but everything else about him was different. He wore a pinstriped double-breasted dark gray coat over a vest and white shirt with a wide similarly striped tie. His pants were pleated. His normally bare feet were covered with black shoes and over them he wore spats. A dark Fedora covered his head, making the sneer on his face appear even more imposing.

"Ewan?" she repeated. "What are you doing?"

"I ain't taking no more sass from youse." He approached her, frowning. "Time youse come with me."

"What?" The new apparel and his words connected at the same time, and she burst into laughter. "Are you trying to be a gangster?"

"I ain't explainin'. And I ain't foolin'."

She eyed his appearance, his delicate Fae features and long hair at odds with the stereotypical 1930s gangster dress. "Are you trying to intimidate me?" If so, he was failing miserably.

"I'm taking charge." He twisted his expression into what Rose assumed was supposed to be a snarl. "And youse gonna do what I say."

She couldn't stop laughing. How ridiculous. "Knock it off, Ewan. It's not going to work." She gasped for breath. "Unless this makes you a faery godfather."

Grinning, she pointed a finger at him. "Or a hit faery."

She knew he wouldn't harm her, which made this situation all the more ludicrous. James Cagney he wasn't.

He scowled. "You're coming with me." He no longer mimicked Cagney's speech.

"No, I'm not." Rose straightened and struggled to bring her breathing under control. She hadn't laughed like that in years.

"Yes, you are." He moved so quickly he caught her unaware, wrapping his arms around her, holding her close to him. "And we're going now."

Panic flared. If he transported them into the magical realm . . . Not taking time to think, she smashed her spiked heel into his foot. His grip loosened and she drew back far enough to drive her knee into his groin.

His eyes widened and he emitted a squeak, then sank slowly to the floor in a heap.

Rose took several steps backward, putting a safe amount of distance between them, even as her conscience flared. He really appeared to be in pain. But she couldn't let him take her away.

"I'm sorry," she murmured.

"Rose?"

She glanced at the door to the stage as Sequoia appeared. Her cousin's gaze immediately went past Rose to Ewan. "Dear Lord, what happened?" She rushed to Ewan and knelt beside him. "Are you all right?"

"He grabbed me and was going to transport me to the magical realm." Rose shrugged, hoping she appeared more nonchalant than she felt about it. "I had to get away."

Sequoia shot Rose a dry glance, then turned back to Ewan and touched his face. "Can you speak?"

He drew in a deep breath. "The . . . the pain is ebbing."

Rose shared Sequoia's sigh of relief. She'd never had to knee a man in the groin before. It definitely worked, but the aftereffect was a bit unnerving. "Is Brand around?" she asked, anxious to escape.

"Just inside." Sequoia didn't turn but continued to fuss over Ewan.

Fine with me. The more her cousin kept the hit fairy occupied, the less chance he'd be bothering her.

Rose yanked open the stage door and stepped inside. The sound of excited voices reached her at once, and she allowed herself a small smile. Were they still wondering about Brand's flying act?

After a couple of tentative steps, she hesitated. Brand had made it clear he didn't want her backstage. With a sigh, she scanned the area, broken by wing curtains and stacked boxes. "Brand?"

"Rose?"

The man must have radar ears as Rose could barely hear herself above the chatter and thud of moving scenery. Brand appeared from behind a wing curtain and moved toward her purposefully.

Rose's throat tightened. What now? Was she going to get blamed for this latest episode of escaped magic?

"Rose." His eyes gleamed with excitement as he seized her shoulders. Before she could do anything more than stare at him, he bent . . .

And kissed her.

Seven

Brand only meant to give Rose a quick kiss, an exchange between friends, a thank you for the gift of flight he'd received, but one touch of her soft lips sent a sizzle of energy through his veins that demanded more. He slid his arms down her back, pulling her closer, deepening the kiss, savoring the taste and texture of her exquisite mouth.

Kissing her, holding her, surpassed the fantasies from long ago. She was sweet and hot, molding against him as if designed to fit there, her response fueling dangerous desires.

The sound of voices in the distance jerked him back to reality, and he eased away from her. Eyes wide, lips trembling and swollen, she looked as shocked as he felt.

"I . . ." He had to clear his throat to continue. "I just wanted to thank you."

"Thank me?" Her voice sounded unsteady as well. "For what?"

"For the flying." He couldn't resist rising a few inches off the floor just to test that he still could. What an awesome sensation—a tingle similar to hitting his funny bone filled his veins whenever he defied gravity.

"Stop it." Rose caught his arm and tugged him down to the floor. "You'll have a hell of a time explaining this if someone sees you."

He grinned. "I already had a hell of a time trying to explain it to my crew. I finally told them Sequoia and I had worked it out as a surprise."

"A surprise for you, too, I bet." Mischief danced in Rose's eyes. "A boy sitting behind me made the wish."

"And a wonderful wish it was. I've been trying to duplicate Copperfield's flying for years." But what he'd achieved thus far hadn't even come close to what he'd experienced tonight.

"You handled it beautifully." Her warm smile triggered an answering warmth within him.

Brand took her hand, eyeing her dress. While not as alluring as her red one, it accented her very appealing curves just as well. "Are you ready for dinner?" The words erupted from him, overruling his common sense once again.

She blinked, but didn't pull her hand free. "I wasn't sure you meant it. Besides, what kind of place is going to be open at this hour?"

"I know of one." Where they'd have a chance to talk, where'd they wouldn't be disturbed.

Where they would be alone.

Sequoia pushed Ewan's hair away from his face as his breathing finally settled into a less stressful rhythm, easing the ache in her chest as well. "Your color is better," she told him. "Give it a little while more before you try to move."

"I can stand." He struggled to his feet, then swayed unsteadily.

Sequoia wrapped her arm around his waist to keep him from falling over. Just like a man to ignore sensible advice, human or Fae. "I don't think you're all the way there yet." She steered him down the hall, very much aware of his muscles rippling along his back. "Come on. You can rest in my room."

"At the hotel?" When she nodded, he tightened his arm around her shoulders. "Very well."

A momentary dizziness swept over Sequoia. She blinked, then found herself standing in her hotel room, Ewan by her side. "Wow." Good thing growing up with Rose had exposed her to some of this stuff, or she'd be screaming by now.

Ewan slumped within her hold, and she guided him to the king-sized bed. "Here, put your feet up and rest until you feel better."

Once he was lying flat, she noticed his clothing. How could she have missed it earlier? This was a far cry from his rugged half-naked appearance. "What are you wearing?"

"I was emulating the gangsters from the television. I thought this approach would convince Rose to obey me. She laughed instead and called me a hit faery."

Sequoia had to smother a giggle. "Sounds like Rose."

He moaned and curled into a fetal position. "I didn't think she would hurt me."

"When Rose said she wasn't going with you, she meant it." Sequoia sat on the edge of the bed to remove his hat and shoes, alarmed by his passivity. This was not the same man she'd faced before. "She's not going to change her mind."

"I can't return without her." He shuddered. "You don't know Queen Titania."

"I've heard enough stories." She maneuvered him out of his jacket, then unraveled his tie. "There, that better?"

"Much." Ewan rolled onto his back and took her hand. "I am beginning to think I will live."

He was gorgeous when he smiled like that. Sequoia's pulse tripled as he placed a light kiss on the back of her hand. "I hope so."

"I have never experienced pain like that before. We are much less violent among the Fae."

"Which is why you'd be better off to just go back there." Though she already didn't want to see the last of him. He intrigued her—this gorgeous macho faery who was suddenly so vulnerable.

He released her hand and rolled back onto his side away from her. "I cannot. I was given a task to complete."

She rested her palm on his shoulder, attempting to reassure him. It had nothing to do with the secret thrill she received whenever she touched him. "You can't keep threatening Rose. You'll only get hurt again."

Ewan jerked upright in a sudden movement that had Sequoia drawing back. His face had darkened, his eyes blazed.

Her throat went dry and she went to stand, but he caught her around the wrist, holding her in place. "I have no choice. I will do as I was bid," he said.

He meant it. Damn him. Sequoia knew Rose. Her cousin wasn't about to cooperate with him. That left Sequoia with no choice. In order to protect Rose . . . and Ewan . . . she had to agree to his crazy proposal from earlier.

"Very well," she said. "If you stay away from Rose, I'll teach you what love is."

The fire in his eyes grew even hotter and his too-sexy lips curved in an enticing smile. "Will you?" He continued to hold her wrist while he traced a single line up her arm with his fingertip. "Will that include personal demonstrations?"

The shivers he created shuddered through her body, stirring a longing she hadn't fed in quite some time. The sudden urge to make love to him startled her. He might be devastatingly handsome, but he was far from being her type.

She snatched her arm free and pushed away from the bed. "Not in the way you mean." With some distance between them, she could think better. "But you'll get your first lesson tomorrow morning."

His smile only grew broader. "I am looking forward to learning much from you."

"I'll just bet you are." If she wasn't careful, he might learn more than she intended. "If you're feeling better, you can leave now."

"I am comfortable here." Ewan reclined back against the pillows, a come-hither look in his brilliant eyes that tugged at Sequoia's resistance. "You can join me."

Oh, yeah. That would be smart.

"I don't think so." She'd spend the night in a chair before she climbed into bed beside him. There was foolish and then there was downright stupid.

"As you wish." He snuggled down in the blankets, making himself comfortable.

Sequoia sighed. It was going to be a long night.

Brand kept his hold on Rose's hand during the entire trip back to the hotel, and she made no attempt to pull away. She liked the warmth and strength his grip conveyed.

But she didn't understand his change in attitude. That kiss. Dear Lord, that kiss should be patented. He'd make a fortune. She'd been kissed before, but nothing had ever sent a lightning bolt to her toes like that.

She loved it.

She feared it.

"You're quiet." Brand led her out of the elevator on the penthouse level. "What are you thinking?"

She didn't try to circumvent the truth. "That you could be a dangerous man." Especially where her emotions were concerned.

His face lit with pleasure. "Really? I like that." He keyed open the door to his suite. "Much better than mysterious."

He led her inside, then pushed the door closed. Releasing her hand, he removed his tuxedo coat and tie and tossed them on the nearby couch, then unbuttoned the first few buttons of his almost dry white shirt. "I much preferred when I could perform in jeans and a sweatshirt."

Rose grinned. "You're too famous for that." She found her gaze locked on the hint of dark hair peeking out from the vee of his shirt. Why did he have to look so damned sexy?

"So they tell me." He came toward her. "Feel free to get comfy, take off your shoes."

He knew her well. The first thing Rose liked to do was get rid of her footwear. She hesitated, then bent to remove her heels. "What about dinner?"

"There's time for that yet." The mischievous glint in his eyes should have warned her, but she still gasped when he pulled her into his arms. "Dance with me."

"There's no music."

"I can hum."

He led her into a simple waltz, then slowly levitated so that Rose was forced to link her arms around his neck and rest her feet atop his to keep from sliding to the floor below. "What are you doing?" Acutely aware of his hard body, Rose couldn't stop the shiver of delight that traveled over her skin.

"Dancing with a beautiful woman." He tightened his hold around her waist until a piece of paper wouldn't fit between them. "How about I add this to my act? A spontaneous flying dance with a woman from the audience?"

Rose frowned. He'd get this close to a stranger? "I'm sure it would please your adoring fans," she muttered.

He chuckled. "You don't sound as if you like it. How about if I choose you every time?"

That brought her gaze to his. Despite his levity, his eyes held a dark seriousness that made her breath catch in her throat. She liked that far too much. "I'm not sure that would be wise."

"No, it wouldn't be wise." He bent closer until his breath mingled with hers. "It wouldn't be wise at all."

Anticipation had her raising her lips to his when a sudden knock on the door shattered the moment. Disappointment rose as Brand lowered them to the floor and glanced at his watch. "Right on time."

Huh? Before Rose could question him, he crossed the room to open the door and admit a waiter with a pushcart containing several covered dishes and a wine bucket.

"Excellent." Brand motioned toward the small dining table in the corner. "Set it up there, please."

Rose came to his side. "What's going on?"

"Dinner." He produced his heart-melting smile. "I ordered ahead of time because I knew nothing would be open this late. Besides, there's less chance of leakage."

That made sense, but the thought of remaining in the intimacy of his room for an extended period created a quiver in her belly. She thought she'd hardened herself to his abandonment, eliminated her attraction to him, learned to control her emotions where he was concerned.

And she was rapidly discovering none of that was true.

Once Brand had shown the waiter out, he led Rose to the table. It had been set for two with a single candle burning in the center. "I hope you like it."

He seated her, then lifted the lids off the various dishes—beef tenderloins, rice pilaf, steamed vegetables, and warm bread with steam rising from it. The mixture of scents, especially that of the yeasty bread, made Rose's mouth water and her stomach growl in appreciation.

"It looks delicious." She heaped generous portions onto her plate. Brand lifted the bottle from the ice bucket. "And champagne."

Rose raised an eyebrow as he worked the cork free. "Are you celebrating?"

"I am now." He poured the bubbly into two tall narrow wine flutes, then handed one to Rose. Lifting his glass, he held it out. "To a successful show."

"I'll drink to that." Rose clinked her glass against his, then sipped. The bubbles tickled her nose and she sneezed. As Brand grinned at her, she grimaced. "It's been a long time since I've had champagne."

Brand settled into his seat and served himself. "I thought you lived the high life."

"Me?" She had to laugh at that. "Where do you get

your information? I work and go home. That's it."

"What about your flock of admirers?" Though Brand's tone was nonchalant, something in his expression caught her attention.

"What admirers?" Did he know something she didn't?

"You always had several around you in high school."

"Oh, that." She shrugged. "I never took them seriously. They were drawn to the magic, not to me."

"And now?"

At the intensity of his voice, she lowered her fork and met his gaze. "Men are drawn to me sometimes." But none had held her interest longer than ten minutes. "I haven't found one I wanted to keep."

A glimmer flickered in his eyes before he resumed eating. "I'm surprised."

"I don't have time for men. My work is more important." Through her work she could prove she was something more than her magic.

"Writing exposés?" Brand didn't look at her as he spoke.

She frowned. Was this wonderful evening going to deteriorate right now? "Among other things."

"Did you learn anything interesting during tonight's show?"

"Not much." When he glanced at her, she smiled. "I was too caught up in the performance to pay attention like I should have."

The tension left his features. "That's quite a compliment."

"Though I'm pretty sure I know how that flying act was done," she added.

He laughed and raised his glass to her. "Touché, Rose. I could always count on you to make me laugh."

"You need to laugh more." His entire countenance changed when he did, reminding her of the boy she'd once adored.

"I haven't had much reason to do so," he said.

Rose tilted her head. "You have Sequoia working for

you. How can you not be laughing on a daily basis?"

"Good point." He glanced at his plate, then up again. "But she's not you. With you every day was an adventure."

His words added a twist to her gut. "Only because you never told me how stupid most of my ideas were." She struggled to keep her tone light even while she avoided his gaze.

"Because I didn't think they were stupid." Brand grinned. "Okay, the time you had us tie our bikes together to ride side-by-side down Dead Man's Hill was stupid, but other than that . . ."

She remembered that particular feat well. They'd ended up somersaulting over their handlebars and landing in a tangled mass of arms and legs. "At least we didn't break anything." Which her mother had claimed was a miracle in itself.

"No breaks," he agreed. "But I had enough bruises to pass for a Dalmatian."

She'd been covered with them as well, but she dismissed his comment with a wave of her hand. "Builds character."

"So I've heard." He hefted the champagne bottle. "More?"

"Please." She never even became light-headed while drinking liquor. It was Coca-Cola that made her drunk—a common affliction among the Fae, from what she'd been told.

Taking her glass, she pushed away from the table and meandered to the wide windows where she could watch the lights twinkle among the darkened city. Despite the evidence of so much life, she felt very much alone.

And very aware of Brand's presence.

"I need to get going," she said. "Thank you for dinner." She turned, then gasped when she realized that Brand had moved silently to stand behind her.

He caught her hands. "You don't have to go yet." He

floated toward the ceiling, tugging at her to join him. "Come fly with me."

She pulled her hands free. "I'd have to use magic to do that." And she'd lost the thrill of flying years ago. She couldn't very well do it openly. Transporting was easier and saved time.

As he soared around the room, she shook her head with a wry smile. "I'm going to call you Peter Pan from now on. You lost your sense when you gained the ability to fly."

"Don't begrudge me this, Rose. It's a dream come true." He dived at her, tapping her shoulders before rising to the ceiling again. "I'm getting better at controlling it, too."

His delight in this ability radiated from him as he darted around the suite, diving in to tease her before sailing off again. If she allowed herself to join him, he'd be in serious trouble.

As it was, she burst into laughter as he twirled, nearly taking out a lamp in the process. "Come down from there," she ordered. "You're going to break something."

He flew over her head, mussing her hair as he passed. She giggled and ducked when he returned. Watching his next approach, she jumped up and caught his shirt, yanking him down.

He fell hard, the force of his flight behind him, tumbling them both to the bed, his body plastered on top of hers. The initial blow stole her breath, but she found it didn't return very easily as his gaze locked with hers.

The glimmer in his eyes darkened and flared with heat, his smile fading as he caressed her hair. He dipped closer, his intent obvious, giving her time to turn away, but she didn't . . . couldn't.

The touch of his lips against hers answered a yearning she hadn't even realized she possessed. He began gentle, tasting, teasing, seducing, forcing a response. When she opened to him, he plundered with an urgency that sparked fire in her blood.

He wove his fingers into her hair, holding her still as he claimed her mouth, the taste of champagne adding to Rose's headiness.

She shouldn't be doing this. She should stop. Instead she clutched his shoulders, holding him close, meeting the fierceness of his lips with her own. Nothing in her life had ever been this good.

Shifting, Brand nestled his rock-hard erection between her legs, the feel of him—so close, so solid, so hot— building the tight knot within her. She wanted him. Oh, Lord, he made her want him with a desperation that terrified her.

He continued to kiss her, seducing her, while he tightened his hold in her hair. When she moaned, wanting him to stop, wanting him to continue, he finally drew back, his breathing ragged.

"Rose?" He brushed the back of his fingers across her cheek.

"I . . . I can't do this." No matter how much her body wanted it, she'd regret it later. "It . . . it's not right."

He flinched, his ego obviously affected, then jumped to his feet and crossed the room. "Then why kiss me back? Do you intend to make me desire you enough to give you all my illusions?"

She sat up, her body still trembling with need. "You know I wouldn't do that."

"What, then?" He whirled around, fire blazing in his eyes. "Why do I want you so badly? Leaking magic?"

"Perhaps." On his part, maybe, but her response had come from deep within, which frightened her all the more. She couldn't allow him to have that kind of power over her. She stood. "If it makes you feel better to believe that."

"What do you call it, then?"

"Gratitude, perhaps, for the gift of flight." She retrieved her shoes. "How will you feel if it goes away?"

His eyes widened with momentary alarm, then he quickly regained his composure. "Will it?"

"I don't know. If I had cast the spell, probably not, but a wish from someone else . . ." She shook her head. "I honestly don't know."

"My clothing never returned after Sequoia wished it away." He said it as if trying to convince himself.

"I don't know, Brand." She'd never been through anything like this before.

Sparks flared as he stepped closer. "Why don't we test it, then? How about I wish for you to be in your underwear, and we see how long it takes your dress to return?"

She gasped, feeling her dress evaporate before he'd even finished speaking. Thank goodness she had worn a bra with this one, though the flimsy bits of lace on her bra and panties revealed as much as they covered.

Her first instinct was to cover herself, but she forced her hands to remain at her side as she defiantly met Brand's gaze.

He was staring, his pupils wide, his face flushed. "Oh, my God, Rose."

The deep rasp of his voice sent a shudder through her. He extended a hand as if to touch her, then curled it into a fist and dropped it again.

Her nipples tightened into hard nubs. She wanted his touch, craved it so much so that she took a step toward him before she caught herself. "Could I get my clothes back?"

He didn't answer, his gaze lingering on her revealed flesh, his hunger obvious. And the more he stared, the tighter the knot in her gut grew and the more her breasts swelled and ached. Only a few feet separated them, filled with a longing and tension that lurked as a nearly tangible presence.

In another few minutes she'd go to him, give him what he wanted . . . what she wanted. "Brand." Her panic sounded in her voice. "Please."

He jerked his head up as if she'd slapped him. "I'm sorry." He shook his head. "No, I'm not. You're exquisite, Rose."

She didn't respond, but she trembled, the longing more difficult to control.

"How about if I wish I were in my underwear, too?"

His clothing vanished, leaving him in hip-hugging navy bikini underwear that did nothing to hide the evidence of his need.

"Oh, God." Rose groaned and closed her eyes. "Brand, I can't." She blindly turned for the door. She'd run through the hotel half naked if she had to. To remain was to give Brand a power stronger than any magic.

She had her hand on the handle when he spoke. "I wish we were dressed again."

She felt the tug on her magic as her dress reappeared, though the neck was scooped lower and the hem shortened from what it had been. Turning back to glance at Brand, she noticed only his pants had returned. His excellent chest was still bare, as if her power hadn't been able to fulfill the entire request.

"Thank you," she murmured.

He shook his head. "Don't thank me. Just go. Now."

The roughness of his tone spurred her into action, and she fled to the elevator, escaping the room, escaping Brand.

But she still couldn't escape what he made her feel.

Eight

"What's he doing here?" Rose asked as she spotted Ewan sitting at Sequoia's table in the hotel restaurant the next morning. She still retained a niggle of guilt over seeing him lying on the theater floor last night, but he looked fully recovered today. In fact, the sparkle in his eyes contrasted sharply with the dark circles under her cousin's eyes.

"He's promised not to bother you," Sequoia said. "We've made a deal."

Rose raised an eyebrow as she slid into an empty chair. "A deal?" A faery raised by mortals, she didn't trust any of the Fae. Not while Titania was their queen. "What kind of deal?" Did it have anything to do with Sequoia's haggard appearance?

"I've agreed to teach him what love is."

Rose frowned. What did that mean? "I hope you're not—"

"Oh, no. Nothing like that."

"You sure?" Rose was not going to have her cousin sacrificing herself. "You look like crap. Did you sleep last night?"

Sequoia directed a cool stare at Ewan. "Not well."

He grinned in response, then turned his attention to Rose. "I have not yet made love to Sequoia. Is that what you wish to know?"

"Close enough." Rose couldn't help but notice his use of *yet*. Had her cousin? A quick glance at Sequoia confirmed a bright flame in her eyes. Yep, she'd noticed.

"I am *not* a part of this deal," Sequoia said.

Ewan only smiled and resumed reading the menu.

"Argh. Men."

"Rather early for that attitude, Sequoia." Brand approached their table and took the sole remaining chair.

Rose tensed. After a restless night in which her body had argued with her mind, she wasn't sure she was ready to deal with Brand.

As if she had a choice.

He glanced at her, his expression bland, but the gleam in his eyes brought a warm flush to her cheeks. "Good morning, Rose."

"Good morning." She devoted her attention to the menu and was grateful when the waitress appeared to take their orders. After several hours of sleeplessness last night, she'd convinced herself that her reaction to Brand had been an anomaly, a temporary aberration of her behavior. She'd never allowed a man to affect her like that before, and she didn't intend to start now—especially not with this story. It was too important to her future.

"What are your plans for today, Tree?" she asked, attempting to ignore Brand. None of them had to be at the theater until later that afternoon, and Rose always enjoyed her cousin's company.

"I have a visit to the hospital scheduled."

Rose smiled. Sequoia made it a point to visit the children's wards wherever she stopped for more than a day. "Care for company?"

"I'm taking Ewan with me." Sequoia grimaced. "It's part of his training."

"That's okay as long as he behaves." Rose didn't want

to injure Ewan again, but she would if she had to.

"I have given my word," he said, his eyes frosty, his tone imperious.

"See that you keep it, then." If Sequoia thought she could teach Titania's errand boy *any*thing, more power to her, but Rose had her doubts. The Fae didn't normally experience extreme emotions such as love or hate. Which could work to her benefit, she supposed. The longer it took Ewan to grasp the concept of love—if he could grasp it all—the longer he wouldn't be bugging her.

"When are you leaving?" Rose added. "After breakfast?"

Sequoia nodded. "I told them I'd be there by nine-thirty."

Sequoia and her children. Did Sequoia's parents know how much she did for others? Where her true ambition lay? Would they still be nagging her to go to college if they did?

A cry caught Rose's attention as a young family was seated at a table beside theirs, consisting of a mother, father, and young boy of about six, who whined all the way to the table and continued after he took his chair.

Rose rolled her eyes and exchanged a dry grin with her cousin. After growing up among a multitude of cousins, this type of behavior was nothing new.

"I don't wanna see the river," the boy said, slumping in his seat.

"You'll like it, Jeffrey." His mother aimed a quelling glance at the boy. "We're going up in the Arch, too. You can see for miles from up there."

"I don't wanna go to the Arch. I wanna go to Disney World."

"Sounds like Val," Rose said, referring to Sequoia's youngest brother.

Sequoia grinned. "Naw, Val was worse."

"I wanna go to Disney World," Jeffrey said again. "Kyle got to go there."

"That is enough." His father pointed a finger at him. "I don't want to hear another word."

His mother gave Jeffrey the children's menu. "Why don't you decide what you want to eat?"

He took the menu, his expression fixed in a pout. "I don't wanna see any stupid arch," he muttered under his breath. "I wish we were at Disney World."

Rose gasped, feeling the power being pulled from her as the family disappeared.

It took a moment for anyone at Rose's table to react. She couldn't stop staring at the spot where the family had been as the child's menu drifted to the floor.

"Dear Lord," she whispered. This was much worse than a boy wishing for a candy bar. "Wish them back, Tree."

Her cousin smiled. "Why not let him have some fun?"

Rose sent her a pointed look. This was not funny. She turned to Brand. He'd do it. "Brand . . ."

Before he could respond, Sequoia held up her hand. "I'll do it. I wish for that family to have a great time at Disney World, then return to their seats at that table five minutes after they left."

"Could you be more precise?" Rose asked with a shake of her head.

The family popped back in their seats just as suddenly as they had vanished. The parents appeared shell-shocked, but the boy was ecstatic, his smile splitting his face. They wore the same clothing, but now Jeffrey sported Mickey Mouse ears.

The father stared at his wife. "There was a mouse . . ."

"And a duck. With pants." Her face was pale. "It looked like Disney World."

"It couldn't have been."

"That was great, Mom, Dad. Can we do it again?" Jeffrey asked.

The father pushed back his chair. "I think we need to get out of here." He ushered his family out, waving off the waitress who approached.

Ewan chuckled and turned to Sequoia, his admiration

obvious. "That is the most precise wish I've ever heard. Have you done that before?"

Sequoia grinned as she glanced at Rose and raised her eyebrows. "Oh, once or twice."

"A long time ago," Rose added. They'd been young. Shortly after Rose had discovered her magical abilities, she and Sequoia had played a game they called fairy godmother in which Sequoia had received three wishes and no more. After Rose had teasingly translated Sequoia's requests into something slightly different, her cousin had learned to be very exact about what she wanted.

"I suggest we eat quickly before anything else happens," Brand said. His gaze had cooled considerably, and the look he gave Rose held condemnation.

How dare he make this out to be her fault? Rose pushed back her chair, nearly toppling it over. "Excuse me. I find I'm no longer hungry." She hurried out, ignoring Sequoia's cry of protest.

When someone grabbed her arm, she turned to glare at Brand. "What do you want?"

"You don't have to leave," he said, not releasing her arm.

"Don't I?" She jerked free. "Why is it when my magic gives you what you want, it's wonderful, but any other time it's a sin?"

He hesitated. "I—"

"Don't bother to explain. You're the same as everyone else. All you see is my magic. You still don't see *me*." Whirling around, she stalked from the restaurant.

He didn't follow her. Which was a good thing.

Or so she told herself.

Thankfully, Brand didn't accompany Sequoia, Ewan, and Rose to the hospital, so Rose could enjoy listening to Sequoia try to explain love for others to Ewan. Caring for others was a totally foreign concept to him, but Rose had to give her cousin credit for trying.

"It's more than what you see between a man and

woman," Sequoia said to Ewan as they rode up to the children's ward in the elevator. "It's the way you feel about others as well. It's caring what happens to them, wanting them to be happy."

"Why?" Ewan shook his head. "Where is the gain in that?"

"Why does there have to be gain? It makes you feel good, too."

When Ewan only stared at her, obviously not getting it, Rose laughed and put an arm around her cousin's shoulders. "He just doesn't know what he's missing," she said.

"He will." The determined set of Sequoia's mouth would have frightened a lesser man, but a glance at Ewan gave evidence of the sparkle in his eyes.

From the looks of it, he liked thwarting Sequoia. Rose grinned. He'd learn.

Reaching the nurse's desk, Sequoia took charge, introducing them and asking for the head nurse to whom she'd spoken the day before. The woman came toward them, wearing dark blue scrubs decorated with glow-in-the dark spacemen, her stride and manner firm, but the tendrils of dark brown hair that escaped from the bun on her head softened her appearance. When she smiled and held out her hand, Rose chose to believe the tendrils.

"I'm Maureen Travers. Call me Mo." She turned to lead them to a large open room at the end of the hallway. "Most of the children who feel well enough will be in here right now. How long do you expect to be, Miss Adams?"

"Usually I only take an hour or so."

"That's fine."

Sequoia paused outside the doorway and set down the gym bag she'd carried in. "Let me change before I go in."

"What are you doing?" Ewan asked as Sequoia donned a swirling black cape and top hat.

"She's going to entertain the sick children." Rose had known for years that her cousin did this on a regular basis, but this would the first time she'd be able to witness it for herself.

Sequoia applied a bright red lipstick that totally changed her appearance, somehow making her appear more vivid. Straightening, she tossed back the cape and held her head high. "The Sensational Sequoia is ready," she announced.

Mo smiled and pushed through the doors. "Children. Your attention, please. Come this way. We have a special treat this afternoon." With a sweep of her arm, she indicated the doorway. "May I present the Sensational Sequoia."

Sequoia burst into the room, juggling three balls even as she launched into a teasing repartee with the kids. She captured their attention immediately, especially when she captured each ball on a down spin and made it disappear.

Everyone crowded closer. "How did you do that?" "Where did they go?"

Rose and Ewan slipped in to stand by the door in the background. Sequoia was good. Better than Rose had expected—not that she'd tell her cousin that. The magic tricks she performed were fairly simple—standard magician fare—but it was her attitude that made the difference.

"That's love at work," Rose said.

Ewan turned his gaze from Sequoia. "What does that mean?"

"You can practically see it. You have to feel it. Sequoia loves these children. She wants them to be happy. That's why she does this."

"Does she know them?"

"No. You're missing the point."

"I have no doubt," he said dryly.

"These kids are very ill with cancer. Some may die. If she can brighten up their lives for even a short while, they'll feel better and so will she."

"How will this make a difference? Will her love heal them?"

Rose paused. "It might." Laughter and love, like prayer, was always underrated.

"She's pretty good, isn't she?"

Rose jumped as Brand spoke, and turned to see him standing in the doorway. "What are you doing here?" she asked. There went her enjoyment of the morning.

"I finished my errands and wanted to see Sequoia at work." He came over to stand beside them. "She's always bugging me to teach her new illusions. Now I finally get to see her putting them to use." His expression softened. "They really love her, don't they?"

"Love again." Ewan rolled his eyes. "Is that all you mortals think about?"

"It's part of who we are," Rose said.

"But you are Fae."

That made her smile. She sometimes forgot that fact. "True, but I was raised as a mortal, and I wouldn't trade that for anything."

"Life is far simpler in the magical realm," Ewan said.

"You would think that. You have no real emotions other than fear." She'd rather deal with the highs and lows of emotions than exist without them.

Ewan frowned. "We don't fear anyone."

"You fear Titania." When Ewan started to protest, Rose continued. "Come on. You're afraid to go back and tell her I refused to come with you."

"That is not fear." He held himself stiffly. "That is obedience."

"Yeah, right." Rose turned her attention back to Sequoia, careful to avoid looking at Brand. Without trying, she could still feel the touch of his lips on hers. Talk about emotions. He'd turned hers upside down and she hated it. Especially when he was no different than all the other men drawn to her because of her magic.

"I can't see it."

A soft voice caught Rose's attention, and she skirted the crowd of children gathered around Sequoia to see a tiny little girl at the edge, her head bald, her eyes large.

"Need help?" Rose asked.

When the girl nodded, Rose lifted her in her arms and moved to a good vantage point. The child weighed practically nothing. Rose could feel the sharp edges of her bones beneath her skin. It wasn't fair. Why did children have to suffer this way?

The girl giggled as Sequoia performed another illusion, and the smile made all the difference. Rose's chest tightened. Now she understood why her cousin worked hard to do this in every city she visited. For a short time, it mattered to these children. It made them forget for just a moment the reality of their lives.

"Now I will make a rabbit appear," Sequoia declared. She held up her hands and tugged at her sleeve and pulled out . . . an umbrella. Frowning, she tossed it aside. "That's not it." She examined her other sleeve and pulled out a long string of tied scarves. "Hmmm."

The children roared with laughter, and Sequoia kept trying to produce a rabbit and ended up with everything but. Until abruptly a small white bunny hopped out from between her legs.

Sequoia's eyes widened and she glanced at Rose. Rose shook her head. She hadn't done anything. Together, they turned to Ewan, who had a broad grin on his face.

Being a professional, Sequoia managed to work the live rabbit into her act, then handed it to Ewan with a few quiet words. Rose didn't have to overhear to guess what they were. She doubted he'd interfere again.

Too soon, Sequoia finished her performance, but remained to chat with the children. She finally joined Rose, who still held the little girl, and presented the child with a bouquet of silk flowers.

The girl smiled as she accepted them. "Thank you."

"What's your name?" Sequoia asked.

"Cindy." She held up four fingers. "I'm four."

Only four? Rose blinked back threatening tears. "You're a very pretty girl, Cindy."

Cindy shook her head. "My hair fell out." Her voice shook as she continued. "I'm sick."

Sequoia ran her hand over Cindy's shoulder. "I'm sorry, Cindy. I wish you weren't sick."

The tug on Rose's power brought with it a slice of pain as if someone had ripped off her fingernails, but she didn't mind as she watched healthy color return to Cindy's cheeks. The girl struggled in her arms, her energy returning, and Rose set her down.

Was it possible? She'd been able to heal broken bones and cuts before, but nothing like this. Could her magic actually cure someone of cancer?

As she exchanged glances with her cousin, she saw Sequoia's question and nodded. "Do it, Tree." She had no qualms about this. "Heal them all."

Sequoia scanned the room. At least eight children were present. "I wish for all these children to be cured of their diseases."

The magic left Rose in a rush, creating painful agony, ripping the power from her gut. "Dear Lord." She could barely breathe. Her knees felt weak. Using magic had never affected her like this before.

"No, Sequoia."

She heard Ewan dimly as if from far away, his words barely making sense. The room spun now, growing black around the edges. Something was wrong.

Rose reached out for her cousin, but the effort of lifting her arm was too much. It hardly moved at all, almost as if encased in mud. "I . . ."

The last thing she heard was Brand's shout. "Rose!"

She sank to her knees, unable to breathe, unable to think, unable to move. What was happening to her?

No answer came. Only darkness.

Nine

Brand caught Rose in his arms before her head could hit the floor, his heart in his throat. "Rose." What was wrong? She'd gone deathly white and collapsed in a matter of seconds after Sequoia had made that wish. He searched for the head nurse, but she was fussing over the suddenly rambunctious children, trying to calm them.

"What happened?" Sequoia knelt beside him.

"I don't know." But he had to help Rose. Somehow. "We need to do something. Get the nurse."

"Cancel the wish," Ewan ordered as he joined them, his expression grave. "Now."

Sequoia blanched. "Cancel it?" She glanced at the children regaining their health by the moment.

"You have a choice. The children can live or Rose can live, but not both."

From the grimness of Ewan's tone, he wasn't joking. Brand grabbed Sequoia's hand. "Either you do it or I will." He wasn't about to let Rose die.

Sequoia nodded and stood. "I wish I'd never made my last wish." The children abruptly collapsed, calling for the nurse, their former exuberance fading. Sequoia closed her eyes, her fists clenched by her side.

Brand cradled Rose in his arms. Was she still breathing? Shouldn't she recover now? He darted a glance at Ewan. "What's wrong?"

"She's lost too much life force."

"No." That was unacceptable. They were in a hospital. Surely modern medicine could do something. Brand grabbed Ewan's arm. "Can the doctors here help her?"

"Only magic will save her."

"Then take us to my suite." If saving Rose was going to require magic, they'd be better off out of here. At this point they could vanish unnoticed. The head nurse was more concerned with the children right now.

Ewan gripped Brand and Sequoia's wrists with a dry twist of his lips. "As you command."

They reappeared in Brand's suite, and he placed Rose on his bed. "What do we have to do?" he asked Ewan. The man was Fae. He had to know what to do to save Rose.

"She needs her life force restored."

"But I canceled the wish." Sequoia's face was nearly as white as Rose's.

"Not in time. Too much of her power went into the children."

This couldn't be happening. Brand ran his hand over Rose's tousled hair. To see her so still, so quiet, tore at his heart. "I thought faeries were immortal."

"We are. The Fae are not foolish enough to give away their life force to others."

Sequoia touched Ewan's arm. "You can save her, can't you?"

He eyed her with a haughtiness that made Brand want to strangle him. "Only by doing what I told you was foolish. I have no desire to end my existence."

"Please, Ewan." Tears trickled down her cheeks. "She didn't know this would happen. Don't let her die. Please."

Brand straightened. If Sequoia's pleas didn't work, he intended to beat the faery into agreement.

When Ewan hesitated, Sequoia placed her palm against his chest. "Please."

With a sigh Ewan bent over Rose and placed his hand over her forehead. "There's not much life left."

"She's Fae, too. Won't giving her some of your magic spark the rest?" Sequoia asked.

"Perhaps. I have never done this before." Ewan closed his eyes, his expression calm at first. After a moment he groaned and his face crumpled with pain and effort.

Sequoia went to wrap her arm around his waist, but Brand kept his gaze on Rose. Was the color returning to her cheeks? Was her breathing stronger?

With a cry, Ewan pulled his hand free and sagged against Sequoia. "I can do no more."

As Ewan stepped away, Brand settled on the edge of the bed and felt for Rose's pulse. It beat stronger now and some color had returned to her cheeks. "Is she going to be all right?"

"I believe she'll be fine. As Sequoia said, once I shared my energy with her life force, it began to revive on its own, but she'll need a lot of rest."

"I think you need some rest, too." Sequoia steered Ewan to the doorway. "Come with me. Call me if there's any change, Brand. We'll be in my room."

Brand nodded, only dimly listening to her, too intent on watching Rose for some sign of improvement. Trust Rose to give her all . . . even if it killed her. She'd always been selfless like that as a child, giving her lunch to someone who didn't have one, searching tirelessly for the home of a stray dog.

Taking her hand in his, Brand sought solace in the warmth it contained. Had Ewan truly healed her? What if he'd quit too soon?

Brand closed his eyes. Damn this magic. If Rose had been an ordinary woman . . . No, she'd never be an ordinary woman.

Opening his eyes, he smoothed back the tendrils of hair along the edge of her face, needing to touch her, aching for some kind of response. Even if she revealed every illusion he'd ever created, he wouldn't want her dead.

She . . . mattered.

"Damn you, Rose," he whispered. In a few short days she'd managed to turn his well-ordered life upside-down. He'd always taken pride in his methodical approach to his illusions, his performances, his life.

Now . . . now all he could think about was Rose. Holding her, kissing her—Lord help him, making love to her. Was it her magic, as she claimed, or was it because he remembered her impish smile when they'd put a garter snake in Sequoia's sleeping bag?

He shook his head. She was magical—in so many ways—and he was not. Nothing was going to change that.

Her hand jerked in his and he tensed. "Rose?"

Her eyelashes fluttered again her cheeks several times before she opened her eyes. "Brand?"

"I'm here." He squeezed her hand. "You're going to be all right." Saying it made it so, didn't it?

"Tired." She shifted in the bed, her eyes drooping closed again. "So tired."

"Then sleep. Build up your strength."

She drifted off again, but the tight band around Brand's chest eased. She *would* be all right. After a few hours' rest she'd probably be her feisty self again.

Knowing her, she'd be up and around by the time his evening show started. For the first time, Brand wanted to see her sitting in his audience. Needed to see her there.

Otherwise, his biggest illusion tonight would be his smile.

Sequoia lowered Ewan to the edge of her bed, then placed her palm over his forehead. He still felt cool and clammy. "Let me get you some water."

Returning from the bathroom, she pressed the glass into

his hand, then watched as he drained it. "Do you feel any better?" she asked.

"I will recover shortly. I was not so foolish as to give away a large portion of my life force."

"I can never thank you enough for helping Rose. If she had died . . ." Tears welled up, ever near the surface. She'd almost killed her cousin.

"It seemed to be important to you," he said with a calmness that didn't match the intensity of his gaze.

"It is important. Rose is my best friend as well as my cousin. I love her."

"Love?" Ewan cocked his head. "Yet you are crying when you know she is healed?"

"I nearly killed her," she murmured, sending a shiver through her. "It was all my fault." Her voice broke, the enormity of her wish washing over her.

She turned away, but Ewan caught her hand and held her in place. "She told you to make the wish."

"But I should have known." Tears trickled down her cheeks, and she swiped at them with the back of her hand. "Rose healed my arm when I broke it falling off my bike. That exhausted her. Why did I expect she could cure a room full of dying children?"

"Why even try?"

Sequoia stared at him. Could he truly be that unfeeling? "They're innocent children. They don't deserve to die so young."

He shrugged. "All mortals die sooner or later. It is part of the circle of nature."

"But they're children." Didn't he understand? "They've hardly begun to live."

His expression remained puzzled. "Is this part of your love?"

"You're impossible." Sequoia tried to jerk her hand free. "You'll never understand."

He only held her tighter and stood, forcing her to face him. "Then make me understand, Sequoia."

"I only wanted to help the kids. To stop the suffering." The words tumbled out as guilt ravaged Sequoia. "I didn't know . . . Rose said . . . then she fell . . . I didn't mean . . ." Sobs ripped from her chest. What if Ewan hadn't been here?

To her surprise, he drew her into his embrace, allowing her to bury her face into his shoulder until her heart-wrenching sobs finally eased. "What have I done?"

"There is no fault." Ewan touched her hair, then slowly drew his hand over it. "Rose was unaware of the danger to herself, as were you. Would she want you to suffer like this over an innocent mistake?"

He had a point. Sequoia sniffled and lifted her face from his shirt. "No."

"Very well. Rose will be fine in a matter of hours." He caught her chin, lifting her gaze to his. "Remember, I cannot lie."

Sequoia produced a watery smile. For someone who didn't understand love, he was doing a great job of calming her anxiety. "I might just make a good mortal out of you yet."

He shuddered. "I don't think so."

Surprised that she could laugh, Sequoia placed a light kiss beside his mouth. "Thank you, Ewan."

"For what?" His puzzlement made her laugh again.

"For being you." This irritating faery was turning out to have more facets than she'd expected.

A slow smile crossed his face as he pulled her closer, his eyes twinkling. "And thank you, Sequoia."

Despite the aching heat that pulsed through her, Sequoia managed to speak. "For what?"

He kissed her, long, slow, deep, drawing her into a pool of sensuality where she'd gladly drown. Just as her hands moved to link around his neck, he drew away.

Flames blazed in his eyes and his smile held a mixture of heat and humor. "For making love with me."

She blinked. "What?" True, one single kiss had her halfway there, but she wasn't about to jump into bed with him. "I'm not making love with you."

He let her draw away from him, but his gaze continued to hold her. "Perhaps not now. But you will."

"I'm not about—" Sequoia stopped herself. Why bother talking to an empty room?

He was gone.

Rose groaned as the mantle of sleep eased. Every muscle in her body ached. Hell, everything ached. She'd been hit by a truck—a truck that had had the nerve to back up and do it again.

Wincing, she opened her eyes but saw only blackness. Had she gone blind?

She blinked several times, then eased out a breath as the darkness molded into shades of gray and vague shapes. Okay, it was night. What was going on? Where was she?

As she shifted, she realized a heavy arm was thrown over her waist. Gasping, she slid from the bed, landing with a plop on the floor. She hadn't done anything stupid . . . had she?

She struggled to remember. The last thing she could recall was going to the hospital with Sequoia, the children . . . the wish.

"Rose?" Brand switched on the lamp by the bed as he sat up. He wore his tuxedo shirt and pants, and his expression was haggard. "You're awake?"

"I think so." There had better be a rational explanation for why she was in Brand's bed and he was lying beside her. "Why am I here?"

"We brought you here after you collapsed so Ewan could heal you."

"Heal me?"

Brand leaned toward the edge of the bed. "Why are you on the floor?"

"I . . . ah . . . no reason." Rose pushed herself to her unsteady feet. She wasn't about to admit her fears to him. "What do you mean by heal me?"

"By wishing to heal those children, you gave away your

life force to replenish theirs. You almost died."

"Died?" Rose sank onto the edge of the bed. "I remember feeling weak, dizzy, like I had no energy."

"You collapsed." Brand's eyes were dark despite the nightstand lamp. "Fortunately Ewan knew what was wrong and managed to save you."

She'd almost died? True, her body ached something fierce, but she hadn't seen any bright light, didn't even feel weak any longer. "I guess I owe Ewan, then." She grimaced. "But I'm still not going with him."

Brand laughed and rested his hand on her shoulder. "You scared me half to death, Rose."

His touch was warm, sending slow ripples of heat through her veins. "I would think you'd be glad to get rid of me." She tried to keep her tone light, but failed.

"Do you really think that of me?"

She met his gaze, then shook her head. He would no doubt be thrilled to see her leave him alone, but he wouldn't wish her dead. Her pulse jumped as he continued to look at her, and she searched for a change of subject.

"What time is it?" He sat between her and the clock.

He glanced around. "Almost two."

"In the morning?" Had she slept over twelve hours?

"You needed to rest." Brand ran his hand down her arm, pausing to hold her hand.

How was she supposed to think coherently when he did that? "But your show?"

"I showed up, though I consider it among my worst performances. I was distracted."

His meaning was clear, but she chose to ignore it. Her heart was already racing. "Did you . . . did you fly?"

"I did." He smiled. "It hasn't worn off yet."

"That's good." She eased her hand free of his and scooted a couple inches away. Any distance had to help at this point.

"I'm sorry, Rose," he said abruptly.

She frowned. "Sorry?" What had he done now? Her

eyes widened. Had he taken advantage of her unconscious state? "You didn't . . . ?"

"What? No, oh, no." He produced a wry smile. "I'm not quite that desperate. I want to apologize for this morning."

The morning seemed like years away. Rose had to struggle to recall the events.

"You were right. I was thrilled when your magic worked for me and condemning when it worked elsewhere. That was hypocritical of me."

For a moment she couldn't speak. He was actually admitting it? "I . . . I'm glad you realize it," she said finally. "Does that mean you're not going to hate me for having magic anymore?"

"It means I'm going to try." Brand pushed off the bed and walked around to stand before her. "And this . . . this thing today made me think."

"Isn't that dangerous?" She tried to tease, to break the seriousness of the mood, but the slight smile he gave her in response wasn't enough to do so.

"Usually." Brand captured her head between his hands, his hold gentle. She dreaded his next words. "This deal of ours is stupid."

"I won't argue that." But it was necessary for her to gain entry into his world.

He grinned and kissed her, a brief caress that nearly caused her to dissolve into a puddle right there. "I want to cancel the bet."

"But . . . but . . ." Was he throwing her out? Again?

"You can stay. Do your worst." He dropped his hands and turned to face the patio windows. "But you don't have to leak magic anymore."

Rose stood. Was she hearing correctly? "What are you saying?"

"I'm saying the deal is off." Brand pivoted to face her across the dimly lit room. "You can use your magic."

Ten

~

Gratitude warmed Rose. He meant it. He'd actually let her use her magic and stay to get her story. "Have I told you what a special man you are, Brandon Goodfellow?"

His slow answering smile triggered a warmth of a different kind. "Not in the past seventeen years or so."

She was half tempted to accept his generous offer, but this had gone past proving herself to him. She had to prove she could exist without using magic to herself. "I never thought I'd hear you say something even close to this, which makes me even more reluctant to refuse."

"What?" He closed the distance between them. "Are you nuts? This is a win-win for you, Rose."

"It would be, I agree, but I can't do it."

"Why not?" Anger mixed with his puzzlement.

"Because you dared me into this and we both know it. You were angry. I was angry." Which had always been a dangerous situation for them.

"Which is why I admitted it was a stupid bet. Why stick with it?"

"I started out having to prove to you I could make it

without my magic, but it's gone beyond that. I have to prove it to me now, Brand. Until you forced me into this, I didn't realize how much I did use my gift."

His jaw tightened. "You have it to use. Might as well."

"True." But he still hated that she had it. "And I'll use it again, but not now. *This* story I'm going to get like an ordinary person."

He started to respond, then paused. When he finally spoke, she had the feeling it wasn't what he'd originally meant to say. "What about your leaking magic? You're risking your life by not using your power."

"This was an isolated incident." At least, she hoped it was. After all, how many people would wish to cure an entire ward? "I'll be more careful and avoid people when possible."

Rule number one—no hospitals.

"Will that be enough?"

"It'll have to be." His concern came through clearly and Rose smiled, enjoying the knowledge that he cared enough to be concerned. It had been a long time since she'd felt that. "I'll be fine. I promise."

"Will you?" Brand ran his hand along the edge of her hair, his fingertips brushing her face. "You almost died, Rose."

She had to swallow before she could answer, a quiver vibrating in her belly. "I should have known better. I won't let it happen again."

He shook his head. "You're going to give me gray hair."

Her chest tightened at the impact of his words. "I . . ." She had to stop and start over. "I come by it naturally. My father always tells my mother that."

Brand's eyes darkened, but his lips lifted in a half smile. "Knowing you and your mother, I completely understand." He dropped his hands to her shoulders, holding her in place when she would have retreated. "What am I going to do with you?"

His gaze focused on her lips, completely stealing her

breath away. Aching need crossed his face, but she barely had time to recognize it before he claimed her mouth with a ferocity that startled her.

His lips demanded a response—one she was only too willing to give, any resistance gone at the first touch of his sensual mouth. A person would be willing to die in order to have him revive her.

He crushed her to him, flattening her breasts against his chest, as he devoured her mouth with an expertise that turned her legs to Silly Putty. Brand's kiss held a magic all its own—far superior to anything she possessed—and she succumbed to his spell.

Linking her arms around his neck, she met him kiss for kiss, wanting more, demanding more. Reason fled, overwhelmed by the ache building within her, the sensations flooding her mind and body.

He left her mouth and dotted kisses over her face and throat—feather-light touches that only added to her inner turmoil. She leaned back her head to allow him better access, her heart pounding so rapidly she feared it might jump from her chest.

In high school she'd always been envious—no, dammit, jealous—when he was linked with other girls. She'd imagined him kissing them like this, but the reality eclipsed her daydreams. His kiss managed to say more than any words—communicating his desire, his need, while making Rose feel as if she were the only woman in the world he would give it to.

When he cupped her breasts, she gasped, his touch creating a larger shock than being hit by lightning. Her breast swelled, filling his palm, the nipple pebbling, aching for more.

To her surprise, he gripped her shoulders and pushed her gently away from him. Dropping his hands, he took a step backward. "Go, Rose. Go now before we both regret it."

The huskiness of his voice plucked at the taut strands of need inside her. She wanted to go back to him, to experience that devastating kiss again, but slowly his words reached the small part of sanity that remained.

Regret? Her body insisted there would be no regret, but her mind couldn't deny it. She was here to reveal his secrets, not make love with him. Brand was a complication she didn't need in her already chaotic life.

Rose swallowed and backed toward the door, unable to look away from his blazing gaze. "I'm sorry," she whispered, hating his look of pain.

He gave a rough laugh. "Not nearly as much as I am." With obvious effort he turned back to face the windows. "The bus leaves in the morning," he added.

"I'll be there." She wasn't going to give up now despite the small voice in her head that screamed at her to run as far away as she could get.

Fleeing his room, she told herself she wasn't running from Brand or the incredible pleasure he could provide. No, it was worse, for she could never escape. Not from herself. Not from the sudden need to take what Brand offered.

She'd never wanted a man, never needed a man. Being Fae, she knew better than to fall for someone who would age and die while she remained eternally young. And especially not someone like Brand, who still resented her magic, no matter what he said. Yet she couldn't deny how alive he made her feel, the ache boiling in her gut.

Damn Brand. He was going to mess up her life.

Reaching her room, she closed the door and leaned against it. *Going* to mess up her life?

Hell, he already had.

The moment Rose stepped from her room in the morning, Sequoia enveloped her in an enthusiastic hug. "How are you? Are you okay? I'm so sorry. I was so dumb."

Sequoia's words tumbled out, overrunning each other, until Rose laughed. How like her cousin. "I'm fine. Don't worry about it, Tree. It wasn't your fault."

"You sure? You're okay?"

"Positive." True, Rose hadn't been able to sleep after returning to her room, but considering she'd just slept about fifteen hours, she wasn't concerned with that. And she did feel fine—energetic and ready to go. As far as she could tell, she'd suffered no lasting ill effects as a result of the previous day's episode.

"But I feel so responsible. . . ."

"It wasn't your fault." Rose hugged her cousin's shoulders. "Neither of us knew what would happen. I was fortunate that Ewan was there." She grimaced. "I guess I owe him a thank-you. Is he around?"

A strange look drifted across Sequoia's face. "I don't know. He disappeared last night and I haven't seen him since."

"Not a great loss." Though she did owe him a sincere debt of gratitude, Rose didn't want to argue any more over going to the magical realm, which he'd undoubtedly insist was the payment for her life.

"Yeah." Sequoia agreed, but her tone and expression reflected just the opposite.

Rose frowned. Was Tree actually falling for him? "You all right?" She was going to have to explain to Sequoia about the Fae sensuality. They exuded it naturally and looked upon lovemaking as an extracurricular activity. Few even grasped the concept of commitment.

"I'm fine." Sequoia produced a faint smile. "Want some breakfast?"

Rose shook her head. "We need to get going or we'll be late for the bus." She still preferred transporting to walking from place to place, but traveling with Brand was doing great things for her legs.

"We've plenty of time. You're actually early for a change."

Lifting one eyebrow, Rose grinned. "I'd rather play it safe." Especially after last night. Brand would want her to leave. A part of her wanted to flee as well.

But she had a story to get—a story that was becoming more difficult to do every day. But she would get it. All she had to do was resist the temptation Brand provided.

Yeah, easier said than done.

Just thinking about his kiss made her go achy and tingly. Not a good sign.

Even worse, her heart skipped a beat when she saw Brand standing on the bus steps. He produced a welcoming smile as they approached, and she found herself automatically smiling in return.

"It's about time you two showed up," he said.

"Hey, we're not late," Sequoia protested.

"Almost." He waved them inside. "I have breakfast ready."

"Breakfast?" He cooked? Rose smelled cinnamon rolls and bacon as soon as she entered the bus. "What's going on?"

"I knew you'd be better off not dining around other people," Brand said over his shoulder as he led back to the table. "And I also knew you'd be here, so I ordered breakfast to go." He opened the white Styrofoam containers on the table to reveal masses of pancakes, hash browns, eggs, cinnamon rolls, bacon, and sausage. "Think I got enough?"

"How many you expecting to feed?" Sequoia asked. "The entire crew?"

"Just us." Brand waved them into seats and placed glasses of juice before them. "And Carter, though I'm willing to bet after the partying he did last night, he's not going to be much company today."

Rose's stomach grumbled, reminding her she hadn't eaten in over twenty-four hours. She spooned piles of food onto her plate. "Looks just about right to me. Come on, Tree. Dig in."

They'd all served themselves and were eating heartily when Carter stumbled onto the bus, his eyes red, his chin unshaven, his face pale.

"Looks like the living dead do exist," Sequoia murmured.

"Want some breakfast, Carter?" Brand asked.

Carter's complexion took on a slight green shade as he shook his head. "I think I'll just sleep a while longer." With a halfhearted attempt at a smile, he staggered over to a far couch and stretched out upon it. Within moments his light snores were the only sign of life.

"Just as well." Rose was anxious to share the idea she'd developed during her hours of early morning contemplation. "I think I know a way to solve my leaking magic."

She glanced over her shoulder as the driver came in, then set the bus in motion. "Will he hear us?" she whispered.

"Doubtful. It's pretty noisy in here," Brand said.

Sequoia spoke around a mouthful of hash browns. "What's your idea?"

"I've noticed that if several wishes are done close together, they become less accurate, sort of diluted." She clearly recalled her dress reappearing much shorter than it had started, and from the slow smile on Brand's face, so did he.

"What if the leakage has a finite amount of magic?" she continued.

Sequoia stopped eating. "Huh?"

"What if my magic has to build to a certain level to start leaking?" Rose built a dam with her pancakes, then poured syrup into the pool until it overflowed. "Right now, my magic is being pulled from me. I think each wish drains some of the backup off."

She spooned the syrup out of the pool. "One wish. Two wish. Three wish."

Brand nodded, watching her closely. "Go on."

"Perhaps by making several wishes in a row, you can drain my leaking magic out so that it won't work for a while." Rose couldn't contain the excitement in her voice. If this worked, she'd be able to operate almost normally for the duration of this story.

"For how long?" Sequoia asked.

"I don't know." Never having experienced anything like this before, Rose was operating on conjecture and slim logic. "I was thinking you could make a wish every hour after my magic stops working until it kicks in again. Then we'll know."

Brand lifted his glass to Rose. "That's actually a good idea."

"You don't have to sound so surprised." Rose wrinkled her nose at him. "If you're both willing, we could try it now. My guess is bigger wishes will drain it faster than smaller wishes."

Sequoia frowned. "What's the difference?"

"A big wish is something like sending that family to Disney World. I felt that power leave me. A small wish is something like . . . say, wishing for Aunt Lizzie's coffee cake."

"Oh, yes." Sequoia practically drooled. "My mom's coffee cake. I wish for Mom's coffee cake, fresh from the oven, right here, right now."

Rose barely felt the pull at her magic, but the item appeared on the table, steam rising from the pan. Sequoia didn't hesitate to dig into it. "Oh, Lord, it's warm."

Rose didn't hesitate to follow her cousin's lead. Her aunt's coffee cake was exceptional and requested for every family gathering. But Rose had missed many family gatherings in the past few years.

She closed her eyes at the explosion of butter and cinnamon on her tongue. "Oh, my, it's heaven. Try some, Brand."

As he took a piece, she waved her sticky hand at him. "Your turn."

He shook his head. "I prefer to avoid making wishes."

The tone of his voice made Rose frown, but he didn't look as if he were angry with her. "Okay, then, Sequoia, go on."

"I wish for a pitcher of cold milk. Two percent. And three glasses."

As the pitcher and glasses appeared, Rose sighed. She was hardly feeling the effect of these wishes. "It's going to take forever at this rate."

"Then we'll count how many small wishes it takes." Sequoia continued to make simple requests, but on her fourth try she only received eight red roses instead of the dozen she'd wished for.

Her fifth wish for a vase to put them in resulted in a shapeless lump of glass, and her sixth wish went unanswered, as Rose expected when she felt absolutely nothing tug at her.

"Well, now we know." Rose beamed. It had worked. Six small wishes could deplete the backlog. "Now you can make a wish every hour until it comes true so we know how long it takes to build up again."

"Very clever, Rose."

Brand's approval warmed Rose. It had been a long time since he'd told her anything like that. "I had to come up with something. It was too dangerous to run around leaking. Who knows what someone could wish for?"

"Exactly." Brand met her gaze, the intensity of his reminding her of his concern last night. "Now you should be safe."

"As well as everyone around me." She grinned and his answering smile spoke more clearly than words. He understood. He cared.

Her internal alarm went off as something soft weakened her defenses. *Danger. Danger.* This wouldn't do.

Lowering her gaze, Rose devoted herself to her plate. "Yum. Good."

With the meal finished and the table cleaned, they all retired to the easy chairs and couch, groaning about how much they'd eaten. "I think Carter has the right idea." Brand stretched out on the couch.

"Slug," Rose muttered, envying him the couch. She couldn't sprawl nearly as comfortably in the chair.

"It's going to be a long drive to Dallas. Why not sleep through some of it?" With that, he closed his eyes.

"Actually that sounds great." Sequoia was petite enough to fit in her chair, but even with trying to tuck her feet beneath her, Rose couldn't relax enough to sleep.

"Fine, you guys go ahead and sleep without me," she muttered.

Brand cracked open one eye. "Want to share?" He pushed against the back of the couch leaving a sliver of space beside him.

For a moment Rose was tempted. To feel his hardness against her again, to smell the scent of his aftershave, to touch . . . She shook her head vehemently. "I'll be fine right here."

His crooked smile twisted her gut. "Coward. Suit yourself."

Closing his eyes again, he drifted off into rhythmic breathing, Sequoia only a minute ahead of him. Rose grimaced, set her watch for one hour, then stared out the window, struggling to keep her gaze off Brand's slumbering form.

Even asleep, he was handsome, with a relaxed innocence that reminded her of the boy he'd once been— loyal, caring, steadfast with a total devotion to the art of illusion. What fates had directed that desire in his life? Had they known she would one day develop the power he longed for?

She yawned, smothering it with her palm. Had the fates ordained that she would lose her best friend over something neither of them could control?

Stupid fates.

She yawned again, then slept.

Her watch alarm woke her up, jarring her from the fringes of a dream she wanted to rediscover. Jabbing the alarm into silence, she went to shake Sequoia.

"Hey, Tree. Time for a wish."

"Go 'way," her cousin mumbled.

"Come on. Just one quick wish."

"I wish Ewan was here." Sequoia rolled onto her side and retreated into a slumber again while Rose stared at her.

Thank goodness that wish hadn't come true. They were better off without Titania's messenger in their midst. No doubt he was off conjuring up some sort of spell to trick Rose to return with him.

Or he was planning to use Sequoia to force Rose into compliance.

Rose narrowed her eyes. Tonight she'd have a long talk with her cousin and clear up this infatuation. Ewan was bad news and Sequoia needed to realize that.

After a couple of hours Brand and Sequoia awakened, though Carter continued to snooze away. As the bus covered the miles to their destination, Brand, Sequoia, and Rose reminisced over their childhood days, pausing each hour to let Sequoia make some crazy wish.

At six hours and counting since last magic, nothing yet had happened, which thrilled Rose. The longer, the better. She'd be able to attend Brand's show now without fear of her magic being used.

Sequoia sighed and gazed out the window at the passing scenery. "I'm already getting tired of being on this bus. Can we stop for dinner, Brand?"

"Definitely. I expect we'll reach Dallas about midday tomorrow. We'll pull in somewhere tonight for a rest."

Rose stood and stretched. "At least the bus is comfy. It could be worse."

"Oh, I know." Sequoia gave a wry grin. "I just don't like the riding part of it. I want to be where I'm going now."

Brand chuckled. "Some things never change."

"Hey, I used to get car sick, you know. I've never enjoyed driving." She sighed. "I just wish we were there now instead of having to drive for another day."

Rose felt the pull on her magic even before the driver cried out, "What the hell?"

They all turned toward him. "What is it, Gary?" Brand asked.

"Last sign I saw said Dallas six hundred twenty-seven miles. This one says ten miles. That can't be."

Brand and Rose exchanged glances. It could very well be. As one they focused on Sequoia.

She grimaced. "Oh, crap."

Eleven

"I guess six hours is the time limit, then," Rose muttered. A simpler wish would have worked better, but at least now she knew. "You'd better wish us back to where we were, Tree, or Gary is going to discover he really is that close to Dallas."

"I'm sorry. I didn't think." Sequoia grimaced. "I wish we were back on the highway where we were when I wished us here."

Rose knew without looking that the wish hadn't worked. She hadn't felt even a tiny pull and that constituted a major wish. "We're in trouble. You used all the magic that had built up with that one wish."

"I don't even want to try to explain this," Brand said.

"I don't think you can." For once, Rose wished she had more magic leaking. "But we'd better come up with something. A rift in space, perhaps?"

Brand sent her a dry look and she shrugged. There was no rational explanation for covering over six hundred miles in a minute.

"Now what's going on?" Gary exclaimed.

"What?" Brand went up to stand by the driver.

"Looks like I'm where I was a minute ago. Sign says six hundred twenty-seven miles."

Rose glanced out the window. The tall buildings of Dallas had disappeared from the distance and the mile markers were more what she expected to see. They'd reverted back to their original position. But how? She hadn't felt any pull on her magic.

When Brand glanced at her, she shrugged. She hadn't done this. Who had?

"Must have been a practical joke, Gary." Brand patted the driver's shoulder, then came back to join Sequoia and Rose. "What happened?"

"I happened."

Rose gasped as Ewan appeared beside Sequoia. "Was this not the solution you sought?"

Sequoia beamed a radiant smile at him. "It is. Thank you, Ewan."

As he presented an egotistical bow, Rose noted he'd changed his clothing yet again, but to something far more normal than a gangster's zoot suit. He now wore typical blue jeans, T-shirt, and tennis shoes, the ordinary clothing only enhancing his Faeness even more. He radiated magic and sensuality that even she noticed. No wonder Sequoia was infatuated with him.

"Yes, thank you, Ewan," Rose added, succeeding in diverting his gaze from her cousin.

"Experimenting with your magic, eh?" he asked as he lowered himself into a nearby chair.

"Something like that."

"Not a bad idea. I doubt Titania expected you to handle it this way."

Rose sank onto the couch and leaned forward. "That's because Titania doesn't have the first idea of who I am. She snaps her fingers and all you minions leap to obey, never questioning whether she's right or not."

Ewan tensed. "I am not a minion. I am Fae."

"Same thing."

Sparks lit Ewan's eyes and Rose drew back. Okay, maybe she'd gone a bit too far. Before the faery could speak, Brand sat beside Rose and reached out to clasp Ewan's hand.

"I forgot to thank you for what you did for Rose," Brand said. "It means a lot to me."

"It was important to Sequoia." Ewan locked gazes with Rose. "Which is the only reason you are now alive. Have you no sense? Even foolish pixies know not to give away their life force."

She winced. "I didn't know I could give it away. I missed Faery 101."

"If you would come to the magical realm, you would learn many things you do not know."

"No." Rose drew in a breath and tried again in a calmer voice. "It's not that I don't appreciate what you did for me, Ewan, but I don't want to go. There is nothing there for me."

"Yet there is here?"

Rose waved her hand at Sequoia and Brand. "I have my family, my friends, my work. Those are all important to me."

"And in a millenium when they are all gone, what then?"

Pain pierced Rose's heart. She didn't want to think about a future in which all those she cared about aged and died. Part of being Fae was being immortal. Even Robin Goodfellow had been gifted with it, despite being half-human, before he gave up all his magic to be with Brand's mother.

"I'll deal with that then," she said, hating how her voice shook slightly.

Brand took Rose's hand and squeezed it—a simple gesture that chased away the chills of the future while Sequoia touched Ewan's shoulder.

"We have a deal, remember, Ewan?" Sequoia asked.

His eyes gleamed. "I remember and await my next lesson. Tonight, perhaps?" His tone alluded to horizontal activities that had Rose ready to slap him, but her cousin lifted her chin defiantly.

"Definitely tonight. I'm taking you on a walk through town."

Ewan frowned. "How will that teach me about love?"

"You'll see." Sequoia settled into the chair beside him with a smug grin.

"Are you sure you want to do that, Tree?" Rose didn't trust Ewan alone with her cousin.

"Very sure." The sparkle in Sequoia's eyes promised a dire fate for Ewan, easing Rose's fears. Perhaps Sequoia wasn't as affected as Rose had assumed. "I can handle Ewan. Don't worry about me."

"What, me, worry?" Rose responded.

"I didn't say not to worry at all." A wicked grin crossed Sequoia's face. "You'll be stuck with Brand, after all."

Rose made a flippant gesture with her hand to disguise the sudden drop in her belly. "Oh, that's not a problem."

"You sure about that?" Brand asked, his voice rough, a hint of a smile on his lips.

Meeting his mischievous gaze, Rose forced a brilliant smile. "Of course."

But suddenly she wasn't so sure at all.

Perfect. Sequoia surveyed the tree-lined streets of the small town where they'd taken rooms for the night. With luck, she'd find good examples here to show Ewan.

She glanced at him, standing beside her, too good-looking to be true. Mostly because he wasn't true, not in her world. He belonged in fairy tales and dreams.

Especially her dreams, where he'd played a major role lately.

"Come on. Let's walk." She nudged him into movement, leading the way toward the small park she'd spotted as the bus passed through town.

Evening crept through the trees, the light fading, the air gathering the slight chill that hinted at an approaching winter. Leaves of gold and brown still clung to the trees, slowly losing their battle to remain a while longer. Those that had already fallen crunched beneath her feet as she and Ewan walked along the sidewalk, adding to the unique scent and sounds of autumn.

"What am I supposed to see?" Ewan asked.

"I'm not exactly sure." Sequoia shot him a grin. "But I'll know when I see it."

He only shook his head, but luck was with her. As soon as they entered the park, she spotted an elderly couple walking hand-in-hand. Though they didn't speak to each other, they still managed to communicate in a single look, a nod of the head.

"See them?" she told Ewan. "That's love that's endured, grown stronger for weathering what life has to offer."

"I see no love, only ancient mortals soon to return to nature."

Sequoia sighed. "You're trying to be deliberately dense, aren't you?"

His expression didn't change, but she thought she detected a hint of mischief in his eyes. "What do you mean?"

"Watch them." She turned to do so. "See how comfortable they are with each other. Can you feel the affection between them? Notice how he watches where they walk and leads her around cracks that might make her stumble."

"And this is love?" Ewan sounded dubious at best.

"It's part of it. Love is a bond between two people, between many people, that endures no matter what happens. If she were to return to nature, as you put it, he wouldn't love her any less. He'd keep his love and her memory alive in his heart."

Ewan placed his hand over his chest. "You make this simple heart out to be more than just a physical organ."

"Because it *is* more." How could she make him understand? "Loving someone can bring you more joy—and sometimes more pain—than anything else in this world."

"Pain?"

"To lose someone you love can bring physical pain. You can't touch them anymore, can't talk to them. It leaves a hole in your life that can never be filled, not in the same way." Remembering how she'd felt when the only grandfather she'd known had died brought tears to her eyes. "Yet because you loved them, a bit of them remains alive inside you. They're never completely gone." Even now, she could still recall the licorice bits he kept in his pocket and the scent of his favorite pipe tobacco.

"Would you feel pain if I went away?" Ewan asked abruptly.

Sequoia shot him a puzzled look. "Some," she admitted. She liked him. Despite his arrogance, he did make life interesting.

"And would you remember me?"

"I doubt I'll ever forget you." Her adventure with him would be a tale for her grandchildren.

He stopped and faced her. "Then you love me?"

His words sent a stone plummeting to her stomach. "I can't." She answered quickly without thought, afraid to examine that question. "I don't even know you."

"Yet you just said I meet the criteria you laid out for love."

His logic made her want to scream. "There's more to it than that. Love is more than physical attraction and kisses. It's knowing another person—good and bad—and still caring." She placed her palm over her chest. "Who they are inside."

She stared at him. Did she know who he was? A magical man, of course, and sexy as sin, but kind despite his attempts to be macho and overbearing. He made her laugh, made her feel more intensely than she'd ever experienced before. She enjoyed his company. Worse, she actually liked him.

He remained quiet as well, apparently considering her words. When he spoke again, he surprised her. "And who are you inside, Sequoia? I know you are a woman who cares about a great many people. Are you more than that?"

"I hope so." Sequoia paused. Who was she? "I enjoy the illusions Brand has taught me. I think I could be good at it if I practiced more. But my parents want me to go to college and get a degree in something 'worthwhile.' "

"Do you not wish to go?"

"Not really. I like what I'm doing. Brand is a great boss, the job is fun, and I get to travel." But she was sometimes lonely, not that she'd admit that. Many a night alone in another anonymous hotel room, she'd stared at the city lights and wondered if there was something more she was missing.

"Can you not tell your parents that?"

She smiled wryly. "I've tried. They think I'm going through a phase. No matter how famous Brand is, they want me to be more than his assistant."

"Why?"

"Because they love me, they want what's best for me."

"But is it best for you?"

Sequoia had to laugh. "I wish I knew."

Ewan resumed walking. "I am certain I will never comprehend love. It is too complex and illogical."

"True enough, Spock." Sequoia stopped abruptly, her gaze caught by the sight of angry flames leaping into the air in the distance. "Fire. Come on, Ewan."

She ran toward the flames, not waiting to see if Ewan followed. Had the fire department been called? She hadn't heard sirens recently. Or had she been too wrapped up in Ewan to not notice? Did someone need help?

A two-story house on a corner opposite the park was on fire, flames reaching greedy fingers out the windows and through the roof. Two fire trucks were set up with hoses aimed at the blaze, but as far as Sequoia could tell, the water wasn't doing much good yet. Even from across the street, she could feel the heat.

"Oh my God!" She pointed to a window on the second story, where a fireman stood, a small child cradled in his arms. "How can anyone still be alive in that?"

"He will never make it out safely," Ewan said with a calmness that made her want to hit him. "The fire is shooting out around his ladder."

Flames shot out of lower story windows, arcing through the ladder spokes. No way the fireman could descend safely. "They have a net thing, don't they?" But she didn't notice one being set up.

"Catch the kid."

She heard the fireman's shout and gasped as he tossed the child to the ground. Two firefighters caught the child safely and hustled it away from the house.

Sequoia's heart filled her throat. What now? She took a step forward, wanting to do something, anything, but Ewan placed his hand on her shoulder.

"You cannot help."

"But he'll die." She couldn't look away from the man in that window.

"Why did he go inside when it was so dangerous?"

"Because that's what firemen do," she snapped. "They care about people and risk their lives for them on a routine basis."

"Even people they cannot possibly know?"

"Usually people they don't know." She drew in a sharp breath as the fireman swung his legs out the window. He was going to jump. The distance wasn't horrible, but he'd break something at the least. "Oh, no."

She brought her hands to her mouth to hold in the sharp cry that wrenched from her lungs as he leaped toward the ground. He fell swiftly, then abruptly slowed until his descent more resembled a gentle elevator ride. As he touched the soil with a slight bump, he glanced up to where he'd been.

"If that don't beat all!" he exclaimed.

"Looks like your guardian angel is working overtime, Matt," another man said, slapping Matt on the shoulder. "Damnedest thing I ever saw."

A bubble of joy filled Sequoia as she whirled on Ewan

and threw her arms around his neck. "You did that!"

He staggered back a couple steps before he balanced himself, wrapping his arms around her. "It seemed important to you."

"It was. Thank you, Ewan. Thank you." She kissed him with enthusiasm, giving free reign to the rush of passion he incited. He'd saved the fireman for her. Her heart swelled. Had anyone ever done anything just for her?

He quickly took advantage of the situation and claimed ownership of the kiss, of her, his hands lifting her bottom to nestle her firmly against him. She had no doubt of his desire with the physical evidence pressed against her belly and was rapidly giving in to her own beneath his sensuous mouth.

When he left her lips, she moaned, wanting more, then shivered with delight as he nipped her earlobe and whispered words she didn't understand, yet their meaning was perfectly clear. Excitement, heat, and need mixed with something far more dangerous, weaving through her gut until the realization made her cry out.

"Dear Lord, I think I do love you." How could this happen? She wanted to rationalize and couldn't. Nothing about the man was rational.

He paused and caressed the side of her face, his gaze piercing and dark. "Then show me."

They were in her hotel room, which didn't surprise her, though the force of the contained passion in the tiny area did. He radiated sex, and her body, her will responded.

She brought his mouth back to hers. "Yes."

I should have gone with Sequoia. Rose shifted the pizza box she carried from one hand to the other as she stood before the room to Brand's hotel room, trying to convince herself to knock.

She shouldn't be doing this. She knew better. It was dangerous, it was foolish, it was asking for trouble. She'd told herself she needed to explain things to Brand, but truth was she enjoyed his company, wanted to be with him, but what then? "This is insane."

She started to turn away, but the door opened as Brand prepared to step outside. Rose jumped, then managed a smile. "Pizza?"

His eyes, usually the main clue to his feelings, were masked, and he hesitated long enough to bolster her doubts.

"Forget it." She stepped back. "Stupid idea."

"No." He caught her free hand. "I like pizza." Pushing the door wide open, he guided her inside.

Rose swallowed, but went, feeling very similar to the fly heading for the spider's web. "Everything but anchovies," she added.

"My favorite."

Of course, she'd remembered.

This room was much less luxurious than the one in St. Louis, so they ended up placing the pizza box on the bed and sitting cross-legged beside it to eat.

After devouring one slice, Brand paused. "Why did you come here, Rose?"

She considering his question, unable to find a satisfactory answer. At least not one she'd admit to. "Stupidity," she said finally.

He grinned. "I'm not going to argue that."

She wrinkled her nose at him, then continued. "And I want us to talk. Really talk." Something she hadn't realized until that moment. "I don't want to go through the rest of my life knowing you hate me."

"I don't hate you," he said slowly.

"Detest me, then. At best, envy me." When he remained silent, she grimaced. "I don't think you ever realized how much you hurt me when you quit being my friend. That made me feel even more freakish than I already did."

"Freakish?" His head snapped up. "You had magic, power."

"I had a gift that I had no idea how to control; that frightened the hell out of me. When I needed you the most to help me, ground me like you always had, you weren't there." To her horror, her eyes began to water, and she slid off the bed to pace the floor. Even now the memories still had the power to hurt. "Oh, damn."

"I was crazy with jealousy, Rose." Brand didn't move. "All of a sudden you had everything I've always wanted without even asking for it."

"That's right." She whirled to face him. "I didn't ask for it, yet somehow it was still all my fault."

"Not all your fault." Brand met her gaze, his brilliant green eyes sober. "I gave equal credit to my father. Can you imagine how betrayed I felt when I learned he'd once been Fae, that he'd given up everything for my mother?"

"He adores your mother. Even a blind man could see that." After nearly thirty years of marriage, Brand's parents could be spokespersons for enduring love. Rose crossed her arms. "So you believe magic is more important than love?"

"I believe love is highly overrated. It makes a man do things he later regrets."

Good thing she'd learned this now. It made controlling her attraction all the more easy. "I don't think your father regrets anything."

"He's a fool if he doesn't. Look at what he gave up."

Rose stalked toward the door. "You're the fool." She'd hoped that they could clear the air, resolve their differences, but that was not going to happen. Not while magic was the be-all and end-all for him.

He moved swiftly to block her exit. "Damn it, Rose. I have Fae blood in my veins. Why couldn't I have the magic?"

"Do you think I wouldn't give it to you if I could? It doesn't work that way. I can give you some abilities, like flying, but I can't transfer all that makes up my magic." She raised her chin. "What do you want from me?"

"Oh, God." His groan was deep. "I want more than I should even dream about. I want you, Rose."

"No, you don't." She evaded his outstretched hand.

"You want the magic like everyone else. That's all you see. That's all you care about."

"I see you." Angry sparks lit his eyes. The line of his mouth was grim.

"Hardly. If you knew me, you wouldn't have quit being my friend. You wouldn't resent me for something that's no fault of mine." She swallowed the thick lump in her throat. "If you really saw me, you'd know why I have to do this exposé. I've never used magic to write any of them. My *knowledge* of magic, but nothing more. I've worked hard, done honest labor to earn a spot on this magazine, and this story means a promotion. For once in my life, I'll have something I've earned with no magic involved."

"Rose . . ."

She shook her head. "If you knew me at all, you'd know that, Brand. Instead, you assumed I used my abilities to obtain my information. How could I do anything else? Right?"

Two tears fell to the carpet, turning at once into gleaming opals. Rose yanked open the door, detesting her display of weakness, but Brand caught her arm.

"I want to understand," he murmured, pain etched across his rugged features.

"You never will." How could he? "Not until you can realize what it's like to be a faery in a world full of mortals." She tugged her arm free and hurried away. "And *I* can't even do that."

Twelve

Sequoia snuggled against Ewan's shoulder, her body still humming with the aftereffects of excellent lovemaking. She'd heard the legends of the Fae being superb lovers, and now she knew it to be truth. "That was wonderful," she murmured.

"Yes, it was." Ewan sounded surprised, and Sequoia raised up on her elbow to peer down into his face.

"You don't have to sound so shocked. What's the matter? Didn't expect it to be so good with a mere mortal?"

"I have never made love with a mortal before, so I had no expectations." He ran his finger over her bare shoulder, triggering a shiver of delight.

"And?" Was he disappointed? *Don't let him say so even if he was.*

"It was very different."

Talk about bursting a person's bubble. Sequoia sat up now, wrapping the sheet around her. "Different, how? Different good or different bad?"

"I cannot say." He scooted into a sitting position as well, proud, comfortable, and too damned sexy in his nudity. "There were sensations."

"Oh, boy, were there." Though Ewan wasn't her first lover, he was bound to be her last, for no one could hope to compare with him. "Did you see fireworks, too? I'd always thought that was just a stupid phrase."

"No. Yes. That is not what I mean." He frowned as if struggling to put his thoughts into words. "There were . . . feelings I am not accustomed to."

Sequoia couldn't stop her smug smile. "Maybe you're learning how to care, how to love." Which would serve him right for making her fall in love with him.

He drew back sharply. "More likely I was missing the magical stimulation two Fae share during lovemaking."

"Oh." Her heart plummeted to her stomach, and she slid from the bed, tucking the sheet more firmly around herself, feeling strangely vulnerable. A first for her. "I'm so sorry to disappoint you. Maybe you ought to return to the magical realm so you can make love to a faery."

"Is that your plan?"

"What?" As she turned to face him, he left the bed, magnificent in his nakedness, stirring the smoldering embers within her.

"Your declaration of love, your sacrifice of your body was your way to send me back to my home."

Sacrifice of her body? She sure hadn't looked at it that way. Rolling her eyes, Sequoia shook her head. "Yeah, right." Was he really that naive?

"As I suspected." His eyes darkened. "I have been warned never to trust a mortal. I allowed myself to forget that. It will not happen again."

He was serious. She stepped toward him. "Ewan, I didn't . . ."

Once again he disappeared, leaving her alone.

Damn the man. How could a person have a decent argument if he kept doing that?

Sequoia wrapped her arms around herself. "He'll be back." She wasn't sure if she was saying the words aloud to make them true or because she believed it.

She straightened her spine. "He'll be back."

• • •

Rose shifted in her theater seat the next night. The remainder of the ride to Dallas had been strangely quiet. Even Sequoia had been subdued. And now Brand's performance was off.

As Rose watched his evening show, she found it easier to concentrate on discovering his secrets. Most of the audience didn't appear to notice, but she could tell his energy and charm were dimmed from his earlier presentations. Had their argument affected him as well?

She knew she'd been unable to concentrate, to think about anything but Brand's delicious kisses and the way he made her want. Lord help her, she wanted.

Rose shook her head. This was not getting her article done. Forcing herself to focus, she discovered how Brand managed to walk through an apparent brick wall. He was good. If he'd been at his top form, she'd probably still be clueless.

When it came time for him to fly, she held her breath. Did the spell still work? It did and he soared above the audience to thunderous applause and total amazement. The smile he beamed to those below him was real for possibly the first time this night. It faltered briefly when his gaze met Rose's.

She responded with a weak smile and a thumbs-up. If she'd realized flying would make him so happy, she would have placed a spell on him years ago.

But he wouldn't have been ready then.

Even now, his acceptance of magic, of her power, was limited. Until he understood how much her magic was a part of her, he wouldn't ever be ready.

Rose sighed. The only good thing to come from this silly deal thus far was her own acceptance of her magic. Not using it brought home how much a part of her it was. She'd avoid using it until she had the story on Brand so he couldn't accuse her of cheating, then she'd be true to herself. She'd tried to deny it long enough, to deny that she was Fae, that she was anything like Titania.

But she *was* Fae. Nothing she could say or do would change that fact. Perhaps she should go with Ewan, visit the magical realm. Maybe she did fit in better there than here.

Or was she again trying to deny an unavoidable truth?

Meeting Brand's heated gaze as he returned to the stage, she grimaced. Such as the way he made her feel?

With the show over, Rose waited for the crowd to thin before she tried to find Sequoia. They'd decided to visit a local club—just the two of them. No men.

Apparently Sequoia had finally come to her senses in regard to Ewan, but it had left a wound in her cousin's eyes. If that arrogant faery ever appeared again, Rose had a few choice words for him.

"Well, if it isn't Miss Thayer."

The sneer in the voice had Rose stiffening even before she turned to see who spoke. Recognizing the man only added to her tension, but she kept her tone even. "Peter Majestic. What a surprise to see you here. Checking up on your competition?"

"What competition? You put me out of business." His anger came through clearly now.

"You put yourself out of business." True, she'd written the article that exposed his more well-known illusions, but others had survived her exposés. "All you had to do was work up new material."

"Ha. What new material? By the time you're done, there won't be an illusion left to be accomplished."

Rose bit her tongue to keep from saying what she truly wanted to say. Peter Majestic had been going steadily downhill even before she wrote her exposé. He had made a brief splash over fifteen years ago with a single innovative illusion that had been swiftly duplicated by other magicians. Past fifty now, his looks fading, his talent never equal to that of Brand's, he needed a scapegoat to satisfy his ego. Obviously she was it.

"I'm doing my job," she said finally, dismissing him in tone and action by turning her back on him. Before she could go two steps, he snared her arm and jerked her to a halt.

She turned slowly, ensuring he felt the full force of her glare. This might end up being a knee to the groin she wouldn't regret. "I suggest you let go of me."

"I could sue you, you know. You ruined me."

She hesitated. Just how rational was he? "If I had written anything other than the truth, perhaps you'd have a case. As it is, you know you don't."

"You can't be sure of that."

"Yes, I can. If you had a case you would have sued me when I first wrote the exposé five years ago." Rose yanked her arm free of his hold. "Go away, Majestic. Whatever your problems, they have nothing to do with me."

She intended to stalk away, but this time he grabbed for her shoulder and ended up tearing the elbow-length sleeve on her dress. That did it. He was going to be in severe pain very shortly.

Before Rose could round on him with a carefully aimed knee, Brand appeared by her side and stepped between her and the faded magician. "Get the hell out of here, Pete."

Rose could feel the violence radiating from him. "I was handling it," she muttered.

He ignored her, his attention centered on the smaller man. "Go. Just because you're a has been is no reason to take it out on Rose."

Rage burned in Majestic's eyes. "You're protecting that bitch? You'll feel differently after she tells the world how you do that flying illusion."

Brand produced a sardonic grin. "Actually, I can pretty much guarantee that that's one illusion she won't reveal."

Rose grimaced. He had a point there.

A sneer crossed Majestic's face. "I see. She must be pretty damned good in bed, then."

Brand planted his fist into the man's jaw, knocking the magician to the floor, then towered over him, glaring down. "Get out of here. Now." Glancing up, he motioned for a distant security guard to come over.

Holding his hand against his face, Majestic climbed to his feet. "You'll be sorry, Goodfellow. She's just using you to get your secrets. You'll see."

Brand ignored him to glance at the guard. "Escort this person from the building, please."

The guard gripped Majestic's arm in a firm hold. "Yes, sir, Mr. Goodfellow."

Majestic left, but he called out a final comment over his shoulder. "You'll be sorry. You'll see."

His words echoed in the empty theater as Brand finally recognized Rose's presence. Her anger hadn't cooled at all. "Do you feel better now?" she asked. "All macho and stuff? Want to beat your chest?"

His eyes widened before he frowned. "I was trying to help you."

"I was handling it myself." How did Brand think she'd survived the past seventeen years without him?

"I thought you didn't want to use your magic."

She inhaled sharply. "Don't be a jerk." She looked away for a moment, attempting to rein in the urge to punch him, then impaled him with her worst stare. "Why do you assume I need magic? Am I incapable of taking care of myself? I've taken self-defense classes. I've faced worse idiots than him over the past few years and, you know, I haven't turned one of them into a toad yet."

His mouth set in the obstinate line she recognized all too well. "I'm not assuming anything. I thought you needed help."

"Well, I didn't." Spotting Sequoia in the hallway, Rose hurried toward her. "Let's get the hell out of here."

Her cousin glanced from Rose to Brand and produced a wry smile. "Sounds good to me."

"Where are you going?" Brand demanded.

Rose turned her head slowly and glared at him. "Not that it's any of your business, but we're going out."

"Where?"

She sent him an incredulous look, then turned away. That did not deserve an answer, but Sequoia replied anyway. "New nightclub—City Lights."

When Rose glanced at her cousin, Sequoia shrugged. "Well, he is my boss."

Rose shook her head. "He's a man and right now I'm fed up with all of them." Especially Brand Goodfellow. She couldn't decide which she wanted to do more—kiss him or kill him.

Sequoia fell into step beside her. "I'm all for that. To hell with men."

That about summed it up.

Three hours later Brand continued to pace the floor of his suite, only half-listening to the television set. His thoughts, as usual of late, centered on Rose. No other woman could drive him so crazy so quickly.

Try to help her and what did he get? Accusations and anger. Some thanks.

Okay, so she probably could have handled it. She was the most independent, infuriating woman he'd ever met. Once again he'd screwed up where Rose was concerned.

Brand slid open the patio door and stepped out into the warm night. A cool breeze kept it pleasant, disrupting the humidity enough to make it bearable. Lights dotted the area surrounding the hotel—businesses, malls, homes.

Normally after a performance such a sight would relax him, but not tonight. His concentration had been off and his show had suffered because of it. All because of Rose.

Damn her. In a matter of days she had managed to destroy all his carefully built control. Especially tonight. When he'd emerged from backstage to see Majestic rip her dress, Brand hadn't thought, he'd reacted.

Majestic should have been grateful Brand controlled his first impulse to pulverize the has-been, though Brand had needed precious little incentive to swing a satisfying punch at the man.

And it had felt good. He'd protected his woman.

Brand groaned. *His* woman? Where was his brain? Rose belonged to no one, and if he'd doubted that, she'd certainly cleared it up for him right away.

Yet the other magician's comment about Rose being good in bed had hit too close to home. Brand wanted her—in his arms and in his bed. Seventeen years hadn't changed his feelings nearly as much as he'd thought. She only had to reenter his life, and his hormones reacted as if he were still a teenager.

Brand stared into the darkness. He desired her with a ferocity that startled him. If he believed in such vagaries as fate he'd think they were destined to end up in bed together. But he knew better.

No matter what his more primal urges wanted, his common sense knew he and Rose could never be together. Her magic and his longing for it would always be between them.

With a sigh, Brand jammed his fingers through his hair and allowed himself to play a game of what if. What if Rose wasn't Fae? Would they have been a couple through high school? Beyond? Or would he have become bored with her? Moved on to another by now?

Somehow he doubted that. It was every other woman that he'd quickly grown tired of. But Rose had been adventurous and fascinating even before she'd grown into her magic. Every moment spent with her had been exciting.

Which was one thing that hadn't changed over the years. Even now he could truthfully say he hadn't experienced one dull moment since Rose's arrival.

A sudden rumbling in the distance caught his attention, and Brand straightened to examine it more closely. Screams echoed in the darkness as a large plume of dust rose, blotting out the lights. His breath caught as he sensed the terror out there. What was going on?

Where was it? Downtown to be certain, but from this height he couldn't make out any details. He stepped inside and switched the TV to a local station. Maybe they'd have something on.

He'd barely changed channels when a Special Bulletin screen flashed up. Within moments a young woman, her expression strained, appeared. "This just in," she said. "The roof at City Lights, a popular nightclub in downtown Dallas, has collapsed, burying the approximately two hundred customers within. Rescue crews are just now arriving on the scene."

She paused and touched her ear. "We have Paul Leonard at the scene of this tragedy. Go ahead, Paul."

The picture changed to a man standing in front of a half-standing building that looked far worse than what Brand had seen from his balcony. The man spoke, further highlighting the number feared trapped beneath the rubble, but Brand wasn't listening.

City Lights.

That was where Rose and Sequoia had gone.

Bone-chilling terror washed over him before he could move, then he dashed to the balcony to view the disaster. He had to do something. Save them.

He'd risen two feet off the balcony before he realized he had the power to fly there and help. He soared into the air, then stopped as his mind finally tempered his impulses.

Fly there? Flying within the confines of the theater could be explained. If someone saw him now, no explanation would suffice. And what could he do when he did reach the nightclub? The trained personnel had a better chance of saving someone than he did.

Yet the urge to be there, do something, gripped him. If anything happened to Rose or Sequoia . . .

Maybe they'd already returned.

He flew to the balcony of Rose's room and tried the door. Locked.

Not a problem.

Especially for an illusionist trained in escapes.

Within moments he was inside her dark hotel room.

Her scent—a mixture of flowers and freshness—filled the air, but he knew she wasn't there even before he searched the area. His throat tight, he returned to the balcony.

The dust still lingered in the distance, a vision of destruction against the black of night. It took little imagination to feel the collapsed building around him.

Brand wrapped his fingers around the rail, resisting the urge to soar into the sky. Was this what Rose had meant by the restrictions that came with her magic? He could fly, but at this moment he couldn't do anything with it. Had she felt this same frustration when she'd realized she couldn't cure a room full of sick children?

He'd always been so sure that she'd used her magic freely without thought of consequences, but had she really? Had he only noticed because he knew her secret? No one else at school had ever accused Rose of being different, of doing anything unexplainable. Had she actually been more circumspect than he'd imagined?

Closing his eyes, Brand tried to recall those painful days of high school. Had his jealousy magnified her magic use into more than it was? Aside from a few incidents, she'd been coping admirably without using her powers over the past several days.

Yet surely she'd use her magic to save herself and Sequoia. A sense of helplessness squeezed his chest as he stared at the growing dark cloud. But what if she'd hadn't had a chance? The announcer said the roof had collapsed. What if she'd been caught in that with no chance to react?

To hell with it.

Brand rose to the top of the railing. If someone saw him flying, he'd deal with it. Somehow. His fear wouldn't allow him to remain still. He had to do something.

With one foot in mid-air he froze. Was that the door? He pivoted, crouched, and waited.

Thirteen

Rose hesitated inside the door, her hand on the light switch. Something didn't feel right. She shook her head to clear the fogginess. Shouldn't have had that last drink.

Yet she couldn't shake the feeling that someone was there. She squinted at the patio door. Was it open?

She was about to back out of the room when a familiar masculine scent filtered in. "Brand?"

A shadowy figure stepped through the patio door. "Rose?"

Before she could respond, Brand crossed the room and pulled her into his arms, devouring her mouth with a fierce possessive kiss that sent her hormones into overdrive. With her defenses already giddy, she needed no excuse to respond.

Wrapping her arms around his neck, Rose answered in kind, her lips melding with his. Even sober she found Brand's kisses intoxicating. In her present state her passion flared high until all she could think about was touching him, wanting him.

The wildness of his kiss ignited an equal wildness

within her. She ached for him. Dear Lord, she wanted . . .
something . . . anything to ease this knot in her gut. Tugging his shirt up, she slid her hands over his back only to
have him abruptly break away, his breathing ragged.

Resting his hands on her shoulders, Brand leaned his
forehead against hers.

She wrapped her fingers around his arms and actually
whimpered. "Don't stop." She needed more of his diz-
zying kisses, more of Brand.

He shuddered and slowly lifted his head. Flames flared
in his eyes. "Thank God you're all right."

His words eventually penetrated her hazy consciousness. "Why wouldn't I be?"

"The club, City Lights, there's—"

"Oh, we didn't go there." She and Sequoia hadn't felt
like socializing with others. They'd wanted to get drunk
and commiserate about the men in their lives. "We stayed
in the bar downstairs. Good thing, too." She nodded
sagely. "Might not have made it home otherwise."

Brand's gaze grew more penetrating and he lifted her
chin. "What did you drink?"

"Coke, of course." It was the only beverage that could
make her light-headed. "I had four. And Tree polished off
a bottle of wine."

A slight smile framed his lips. "You're drunk."

"I'm not drunk," she protested. She pulled away from
him, then brought her hand to her head as the room
swayed in response. "Well, maybe a little."

"Is Sequoia in as bad a shape as you?"

Rose couldn't stop her grin. She, at least, had retained
enough sense to guide them to their room and pour her
cousin into bed.

"I take it from that goofy smile that Sequoia is drunk,
too," Brand said.

"Oh, she's worse." But they'd had a good time listing
Ewan's and Brand's faults, following each enumeration
with a drink. Caught up now in the tingling glow of

Brand's kiss, Rose couldn't remember a single fault she'd named.

She gave him what she hoped was her most beguiling smile. "Kiss me again. You do that so well."

"Do I?" He appeared pleased, but released a shuddering breath. "Sorry, Rose, I can't while you're like this."

"Like what?" She staggered to the middle of the room and stretched out her arms. "Unafraid to say what I think? Unafraid to admit you make me burn inside?"

"Oh, God." Brand's voice was deep and husky as he clenched his fists by his side. "Don't make this harder than it already is."

"Hard, is it?" She eyed his groin, barely visible in the darkness, but she'd felt the solidness pressed against her during their kiss. There were mysteries there that she understood logically, but had never experienced. Now, suddenly, she wanted to. "Make love to me, Brand."

He made a choking sound and hurried toward the patio. "I need to go."

"No, you don't." Rose stepped toward him, then frowned, realizing they were in her room, not his. "Wait a minute. Isn't this my room? What are you doing here?"

He paused on the balcony. "I was worried about you."

His words sent an irrational warmth surging through her. "Why?"

He motioned her onto the balcony, then turned her to face the pillar of dust in the distance. "A roof collapsed at City Lights. It buried people inside. I was afraid you and Sequoia were among them."

"Dear Lord." The sight of the dark cloud drifting skyward, the black plumes of dust visible against the night sky, brought a sobering clarity to her thoughts. People were dying there. "I need to do something."

Brand squeezed her shoulder. "I doubt there's anything you can do at this point."

Though he made sense, she couldn't ignore the tightening in her chest. "I can try."

"Not without endangering yourself, and I won't allow

that." The finality of his tone indicated his seriousness.

"Still . . ." To be helpless frustrated her. What was the good of having magic if she couldn't save lives?

"I understand." Brand massaged her shoulders. "I think I finally do understand what it's been like for you."

She turned slowly to face him. *Brand* was saying this? "How could you?"

"I wanted to fly there, to save you, and realized it wasn't that easy. I felt useless, frustrated."

He had no idea. "You've been able to fly for several days, and now you know all about me?"

"I said I understand now." A hint of anger lingered in his voice. Was he upset that she wasn't declaring this a marvelous insight?

Rose emitted a sound of disgust. "You understand one little piece of me, that's all. But there's so much more. No matter how many times I've told you, you still don't get it."

"I—"

Words burst forth after years of holding them in, coupled with resentment and irrational anger. "You can't know, Brand, what is was like to receive this power as a child, to be able to suddenly do . . . create anything I wanted. Talk about a kid in a candy store. I went crazy . . . did stupid things."

Brand grimaced. "I know."

The urge to hit him made her stalk back inside, but he followed her. "Do you?" she demanded. "Mom and Dad warned me that I had to keep it a secret or else there would be consequences. I had magic I had to hide. I had a secret I couldn't share."

She drew in a shaky breath. "Do you know how terrified I was in the beginning when a simple sneeze could make something magical happen? How could I guard against that?" She'd stayed close to home for months, avoided her friends and activities until she'd finally learned to control her power.

"Apparently you managed," Brand said dryly.

"Yeah, I managed. What choice did I have?" She met his gaze, tilting her chin. "But I couldn't escape the fact that I was suddenly different, someone to be avoided. After all, you were my best friend and you left me, detested me."

He winced at that. "It was hard for me to accept, Rose."

"For me, too." She sighed. "But the worst part was the apathy that came a few years later. Everything came too easily. How could I feel worthwhile when I never really accomplished anything? I could have whatever I wanted and it wasn't enough."

"Rose—"

"Try to imagine being told never to get involved with anyone because I was fated to live forever . . . alone forever." Despair she usually managed to keep at bay claimed her now, her tears falling into a pile of opals on the carpet. "I can't die, but for a while there I wanted to. What good was a future without family, without friends, without any sense of true worth?"

Brand extended his hand to touch her, but she moved away, giving him her back. "God, Rose, I didn't know."

"You didn't care." She'd needed his friendship, his approval, so badly and never received it. "If not for Sequoia, I don't know what I would have done." But her cousin had convinced her that she did have a future worth exploring, goals to strive toward.

"I went to college," Rose continued. "I earned a degree in journalism using my mind, not magic. The way I felt on graduation day when I received that diploma was far more exciting than any amount of magic. I had accomplished something on my own."

She faced him again. "I wrote my first exposé based on what I knew about magic, what I'd learned, what I saw and heard. I used no Fae magic in obtaining that story— not then, not ever." The dubious look on Brand's face spiked her anger. Hadn't she told him this already? Why couldn't he believe her?

"That's why I write these stories, why the promotion

I'll get after this exposé is important to me. I'll have earned it. My magic is a part of who I am. I can't escape that and I don't know that I want to. But it's not all I am."

"I know that."

"I doubt it. All you see is the magic. Else you never would have deserted me."

Sparks danced in his eyes. "You're never going to forgive me for that, are you?"

"Why should I? You've never forgiven me for being different." She yawned, suddenly exhausted. The Coke was catching up with her. "I'm tired. Go away, Brand."

Thank goodness the bed was close. She fell facedown upon it and closed her eyes.

And sank deep into the oblivion of sleep.

Brand hesitated when he spotted Rose and Sequoia outside the hotel entrance the next morning. Though Rose showed no outward sign of the previous night's partying, Sequoia looked like an illusion gone bad. Her normally tanned skin was pale, accentuating the dark circles beneath her eyes. She moved cautiously like someone testing a limb after removal of a cast.

He grinned. They had a show that night and he had the feeling it was going to be a very long day for his assistant. Yet Rose displayed no unease or ill health. Another benefit of her Fae blood, undoubtedly.

Frowning, Brand approached them. She'd given him a lot to think about last night, and he'd spent most of the night going over her words, hating the truth in them. But he still hadn't reached any conclusion. Knowing more of what life was like for Rose didn't magically make his yearning for it go away.

"Good morning," he said with a bright grin that only broadened when Sequoia shuddered.

"You deserve to be shot," she muttered.

"For wishing you good morning?"

"For yelling it at me."

Brand glanced at Rose, keeping his smile in place. "I didn't think I was yelling."

To his relief, she returned his smile. "In her world you are."

Sequoia groaned. "This is so unfair. I know I had a really good time last night, but I don't remember much of it at all."

"Might not want to finish the bottle next time," Brand said.

The look she gave him could make a man walk through walls without the benefit of illusion. "I am never going to drink again."

Rose laughed and hugged her cousin. "How many times have I heard that through the years?"

"I mean it this time."

Rose guided Sequoia toward the intricate gardens beside the hotel. "Just wish yourself better." She darted a look at Brand when he fell into step beside them. "We were going off to do some small wishes and drain the buildup."

He nodded. If Rose insisted on maintaining her part of the deal, keeping her magic from leaking was a good thing.

"Won't that kind of wish hurt you?" Sequoia asked Rose.

"Healing a headache isn't anywhere close to curing cancer," Rose said. "Go ahead."

"I wish I didn't have a hangover and felt normal." Sequoia missed a step and they paused as she brought her hand to her forehead. "It's gone. Just like that."

"Good." Rose patted her cousin's shoulder. "Now maybe you won't be so grouchy."

Sequoia narrowed her gaze. "How come you don't have a hangover? From what little I remember you were feeling no pain, either."

Brand grinned. He wondered when she'd come to this realization.

"I wasn't." Rose's gaze darted to Brand, then away.

Obviously she did remember something of what she'd said last night. "But I have a faster processing metabolism."

"Unfair," Sequoia muttered.

"Talk about unfair." Rose resumed her stroll. "Who can eat an entire box of chocolates and not gain an ounce? Not me."

"That's different."

Brand shook his head. "I have to agree with Rose. I've seen you put enough food away to feed the entire crew, and you're still a little bit of nothing."

"Fine." Sequoia stomped a short distance ahead.

Rose sighed. "Make wishes, Tree."

"Make wishes," Sequoia repeated. "I never thought that kind of request would become a nuisance."

Brand caught sight of the flicker of pain that crossed Rose's face, a pain that echoed in his chest. "Sequoia," he murmured with a note of warning.

"You don't have to make wishes," Rose added.

Sequoia turned, her eyes wide and threw her arms around Rose. "I'm sorry, Rose. I didn't mean that the way it sounded. I'm just not very creative when it comes to that type of thing."

"Not creative?" Brand raised his eyebrows, wondering if the wine had mutated Sequoia. "This from a woman who asks for a peanut butter, banana, and marshmallow-cream sandwich?"

"Hey, they're good." Sequoia wrinkled her nose at him, then gazed into Rose's face. "You okay?"

"I'm fine, but if you wish for one of those I won't be."

"Well." Sequoia lifted her nose to the sky. "I wish for a Daryl McCall CD." When the item appeared in her hand, she glanced at it. "I have this one."

"Then be more specific."

"I wish for the Daryl McCall *Revelations* CD." When it appeared, she smiled at Rose. "Thank you."

"Anything else?" Rose asked.

They resumed walking along the wide cobblestone path

lined with trees. Though mid-morning, not many others were around them. A good thing, too.

"I don't know."

"What about your nails?" Brand asked. Maybe then he wouldn't have to listen to Sequoia complain before every show about how ragged her fingernails were.

Her face brightened. "Good idea. I wish my fingernails were always this length and unchippable and filed and buffed." She extended her hand to examine her nails. "Awesome."

A mother and her son approached, and Brand stepped onto the grass to allow them room on the path. "There's no such thing as dragons, Jeremy," the mother said.

"That stinks," he muttered. "That one in the movie was so cool."

"They're fictional like elves or fairies."

As Rose giggled, Brand shot her a grin. Fiction wasn't always all it was cracked up to be.

"I wish dragons were real," the boy said with a sigh. "It would be totally awesome."

"Oh, shit," Rose muttered.

Before Brand could question her change of attitude, the reason became clear. A small dragon appeared on the grass near them, gleaming gold and green in the sunlight, its scales brilliant, its eyes luminescent. Fortunately it was only the size of a husky and appeared as surprised to be there as they were to see it.

"Mom, look at that!" the boy exclaimed.

"Oh, Lord, how do I explain this?" Rose whispered.

"I'll handle it." Brand stepped forward. She didn't have to be alone with her magic any longer. "Allow me to introduce myself," he said to the mother and child. "I'm Brand Goodfellow, magician. The dragon you think you see is merely an illusion I'm working on."

"An illusion?" the mother echoed.

He nodded. "Appears real, doesn't it?"

"For sure," the boy said.

Hearing Rose snort behind him, Brand glanced at her. "What?"

Mischief danced in her eyes. "Your illusion just set a trash can on fire."

Brand pivoted to see the dragon sneeze, emitting a single stream of flame that thankfully disintegrated before it reached anything flammable. "I'm going to tackle it." He couldn't allow the creature to run loose.

"I'll help." Rose placed herself opposite him as they circled the dragon.

"No magic left?" Brand had to ask, though he already suspected the answer. After all, the boy had wished for a dragon. Receiving a miniature version was enough to show the diminishing strength of Rose's power.

"Not for wishes." She grimaced. "I'll have to use my magic myself."

"Look out." Brand leaped on the dragon as it charged toward Rose. Wrapping his arms around the thick neck, he hung on as the creature fought with the fierceness of a bucking bull. Unfortunately, Brand was a magician, not a cowboy. He flew from the dragon, skidding across the grass before he finally crashed into a bush.

Rose rushed to his side. "Are you all right?"

The concern in her voice mirrored that in her face, and Brand's chest tightened. This woman was definitely doing things to him. "I think so." He tested each limb before climbing to his feet.

"Are you sure that's an illusion?"

Brand jerked around as the mother spoke. Damn, they were still here. He forced a smile. "Just working out the bugs. Stay back now."

"Need help?"

At the already too familiar accent, Brand focused on Ewan as he appeared beside a tree. The faery dressed more like them now in jeans and a T-shirt, but he still looked Fae. Nothing could change that bone structure or those penetrating eyes.

"Ewan." The joy in Sequoia's voice alarmed Brand.

The last thing he neede was his assistant getting mixed up with this crazy faery.

She stepped toward Ewan, then paused. "Can you help?"

Ewan bowed with a sweep of his arm. "It would be my pleasure." He murmured a few words, and the dragon vanished from where it was munching on a bush.

Brand released a sigh of relief in tandem with Rose, and they grinned at each other. Ewan could come in handy when he wasn't being annoying.

Hearing applause behind him, Brand whirled around to see his audience hadn't left. Producing his most charming grin, he pulled two tickets for his show from his pocket—a habit he was glad he'd formed—and handed them to the mother. "Thank you. It needs work yet, but you can see what else I'm doing by coming to my performance tonight."

"That would be wonderful. Thank you." The mother eyed the tickets with delight. "We'll be there."

The boy asked a few more questions, but soon they left, enthusiastic about coming to the show. "You do good work, Brand," Rose said, coming to his side. "And you, too, Ewan. Thank you."

Ewan nodded his head once in acknowledgment. "Cute fellow, that dragon. I always seem to run into the nasty full-grown ones."

Rose's eyes grew wide as she asked the question in Brand's mind. "They're real?"

"In the magical realm." Ewan eyed her with a thoughtfulness that twisted Brand's gut into a knot. Was he planning to use this to lure Rose there? "They live in the mountains."

"Wow, real dragons," Rose murmured.

"I could take you to see them," Ewan offered.

Dismay crossed Sequoia's face, and Brand curled his hand into a fist. Let the faery try.

But Rose merely twisted her lips in a wry smile. "I'm sure you could, but I don't think so."

Ewan frowned. "I don't understand you."

That was an understatement. Brand had been trying for years.

"Good." Rose took a step toward the hotel. "Now that Sequoia feels better and my magic is drained, let's get some breakfast. I'm starved."

Brand shook his head but fell into step with her, his own stomach rumbling in response. "Are you always hungry?"

She shot him an impish grin. "Of course not. It only appears that way."

Glancing over his shoulder, Brand noted Ewan and Sequoia had remained behind. He was not about to leave the two of them alone together. "Coming, Sequoia?"

She hesitated, then nodded. "Join us, Ewan?"

As if hearing Brand's unvoiced command to refuse, Ewan shook his head. "I will see you later."

He disappeared, but that didn't bother Brand nearly as much as the look that crossed Sequoia's face. Damn, she was involved with him. Or wanted to be.

Brand had enough trouble in his life with Rose. He definitely didn't need his assistant longing for a faery, too. When she joined him, he wrapped his arm around her shoulders. Better to keep her close at hand for the remainder of the day and away from Ewan.

When it came to protecting himself from wanting someone unattainable, Brand was lousy, but he would do his best to save Sequoia from what had to be ultimate heartache.

When dealing with the Fae, there was no other alternative.

Sequoia entered her room, surprised her morning headache hadn't returned after a terminally long day. With the evening performance finally over, she could turn her attention to Ewan's reappearance. Why had he come back? She hadn't seen him since this morning. Would he return?

Dealing with him was going to take careful planning

and control of her emotions. And finally she had the time to do that.

She turned, then gasped when she found Ewan behind her. "What the heck are you doing here?" she demanded, her pulse leaping into overdrive.

For a long minute he didn't say anything, but the intensity of his gaze created the same reaction as if he'd touched her. Her skin warmed and the yearning for him that never quite went away flared.

"I want you," he said finally, his tone flat.

Sequoia's heart added an extra beat, but she managed to keep her expression bland. "What if I don't want you?" Not that she didn't, but what if?

He took a step closer, his body heat mingling with hers. "It doesn't matter. I am Fae. If I want you, I will have you."

She dropped her jaw. Did he realize what he was saying? Did he mean it? "*It doesn't matter*? Boy, you really do come from a different world, don't you?"

His eyes darkened. "You cannot resist me."

Narrowing her gaze, Sequoia released a harsh laugh. Obviously, he didn't know her very well. "Watch me."

She bent her knees slightly, ready to shift her weight, and waited for him to make the next move. This arrogant faery was due a rude awakening.

When he reached for her shoulder, she swept her right foot behind his knees, grateful for the years of kickboxing lessons. She might be small, but she was plenty tough as other—more mortal—men had discovered from time to time.

Ewan crashed to the floor with the grace of collapsing scenery. While he was trying to regain his breath, Sequoia flipped him to his stomach, then sat on his back and twisted his arm behind him.

"That hurts!" he cried.

"It's supposed to hurt." She wrenched his arm a little harder and retained her seat when he tried to buck her off.

"I can destroy you." Anger sizzled in his words, sending a tremor of unease through her.

He probably could, but if he tried, he wasn't worthy of her love, that was for sure. "You're welcome to try." She kept her hold on his arm. "But first you're going to listen to me, Mr. Macho Fae. No man—mortal or Fae—threatens me like that. If I share my body with you or anyone else, it is because I choose to."

"There will not be anyone else."

She sighed. "Are you even listening to me? I'm not some stupid bimbo who's going to be grateful simply because you want to have sex with me."

"No, you're not." He sounded resigned, but before she could question him, he disappeared and she fell to the floor with a thud, her legs splayed.

"Ow." She swung her legs beneath her so she could stand.

"You're very different from Fae women."

She twisted around to see Ewan standing across the room. His eyes blazed with an otherworldly quality—a contrast to his very tight jeans and T-shirt. He was so devastatingly handsome, he made her chest hurt. The trick was to not let him know that.

She eyed him warily. Was this round two? "Why are you here, Ewan?" She spoke with a calmness she was far from feeling. "Really."

"I missed you," he said, his gaze holding hers.

Darn, but he knew the right thing to say. "Did you?"

"You're a mortal. I should not want to be with you. I should not dream of making love to you."

He sounded so disgusted with himself that Sequoia had to grin as she stood. "You say the sweetest things."

"I did not want to come back here."

"Oh?" She stepped closer to him, enjoying the gleam that appeared in his eyes. "Then why did you?"

"I could not return to the magical realm without Rose."

Her heart sank, but she kept her smile in place. "I see."

"And you have not yet taught me what this human love is."

"True." His words said one thing, but his eyes displayed more emotion than he probably realized. He might be closer to learning about love than he thought. "I guess you need to come with me to the hospital tomorrow."

"Perhaps I will."

She stopped in front of him, her insides knotting. Was he just here to make love or was it something more? Was she reading more into his turmoil than there actually was? "I missed you, too, Ewan."

He touched her cheek. "When I am with you, life seems more vibrant, more interesting."

Her throat closed so that she could barely talk. "Welcome to the mortal world."

Dipping his head slowly, cautiously, he kissed her with such tenderness that tears sprang to her eyes. For all of his macho nonsense, he was still the one she loved. She drew back and cupped his face between her hands.

"I'm going to make love to you." She'd known that from the moment he first appeared. She kissed him quickly. "With your permission, of course."

He wrapped his arms around her, molding her to his muscular frame. "Permission granted."

She eased out of his hold and placed his hands by his side. "No touching allowed until I say so. I'm going to make love to you first."

His eyebrows lowered. "That is not the way it is done."

"Humor me." She slid her hands under his shirt. "I intend to have you begging me for more before I'm done."

He straightened. "I am Fae. I do not beg."

Sequoia only smiled and lifted her lips to his. He really did have a lot to learn.

And later—much later—he begged.

Fourteen

There she is. Brand caught sight of Rose leaving the hotel elevator and headed for her. *Damn.* He swiped his damp palms on his pants. This was ridiculous. He had nothing to be nervous about.

"Rose." He linked his arm through hers, not giving her a chance to escape. "Eaten yet?"

"No, I—"

"Good." He steered her to the hotel's restaurant and secured them a table. "I want to talk to you."

She eyed him warily as she sat. "What about?"

Drawing in a deep breath, he sat across from her and waved away the waitress who approached. "Actually I want to apologize."

Rose lifted one eyebrow. "This I definitely have to hear."

"It's about the other night, the things you said." Things that still ate at him even two days later, no matter how much he tried to ignore it.

Her amusement faded. "Then I need to apologize, too. I wasn't myself. I lit into you pretty hard."

And how. Brand quirked his lips. "You evidently needed to get it out."

"Yeah." Rose glanced down at the tablecloth, drawing designs with her fingertip. "Losing your friendship still hurts after all these years. Stupid, but true."

Brand reached across to cover her hand with his. "I never meant to hurt you. I know that's hard to believe, but I was more concerned with me." When she glanced at him from beneath lowered lashes, he gave her a wry smile. "Hey, give me a break. I was thirteen and so jealous I couldn't see straight, let alone think straight."

"We were both young and stupid." Rose turned her hand so that her fingers linked with his, her expression serious, her gaze haunted.

"But we're neither now." Brand glanced at their clasped hands, unable to deny the surge of desire that simple touch created. "What do you say we start over?"

"I'm not sure we can." Rose squeezed his hand, then drew hers away. "I still have magic and you still want it."

"I also want you." No matter how many times he tried to explain his attraction away rationally, he couldn't deny the need to touch her, the fire in his blood when he was near her.

Her smile turned sad. "We don't always get what we want."

He recalled her passionate speech from the other night. She would never be normal, would never fit in completely in this world or the magical realm. "I know, but we—"

The ringing of his cell phone interrupted him and he grimaced. "I probably need to get this. Charlie is supposed to call."

"Go ahead."

He'd been expecting a call from his advance crew at the Las Vegas site, their next stop, but the voice that answered his greeting definitely didn't belong to Charlie. "About time I got to talk to you."

"Mom? Is anything wrong?"

"What? A mother can't call her son without something

being wrong?" He heard the teasing note in her voice. "You haven't called in ages, and I wanted to check if your tour was still on schedule."

"Yep, going smoothly. Dallas tonight, then on the road again to Vegas."

"No last-minute changes? You're still doing your big illusion in Las Vegas?"

"You know I am." Brand smiled at Rose, who wore a broad grin. She'd always fit in with his family until . . . well, until. What was his mother up to? "All right, Mom. Spill it. What's going on?"

She hesitated, then finally released a big sigh. "Your dad and I are coming to Vegas for your show."

"Oh." His smile faded. While he loved his mother, he dreaded every meeting with his father. They hadn't seen eye-to-eye in years. "Oh. Great."

"You're staying at the MGM, right?"

"Yes. We're performing there, too."

"Good. That's where I made the reservations. We'll arrive there about the same time you do."

He winced. That didn't leave him much time to adjust to this. "Okay."

Rose lost her smile and reached across the table to touch his arm. He gave her a wry twitch of his lips in response.

"And tell Sequoia that Lizzie and Michael are coming, too."

"I will."

His mother laughed. "I hear that note of impatience, so I'll say bye for now. Love you, hon."

"Love you, Mom." Brand disconnected his phone and sighed.

"Is everyone all right?" Rose asked.

"They're fine." Brand slid his phone into his pocket, still uneasy with his upcoming family reunion. "Mom and Dad are planning to come to Vegas for my big illusion."

"What's wrong with that? Your folks are great." She studied his face, then sat back in her chair, her expression mirroring her disbelief. "Are *you* still angry with your father? After all these years? That's ridiculous."

Brand frowned. "Aren't you still harboring angry feelings from years ago as well?"

"I . . ." She shook her head. "It's not your father's fault that you don't have magic."

"I see it two ways." He ticked off one finger. "First, he could have told me from the beginning about the Fae, about magic, about you. Maybe if I had always known, I wouldn't have been so blindsided by your power."

"My parents hardly told *me* anything. Why should yours be different?"

She didn't understand what it had been like for him to suddenly have his world turned upside-down. He raised another finger. "Second, he didn't have to give up his magic and immortality, but he did."

"He did that long before you were born, too. For crying out loud, Brand, he gave up everything he was to be with your mother. How could you want anything more than that?"

"I want to be magical. Dad was. I have his blood. If he hadn't given up his magic, he could have passed it on to me."

Rose rolled her eyes. "Now you're being deliberately dense. You know as well as I do that he had no choice if he wanted to be with your mom at all."

"That what he said, but he had *magic*. He could've done anything he wanted." Brand knew the power of magic, had seen it through Rose for years. Things could have been different.

"Then you know nothing about Titania."

"Neither do you. All you know are the stories we've been told." Stories so incredible he still found them difficult to believe.

"I believe my parents and yours," Rose said with an icy glance. "But this only emphasizes what I was telling you before. Magic is much too big of an issue with you, Brand. Until you learn to deal with it and accept what is, there's no future for us. Not together, at least."

He hesitated. This wasn't where he wanted the conversation to go. "It's different when it comes to you. I can adjust."

Her smile was sad. "Probably because I'm female."

There was some truth to that. Lord knew he desired her more than any woman he'd ever known. "Rose, we can—"

"Hey, can we join you?" Sequoia waved at them from the restaurant doorway, then came toward them, Ewan in tow.

Brand grimaced, then glanced at his assistant again. She glowed with vitality and her smile was almost too big for her face. "What's with her?" he murmured.

"Sated. Definitely sated." Rose frowned. "Damn."

"She's making it with the faery?"

"I'd be willing to bet on it."

"Damn." Nothing was going according to plan anymore. Not since Rose had shown up.

"I just said that." Rose grinned slightly, then stood to give Sequoia a hug. "You look great. How did it go at the hospital?"

"Wonderful." Sequoia slid into a chair while Ewan took the one opposite her. "The kids were great. They laughed in all the right places."

"They didn't want her to leave," Ewan added.

The look he gave Sequoia held so much passion that Brand wanted to punch him just on general principle.

"You, either," she added. "The children loved him."

"They did not *love* me."

"Yes, they did." Sequoia beamed at him. "I pulled him into the act, and he did a bit with a live rabbit that had the kids rolling. He was wonderful with them."

Sequoia hadn't been this effusive since Bobby McGregor gave her a handmade Valentine in fifth grade. Brand's heart sank. She had it bad.

Which meant she'd be terribly, horribly hurt when this creep inevitably dumped her.

"I have news," Brand said. Might as well start bursting her bubble now. "My parents are joining us in Vegas."

"That's wonderful. I haven't seen them in months."

"So are yours."

Her face fell so quickly Brand felt as if he'd pulled a plug. "Oh."

"Stand up to them, Tree," Rose said. "Tell them what you want to do."

"It's not that easy." Sequoia nibbled on her fingernail, a sure sign of her distress.

"It should be." Ewan spoke with such authority that Brand blinked in surprise. How would this faery know anything about Sequoia and her relationship with her parents? "They love you, correct?"

"Yes, but—"

"If they love you, they want you to be happy. Isn't that what you've told me?"

"Yes, but—"

"Then tell them what makes you happy." He crossed his arms and nodded as if he'd just achieved world peace.

"They don't understand." Sequoia pushed away from the table with a scowl. "I'm not hungry anymore."

Rose stood as well. "I'll join you."

The women left and Brand turned to look at Ewan only to discover he had disappeared as well. Great.

To top it off, the waitress finally appeared, tablet in hand. "Are you ready to order now?"

Brand sighed. It promised to be a real crappy day.

"Jason, I wish you'd hurry up."

At these words from his mother, a boy scurried past Rose in the theater lobby like a rabbit on pep pills.

"Damn." Rose paused for only a moment, then headed backstage. In all the day's confusion, she'd forgotten to have her magic siphoned off. With Brand's performance due to start soon, the last thing she wanted was the danger of loose wishes.

The security guard by the stage entrance recognized her

and allowed her inside. Thank goodness. Now to find Sequoia.

She located her cousin in a back corner, talking to Ewan of all people. What was he doing here? As Rose drew closer, she grimaced. Arguing, apparently.

"It's my life," Sequoia said.

"You don't act like it." Ewan didn't raise his voice, but the calmness of his tone was every bit as effective. "You're willing to sacrifice yourself for them."

"You don't understand. They're my parents. I love them."

"So you are going to allow their love and your love to ruin your life?"

Ah, yes, Sequoia's parents. They were in reality quite nice people, but were convinced that their only daughter had to have a college degree in order to find a job of any consequence.

Rose hesitated by Sequoia and touched her shoulder. "Tree, do you have a moment?"

"I'm busy," Sequoia snapped, not bothering to glance at Rose, her attention focused solely on Ewan. "When did you become an expert at love?"

"I am not an expert," he said. "But I *do* know you."

"That's what you think."

Rose tried again. "It's important. I need a wish."

Sequoia whirled on her, her eyes blazing. "I wish you'd shut up." Without missing a beat, she faced Ewan again. "You don't know me at all."

The slight tug on her magic warned Rose she was in trouble even before she tried to speak. No words came out. No sound at all. Great.

And from the way Sequoia and Ewan were going at each other, she wasn't going to find much help there.

With a soundless sigh Rose left to find Brand. He had to be here somewhere. Despite his reluctance to make wishes, he'd help with this.

She hoped.

She located him near the back of the stage area talking

to some of his crew and waited for him to notice her. When he did, he frowned, finished his conversation, and then came toward her.

Before he could chastise her for being backstage, she pointed to her throat. His frowned deepened. "Is something wrong?"

She attempted to talk, but no words emerged.

"Can't you speak?" he asked.

She shook her head and the corner of his lips quirked upward. "What happened?"

Rose pointed back toward where Sequoia had been, then at her throat. Brand was intelligent. Surely he'd figure it out.

"What?"

With a sigh she held out her hand to indicate Sequoia's height.

"An elf? A midget? A faery?"

She simulated the wavy curves of a woman and waited for him to get it.

"A sexy elf?"

The sparkle of mischief in his eyes gave him away. Rose propped her hands on her hips and faced him, tapping her foot.

Brand grinned. "Okay, okay. Sequoia wished for you to be quiet."

After she nodded, he chuckled. "I'm surprised it took her this long."

The nerve. Rose swiped at him playfully, then pointed again to her throat. Would he help her?

"You need me to wish your voice back?"

She nodded with enthusiasm. *Exactly.*

"What if I choose not to?" Something darker, deeper, and definitely sexier replaced the humor in his eyes as he stepped toward her.

Rose backed away, her body responding to the heat of his gaze while her mind screamed at her to run. Abruptly she met the stage wall. Trapped.

Brand caught her shoulders in his hold—not forceful

yet firm enough to let her know she wasn't going anywhere. "What if I listen to my primal self?" he asked, his
voice deepening, growing huskier. "The part that wants
you so badly I can barely function? You can't scream."

Her eyes widened. He wouldn't.

Would he?

He raised one hand to cradle the curve of her cheek.
Unbidden, she leaned into it, his touch aggravating an
already misbehaving body. "Rose." He murmured her
name with a groan and kissed her.

All her good intentions disappeared beneath the feel of
his lips. No matter how rational she tried be, how much
she told herself they had no future, she couldn't resist the
way he made her feel, the yearning, the fire through her
veins.

Her breasts swelled, aching for his touch, but he concentrated solely on her mouth, seducing her with ease,
until her legs went wobbly. She clutched at his tuxedo
jacket to remain upright and he raised his head.

His pupils nearly blacked out the green of his eyes, and
the ragged edge to his breathing tugged at her. "Have
dinner with me after the show. In my room."

She shouldn't. They both knew more than dinner would
be involved here. To go was asking for trouble, to jump
into a bottomless pool where everything depended on how
long she could tread water.

Still she nodded. No logic in the world could overcome
the burning inside her, the desire to be with him.

Brand smiled with such warmth, her heart leaped to her
throat. "Good." He stole one more lingering kiss, then
turned to go.

After taking a few steps, he glanced over his shoulder
with an impish smile. "I wish you could talk again."

Good Lord, she'd forgotten all about that. She struggled
to speak, her throat clogged by more than a spell gone
awry. "Thank you." She wasn't completely sure if she was
thanking him for restoring her voice or that devastating
kiss.

Carter joined Brand, leading him away, but Rose continued to stare after them, slow realization dropping her heart to her stomach.

She was in serious trouble here. She'd done the one thing she'd sworn she wouldn't ever do.

She'd fallen in love with Brand.

Her seat was closer to the rear of the theater for this performance, which gave her an opportunity to use the lighting to seek out hidden wires. But she rarely used that opportunity, too caught up in watching Brand create magnificent illusions.

Tonight he was at his finest. Even when she knew all too well how the illusion was performed, she believed. Because he made her want to believe. He had a way of winning over an audience, making them laugh, teasing them, tantalizing them.

And wasn't that what being a master magician was all about?

He took control of the stage, his charm and good looks accentuated. Or was it just the way she felt about him that made him seem that way?

She couldn't love him. Lust was okay. She understood that, but love created a vulnerability she couldn't afford. Her magic simply wasn't going to go away. It was just as unlikely that Brand would ever accept that. Where was the future in that?

"What's so great about him?"

The question jarred her out of her meandering, and she glanced at the young man sitting beside her. "What?" She hadn't caught all his words, but his disparaging tone came through clearly.

"I don't see why everyone raves about this guy. He's pretty standard from what I can see."

The man appeared to be a couple years younger than she and obviously much dumber. "Then you must be blind."

He scowled. "Anyone can saw a woman in half and

make things disappear. That's the usual magician stuff."

"But not everyone flies or makes the moon disappear." Which was one illusion she still had to solve.

"That's just hype. Trouble is, women like you and Samantha believe it."

Ah, now we're getting somewhere. "Who's Samantha?"

"My girlfriend. She thinks this guy is the greatest thing on Earth. She has posters all over her apartment." Some of the man's anger filtered into his voice.

"Sounds to me like you're just jealous over nothing. She's not likely to ever even meet him." Which suited Rose just fine.

"A lot you know. She came to last night's show and hung around afterward until he appeared. Got his autograph and wouldn't stop talking about how hot he was." The man glared at the stage where Brand was finishing his fire illusion. "Said he kissed her. Made it sound like he took her to bed."

Rose had to stifle her own surge of jealousy at the thought of any other woman receiving Brand's intoxicating kisses. "I doubt that."

Yet she didn't know what he'd done after last night's show. She'd come straight back to the hotel, not waiting for either Sequoia or Brand, and had forced herself to work on the exposé that was not coming together.

"Hell, look at him. He thinks he's God's gift to women."

Rose focused on Brand introducing his water escape. He was charming, good-looking, intelligent, and gallant, but in all the years she'd known him, he'd never come across with an oversize ego. "He could be," she murmured. Any woman who landed him would be lucky indeed.

And for a brief, irrational moment she wished it could be her.

"God, women!" The man slumped back in his seat.

"You don't have to stay, you know." When he didn't respond, Rose resumed watching. The water escape was her least favorite of all the illusions Brand performed. He was handcuffed, then locked inside a glass tank filled with water, the lid allowing for no air space. A curtain was drawn across the tank and within moments he escaped and reappeared.

She knew the logic behind it—how the cuffs were unlocked, how Brand slipped from the tank—but knowing didn't ease the tension inside her every time she watched it. The locks were real. The cuffs were real. The water was real. The danger each and every time, was all too real.

Brand waved with his cuffed hands, then crouched in the tank and had the lid padlocked. The curtain was drawn quickly across.

Already he'd be at work unlocking his cuffs. Rose tried to reassure herself. He'd done this hundreds of times. Yet her chest ached as if she were holding her breath with him.

"I wish just once he wouldn't be able to get out of there," the man beside her muttered.

It took her a moment to realize what he'd said. The tug on her magic triggered the horror. She stared at the man. "Oh, God."

On stage, Sequoia stood beside the curtain holding the clock, smiling at the audience, oblivious to any problems. Rose jumped to her feet.

To hell with not using her magic.

She ignored the grumbling around her and murmured the few words to activate her own power.

And nothing happened.

Normally she experienced a tingling through her body when she used her magic, but not this time.

She tried again with the same result.

Dear Lord, had she lost her magic completely?

"Sequoia." She shouted to her cousin, but went unheard. Time clicked by with alarming rapidity. Rose pushed through the seats to the aisle and ran toward the front. "Sequoia! Sequoia!!"

At last her cousin looked at her.

"There was a wish!" Rose shouted.

Sequoia blanched and pushed away the curtain to reveal Brand floating facedown in the tank.

The crowd gasped. Some women screamed. Rose's heart stopped.

Reaching beneath the tank, Sequoia pulled out a large axe and swung it at the glass with all her might. She might be petite, but she was tough.

The glass shattered and watered exploded onto the stage, Brand tumbling free from his glass coffin. Confusion reigned in the theater, making it even more difficult for Rose to get to the stage.

By the time she'd bulldozed her way up there, Carter was administering mouth-to-mouth resuscitation to Brand within a circle of stage crew. Rose ached to help. Brand was pale, his breathing nonexistent.

She stumbled to Sequoia's side. "My magic is gone."

"Gone?" If possible, her cousin went even paler. "How?"

"I don't know. I tried to use it and it failed. Oh, God, Tree, he has to be all right."

"He will be." But Sequoia sounded as if she was trying to convince herself of that as well as Rose.

Rose clenched her fists, her insides churning, her chest tight. Brand was going to die.

And it would be all her fault.

Fifteen

Rose was ready to push Carter aside and take over, when Brand finally stirred, coughing and spitting up water. Carter eased him into a sitting position and held him as Brand continued to choke. The coughing stopped and for several long heartbeats, Brand didn't move.

Finally he placed his hand on the floor and propped himself up, his eyes opening. "I couldn't get the cuffs undone," he gasped. "I felt them give, but they wouldn't open."

Rose closed her eyes for a brief moment. Her fault. All her fault.

What good was having magic when she couldn't use it as needed? Was she doomed just to leak magic for the rest of eternity?

"I found a doctor." A stagehand led an older man onto the stage as Rose noted the curtains had been drawn to hide them from the crowd outside. Thank goodness, the audience chatter outside was diminishing.

The doctor knelt beside Brand and took his pulse. "Good," he declared. "But I still want to check you over.

I called an ambulance. You're going to the ER."

Brand shook his head. "I'm fine."

"Doesn't matter. You're going." The doctor exchanged looks with Carter, who nodded. Brand wasn't going to have any say in this.

The ambulance technicians appeared moments later and accompanied Brand outside. He'd insisted on walking, unencumbered, to prove his survival. The doctor pointed at Sequoia and Carter. "You two come with me. The rest of you will have to remain behind."

Rose took a step forward. "But . . ."

"Who are you?" the doctor asked.

She hesitated. "A friend." *A woman who loves him.*

"Sorry. He doesn't need a mob of groupies around him right now." The doctor hurried after the technicians, and Rose caught Sequoia's hand.

"Tell him I'm sorry."

Her cousin gave her a quick hug. "He already knows that. I'll meet you at the hotel when we get back."

"Okay."

But the wait at the hotel was interminably long. Rose paced in her room, wearing a rut in the carpet. Was Brand really all right? He'd still been pale when they'd taken him away. What if there were complications? What if he caught pneumonia?

One worry after another popped into her mind. She should have gone to the hospital anyhow. But would they have let her near him?

She had no real place in his life. What was she? A journalist trying to write an exposé on his magic. Oh, yeah, that would get her far.

Especially where his friends and fans were concerned. They'd be more likely to shove her in a Dumpster.

But what about a woman who cared deeply about him, who would give of her life force to save him?

She paced across the floor once more. "I hate this." She'd never been a patient person in the best of circumstances. With magic, she usually didn't have to wait.

Crossing the room, she noticed the light flashing on her phone. Had Sequoia called before Rose arrived?

Rose jabbed the message button, then grimaced when she heard her editor's voice.

"It's taking too long, Rose," he said. "You have a week to turn something in or forget it."

Short, sweet, and to the point. Typical.

Rose scowled. Like she gave a damn about writing that article right now.

True, she had enough information to reveal how he managed most of his illusions, but she still hadn't figured out how he intended to make the moon disappear. Her exposé would be incomplete without that.

Or was that the excuse she needed to stay longer with Brand? If she were smart, she'd leave now—before she didn't want to leave at all.

But she couldn't. Especially not until she knew he was okay.

Hearing a rap at her door, she ran to open it. Sequoia spoke before she stepped inside. "He's fine. They figure he only stopped breathing for about a minute."

"That's still too long," Rose said. Any time at all was too long.

Sequoia smiled and wrapped Rose in a hug. "He's okay, Rose. Really okay. By the time we left the hospital, he was annoying everyone."

Rose had to smile at that. "Where is he?"

"Upstairs, in his hotel room. They gave him something to help him sleep, so he's pretty out of it."

"Can I get in?" She had to see him, touch him, listen to him breath. "I won't bother him."

"Of course you can see him. Come on. I have his room card."

Rose's stomach knotted as they approached Brand's room, but relaxed when she finally saw him sprawled beneath the blankets in the middle of the king-sized bed. His clothing hung over the back of a nearby chair.

"Carter accepted the challenge of getting him into bed," Sequoia said. "Appears he succeeded."

Rose only nodded and went to brush her fingers against Brand's cheek. Beneath the stubble, his skin was warm . . . alive.

"If you need anything, call," Sequoia added before she ducked out the door.

Only dimly aware of her cousin leaving, Rose perched beside Brand on the bed and smoothed his dark hair away from his face. He'd almost died all because of her stupid pride and her stupid leaking magic.

Well, no more. *No more*.

She was Fae. As much as she tried to make a place for herself in the mortal world, she was Fae with all that entailed. Including magic.

Sliding from the bed, she stood and raised her arms toward the ceiling. Her magic was a part of her. Time to stop playing games.

She drew from deep within her, searching for that latent core of power. She'd start with something simple—a vase of flowers. "Obey me. Now."

The swell of magic hurt at first, a sudden cramp that flowed along her muscles, then dissolved as a vase of red roses appeared before her. Good.

She didn't hesitate, but created another vase, then another until the scent of intoxicating roses filled the room.

Now for a greater challenge.

She pictured herself across the room and transported there with simply a thought. Then transported herself back.

Her power was back.

Not using it for so long had made it difficult to find, her skill at using it rusty, but that would change. She wasn't giving up her magic again for anybody. She glanced at the bed.

Not even Brand.

She'd admit to losing the bet, even though he'd already

said she didn't have to adhere to it. No bet was worth his life.

She settled into the chair beside the bed, unable to resist linking her fingers through his outstretched hand. She wasn't leaving until he woke up.

Even if that meant staying all night.

Brand came out of a groggy sleep with a sore throat, the memory of his near-drowning returning along with his consciousness. He hadn't had a close call like that in years, especially since he always made it a point to double-check his props and sets before every show.

But how did one double-check against leaky magic?

Turning over, he spotted Rose curled up in the easy chair beside his bed, her cheek pressed against the back of the seat, her legs tucked under her. How could she sleep like that?

The small table lamp was on, creating a dim pool of light in the darkness. A glance at the clock confirmed the time. It was nowhere near the hour he usually awakened. He slid from the bed, then paused, realizing he wore only his black bikini briefs. Well, it wasn't like she hadn't seen him in underwear before.

He scooped her up into his arms, enjoying the feel of her warmth pressed against his bare chest, and her eyes flew open at once. "Wha . . . ? Brand, put me down."

"I was just putting you in bed where you'd be more comfortable." And closer to him . . . an image that had him hardening in response.

She squirmed in his arms. "Put me down."

With reluctance he set her feet on the floor. "Fine."

"Are you all right?" she asked as soon as she steadied herself.

He sighed. If one more person asked him that . . . "Don't I look all right?" He spread his arms for emphasis, then grinned when Rose's eyes widened. Her gaze dropped to his briefs, barely able to cover him in his current condition, then flew back to his face.

"Y . . . yes." Her voice came out slightly hoarse. She cleared her throat. "I am so sorry, Brand."

His smile faded. Leave it to Rose to blame herself. Yet he'd done the same thing when she'd been near death. "I know it wasn't your fault. You have no control over what people wish." He hesitated and frowned. "Though I'd sure like to know who hated me enough to make that kind of wish."

"The guy sitting next to me. He was jealous of you. Apparently you met his girlfriend the other night after your show and kissed her. He also believed you'd slept with her."

Brand blinked. He hadn't slept with a woman in a long, long time and right now only one held any interest for him. "Do you know her name?"

"Samantha."

He'd found several women waiting for him after the show two nights ago and had willingly signed autographs, all the while wishing he was with Rose instead. Noting the intensity of Rose's gaze on him, he smiled. Was she jealous? Good.

"I did meet some fans," he admitted. "And I gave them a quick kiss like this." He bent forward to place a chaste kiss on Rose's cheek, but even that stirred the ever-present longing for her.

"You're leading them on when you do that." Rose sounded like a strict schoolteacher, but the glimmer in her eyes was far from demure.

"Nah. This is leading them on." Not giving Rose a chance to back away, he pulled her into his embrace and claimed her lips. They were so soft, so responsive with a sweetness uniquely Rose. He could kiss her forever.

Her initial surprise gave way to a return of his passion and he dived deeper, mating with her tongue. When he drank a moan from deep in her throat, he clasped her tighter, cradling her head, unwilling to let her turn away.

She was what he wanted . . . needed . . . craved.

The ache in his gut tightened and he swelled even more,

poking out from his briefs now. He held her bottom, pressing her against him, seeking the heat between her thighs.

When she gasped, he left her succulent mouth and nibbled along her throat, behind her ear, lingering at the beat of her erratic pulse. Her head fell back and he cradled her breast. He could feel her taut nipple even through her bra and ached to touch her flesh.

Gliding his fingers over the open skin exposed by the scooped bodice of her turquoise dress, he slid beneath the material into the bra to caress the hot silkiness of her bare breast.

Desire, fevered passion shot through him, drawing a groan. "God, I want you, Rose."

"I . . ." To his surprise, she eased away from him, her breathing ragged, her cheeks flushed, her nipples prominent.

"Rose." He clenched his fists, the urge to touch her overwhelming. Was she going to back away from him again?

"Are . . . are you well enough for this?"

Well enough? He was tired of waiting, tired of wanting. In an impulsive gesture he stripped off his briefs, letting his erection jut forward proudly. "Any more stupid questions?"

Her eyes grew large, her jaw dropped slightly, stroking his ego. She swallowed and brought her gaze back to his face. "There are things you should know first."

"Such as?" He couldn't think of anything to make him change his mind at this point.

"I'm going to use my magic from now on. The deal is over."

"Fine." Then he wouldn't have to worry about leaking wishes anymore.

"But I promise I won't use it to get my story." Her words tumbled out as if she didn't say them fast, she wouldn't say them at all.

"I know." He'd discovered how off-base his assumptions about her were. Rose was as honorable as they came.

Surprise crossed her features. "You're okay with that?"

"I'm very okay with it." At the moment anything to do with magic was far from his mind—other than the magic he wanted to make with Rose. He stepped toward her and she took an equal step backward.

He froze, every muscle tense. "I trust you. Don't you trust me?"

"I do, but—"

"Are you going to make love with me, Rose?"

Her slight hesitation added to the knotting on his gut. "Yes," she whispered. "But I . . . I've never done this before. I don't want you to be disappointed in me."

Disappointed? Not in this lifetime. Her other words slowly filtered in and he jerked his head back. "You're a virgin?" From the way she exuded sex appeal, he hadn't expected that.

At her tentative nod, he took a calming breath. "Why?" The question erupted before he could think. She'd always had men swarming around her. He'd assumed . . . evidently, he'd assumed wrong. Again.

"I've never met anyone I wanted to share my body with." She met his gaze, her blue eyes filled with longing. "Until you."

As proud as that made him, her words also terrified him. He wanted her desperately, but this needed to be special. Very special.

Spotting the vases of roses on the floor, he nodded toward them. "Where did those come from?"

"I made them."

He nodded, then broke the heads off several stems and scattered the petals over the bed, the seductive aroma one he'd always associated with Rose. His Rose.

Turning back to her, he caught a glimpse of her trepidation. "Don't worry," he murmured. He intended for her to be very well satisfied before he was done.

He kissed her thoroughly, banking the passion that wanted to seize control, and unzipped her dress. It slid to the floor, leaving her in scanty black underwear that accented her creamy skin. If possible, his desire increased, the urge to bury himself in her growing even more fierce.

Forcing himself to go slow, he kissed a path down to the slopes of her breasts, then slid first one strap, then the other from her shoulders. Unfastening the clasp, he let the bra fall away, and sucked in a deep breath.

"Perfect." Her silken white breasts were firm, large enough to fill his hand yet small enough to stand proud, the rose-colored nipples puckered into hard nubs.

He had to taste her. Lowering his head, he drew her breast into his mouth, savoring her gasp and moans of pleasure as he teased her tight peak. Sweet, seductive, and sexy.

Moving to her other breast, he slid his hand over her heated skin to the edge of her thigh-high panties. Slipping inside, he found her wet, welcoming, and hot. He located her swollen nub and gave it extra attention until her knees buckled.

He caught her and removed her panties as he set her on the bed. Unbuckling her sandals, he blazed a path up her leg to her inner thigh to her sweet moistness. With his tongue and lips, he nibbled and plunged, giving her a sample of what lay ahead.

Rose twisted on the rose petals, releasing their erotic scent, and reached down to clutch his head, her breathing raspy. Whether to pull him away or forward, he never knew, for he chose that moment to nip at her, and she arched up with a cry of pleasure.

The urge to plunge into her contracting womb had him hard enough to break off, but he managed to retain control and kissed his way back to her breasts, to briefly torment the swollen peaks, then find her lips.

"That's only the beginning," he murmured against her mouth.

"I never . . ." Her pupils were huge, her lips red. He'd never wanted anyone this badly in his entire life, yet he took his time, sliding his hands over every inch of her flesh until she squirmed on the bed, her cries incoherent.

"Brand, please."

He couldn't wait any longer. Kissing her deeply, he positioned himself between her thighs, finding the barrier that blocked his way to paradise. He drew back, bringing a murmur of protest from Rose, then plunged forward to embed himself deep within her tight embrace.

She cried out once and he struggled to keep still, to allow her pain to pass. But she raised her hips against him. "More."

He didn't have to be asked twice. He reined in the fierceness of his desire, yet found her moving with him, answering each stroke with her own. They fit together perfectly, as if she'd been made for him.

When she arched again, crying out his name, and rippled around him, he finally allowed himself to release his passion with a groan. To his surprise, he felt a tingling that spread throughout his body, a pleasant yet odd experience.

Of course, what did he expect? Making love to Rose wouldn't be ordinary.

He remained within her as he bent to kiss her. "You okay?"

"I'm wonderful." Her eyes glowed. "That was magnificent. No wonder sex gets so much press."

She really was good for his ego. "You were pretty magnificent yourself."

"Is it always like that?"

Recalling previous, less exciting experiences, Brand hesitated. "I imagine it is with you."

Her luscious breasts beckoned him and he nibbled first at one, then the other, and her insides clenched around him. "You are very responsive," he murmured.

"Is that because I'm Fae?"

She appeared serious and he grinned. "More likely because you're you."

A slow smile slid across her face and she rocked against him. "Then we ought to test that theory. Several times."

As she moved against him, he stiffened again, surprising himself. Yet he'd never before wanted someone with the urgency he desired Rose.

"You aren't sore?" The last thing he wanted to do was harm her.

Rose gave him a seductive smile and drew him closer for a kiss. "I have magic to take care of that. But you may be aching before long."

"We'll see about that."

He lost himself in her kiss, her touch, in her. Who needed magic when they could share this?

Making love to Rose was a magic all of its own.

Sixteen

Rose jerked awake, startled to find a hand loosely surrounding her breast, then smiled as she recalled the morning's events. If she'd known how wonderful lovemaking could be, she doubted she would have waited this long.

Then again, would it be this wonderful with anyone other than Brand?

She stretched, easing out the slight soreness of her body. A shimmer of internal magic erased it completely. Before she could turn to face Brand, his hand caressed her breast, his thumb teasing her nipple into tight awareness. A ripple of pleasure flooded her body, and she eased back toward Brand to feel his erection press against her thigh.

Rolling onto her back, she smiled up at him. "Are you always this . . . alert?"

"Only for you." The sleepiness left his eyes as he kissed her with enthusiasm.

Her body responded at once, the tight knots of potential pleasure curling within her. She'd never suspected she had such wantonness, yet she wouldn't call it a bad thing.

How could anything that felt this good be bad?

And more than the sensual enticements was the feeling this sharing with Brand created—of safety, of caring, of love. No wonder her mother had warned her against falling in love. It was consuming, almost frightening in its intensity.

She wanted more time with Brand yet knew that time was limited. Sooner or later it would end.

But for now—she moaned as he captured her breast again—for now she would enjoy it.

An abrupt knock of the door startled them both just as she had straddled his hips. "Who is it?" Brand called.

"Carter. We need to talk."

Rose grimaced. She kissed Brand quickly. "Bye." And transported to her room.

The last thing she wanted was to be caught naked in Brand's bed. Thank goodness she could use her magic again.

Now to get dressed.

The phone was ringing when she emerged from the bathroom. "Coward," Brand said, his voice warm and teasing.

"Practical," she responded, her body reacting at once just to the sound of his voice. Boy, she was in bad shape.

"I need for everyone to meet in the restaurant for breakfast, okay?"

She frowned as the serious note. "Everything okay?"

"Wonderful. Excellent. Incredible." He chuckled. "How can you even ask?"

"I . . ." She shook her head. "I'll see you downstairs in a few minutes, then."

"That's already too long."

Brand broke the connection, but Rose caught his eagerness and used her magic to create shorts and a tank top.

Sequoia met her at the restaurant entrance. "You're glowing," she declared.

"I don't glow," Rose said. Not unless she played with fireflies.

"You're glowing," her cousin repeated. She glanced past Rose as Brand approached. "And he's glowing."

"Brand doesn't glow." Yet Rose had to admit he had the look of a man well satisfied.

Sequoia grinned. "It's about time."

Rose gave her a blank look. "I don't know what you're talking about."

"Yeah, right."

As Brand joined them, his heated glance brushed Rose with an intimacy that sent heat to her cheeks.

Sequoia chuckled. "Sure, nothing happened," she said. Her smile faded as she glanced behind Brand. "Good morning, Ewan."

Rose frowned when she saw the faery beside Brand. "Where were you when we needed you last night?"

"Busy." Ewan's gaze locked on Sequoia. "I was told to go away."

"You should have known I didn't mean it," Sequoia said.

"I never know what to believe with you."

Brand clapped Ewan on the back. "Welcome to the real world. Come on. Carter is holding a table for us."

They sat and ordered with casual slowness that had Rose tapping her toe beneath the table. What was going on? An announcement of some kind was pending. But what?

Brand reached beneath the table to run his hand along her leg. When she glanced at him in surprise, he only smiled. Oh, yeah, something was definitely up.

Finally, after the coffee and juice had arrived, Carter spoke. "We held off loading the bus last night in case Brand needed more time here."

Sequoia nodded as if she'd expected as much while Rose waited not so patiently. "So?"

"I'm glad they didn't pack," Brand added. "I intend to

offer another show tonight for those folks who had to leave early last night."

"We have a couple of extra days before we have to be in Vegas, so I've already cleared it with the theater," Carter said. "It's a go."

"No." The word burst from Rose without thought. She couldn't watch Brand do his water escape again.

"Yes." Brand spoke quietly, his gaze holding hers. "I know what I'm doing, Rose."

"But—"

"What happened last night was a freak accident. It won't happen again. I guarantee it."

She bit her lip. True, her leaky magic caused his near demise last night, but other things could go wrong. "Brand—"

"Those folks paid money to see a complete show. They deserve their money's worth."

"But you almost died. Surely they can understand that."

"So you'd prefer them to spread the word that I'm a failure? I don't." The conviction in his voice convinced Rose she couldn't talk him out of this. He directed his gaze at Sequoia. "How about you?"

"I don't like it, but I'll do it," she said.

"Good. Then we'll meet this afternoon to run through things. Carter is arranging for the backup water tank to be brought in."

Rose scowled and only picked at her breakfast when it arrived. She'd found it bad enough to watch the water escape before this. How could she possibly sit during it now? What if her magic still leaked?

True, Ewan had said that if she used her power again, the leaking would stop. But how could she be sure? Perhaps she could experiment with Sequoia later, though with the sidelong glances Sequoia and Ewan sent each other throughout the meal, Rose suspected her cousin might have other plans.

Of course, she could use her magic to save him if she had to. *If* it worked when she needed it.

Unable to eat, Rose pushed back her chair. "I'm not hungry after all. Excuse me, please."

Brand hurried after her and caught her arm before she could leave the restaurant. "It'll be all right, Rose. I know what I'm doing. Trust me."

She trusted him. It was her magic she didn't trust.

By the time the evening show was set to begin, Rose couldn't stay seated. She paced the rear of the theater, eyeing the closed curtains. Part of her had debated staying away entirely while another part insisted she be there in case she was needed.

So she was here, her stomach filled with rocks, her chest wrapped in invisible bands of steel. How was she ever going to survive an entire show?

What good was having magic when it didn't ease the tension within her?

The lights dimmed and her heart jumped into her throat. The curtains opened and Brand took the stage.

"Welcome once again. I apologize for the abrupt dismissal of last night's show, but we experienced some technical difficulties." His charming smile invited the audience to laugh with him, to shake off the fact that he could have died, and they did. Within moments he owned them and their belief.

He seduced them with his humor and charm, mingling with the audience, pulling members onstage to participate in different illusions. No one watching him would guess how close he'd come to losing his life, how deadly this game of illusion could be.

Rose remained standing at the back, watching him. To see him make a small object disappear, then reappear through sleight of hand reminded her of the way he'd touched her throughout the day. Slight touches—a hand on her back, a caress along her arm, a brief lingering touch—had built her blood to a fever pitch, which remained unsatisfied when he'd set off for the theater to rehearse.

At one point she'd been tempted to transport him from rehearsal to her room to ease the longing that he had created, but she'd managed to resist. Barely.

And watching him now—so confident, so smooth, so handsome—didn't help at all. She had been better off not knowing how wonderful sex could be, for now she wanted with a fierceness that startled her.

When he looked at her, finding her unerringly through the dim light in the theater, his gaze filled with passion, her senses leaped to attention. How could he make her feel this way when she was worried about him? How dare she want the feel of him inside her when she feared for his very survival?

No logic, no reason.

Only feeling.

Lord help her.

Throughout the night he sent glances her way, each one filled with the intimacy of a caress. He delivered promises and kisses without a touch, only a motion of his hand, a smile, a heated gaze.

When he flew, he darted near her, blowing a kiss that had women in the audience sighing and Rose nearly swooning. What was he doing to her? Her insides twisted from longing and worry, aching so badly she had to wrap her arms around herself. She wished they were *his* arms, holding her close to the beat of his heart. Then, perhaps, her tension would ease.

He faltered once during an illusion in which he transformed a cat into a tiger. She noticed the hesitation only because she'd seen the act several times. Maintaining his smile, Brand waved his hand once again at the cage. In a flash the cat vanished and the tiger appeared. Success.

When the water tank was wheeled onto the stage, Rose sucked in her breath, sensing an equal tension among the audience. Brand had saved this for last—a grand finale to prove he was capable of completing this escape.

He climbed into the tank with a merry wave, twisting her gut into further turmoil. The moment the curtain was drawn across, Rose counted the seconds. Thirty seconds. One minute. Hadn't it been long enough?

She could tell by the waver of Sequoia's smile that her cousin had reservations as well. Ninety seconds. Rose stepped forward. He'd had long enough.

Brand suddenly appeared on the platform center stage his smile broad, his hair and clothing wet. He located Rose and winked.

Her knees weakened and she sagged against the wall. Damn him. He was going to drive her crazy.

The crowd stood, showering him with thunderous applause. Obviously he'd achieved his goal. They believed in him.

As the show ended, Rose hurried backstage to find Brand surrounded by his stage crew. The first words she heard didn't comfort her.

". . . broken, I tell you," one crew man said.

"Stuck, perhaps," Brand said. "After all, it worked, didn't it?"

"That's just it. After looking at this latch, it shouldn't have worked. The trap wasn't going to open."

"Look, Stan, it worked, so something went right in the end."

Carter shook his head. "Then where's the cat?"

Brand frowned. "What do you mean?"

"I mean the cat wasn't below the trap. Where is it?"

"She has to be here somewhere. Look around. You know how good she is at finding hiding places." Spotting Rose, Brand smiled and eased away. "Great show, guys. Thanks."

"What was that about?" she asked, struggling to keep her tone even. "Something did go wrong?"

"Nothing major." Brand paused before her. "According to Stan, the latch on the trap in the cat-tiger exchange broke. He's saying the trap couldn't have opened, but the illusion worked. That's good enough for me."

He drew one finger along the curve of her jaw. "Are

you okay? I swear I could feel you throughout the entire show, worrying about me."

"And I could feel you trying to seduce me."

He grinned. "Did it work?"

She allowed the passion she'd struggled to keep banked rise. "Far too well."

His eyes lit from within and he pulled her close, his arousal evident. "Take us to the hotel."

"That would require magic. Don't you want to wait for a cab?"

"No. Take us now." He kissed her with such fierce passion that Rose could barely concentrate enough to get them transported to his hotel room, but by the time the erotic kiss ended, they'd arrived.

"Your wish is my command," she murmured when he raised his head.

"Is it?" Fire blazed in his eyes as a slow smile crossed his face. "I've thought of you all day, of touching you, being inside you. You've turned me into a sex-starved idiot, Rose."

Her insides clenched. She wanted him just as badly. "I don't necessarily see that as a bad thing." She ran her hand over the hard bulge in his pants, felt it jerk against her touch.

Brand growled low in his throat and seized her mouth to plunder and pleasure, using his tongue, lips, and teeth to accelerate the desire coiling within her. Would she ever get enough of this? Enough of him?

When he found her breast, tweaking her already hard nipple, she moaned, aching, wanting, needing. He left her lips and nuzzled a tender spot behind her ear. "You aren't wearing a bra."

"No." The spaghetti straps of this dress made that awkward.

"What are you wearing beneath there?" If anything, his voice grew more hoarse.

"Not much." String bikini panties were it.

"Oh, God." His groan echoed her own. "I can't be gentle this time."

"Then don't." She seized his mouth, demanding more.

As his lips responded, he felt beneath her short dress and tore her panties in a sharp movement that only fueled her need. As his fingers explored, she rocked against his hand. "I want you," she said, fumbling for the zipper on his pants. "Now."

He sprang free, hard, full, and ready, and she caressed the long silkiness that promised such exquisite pleasure.

With another growl he lifted her so that she could wrap her legs around his waist as he dived deep inside her. The fullness of him, the sense of completion drove her into an instant eruption, but he gave her no time to recover, holding her bottom in his hands as he took her, demanded more. More that she was eager to give.

She clung to his shoulders, her head thrown back, her breath in gasps. This was what she wanted for the rest of eternity. Brand. Only Brand.

Her next climax coincided with his. She pulsated around him, reveling in the thick steel of him. Nothing she'd encountered in her entire life equaled this.

Opening her eyes, struggling to breath, she gasped. They were floating above the floor. "We're flying."

He grinned, the passion still evident in his gaze. "Seems appropriate, doesn't it?"

"Very." She felt in no danger of falling with her legs around his waist and her arms linked behind his neck. Was this how the Fae made love? Somehow, she doubted it. No, this would be uniquely Brand. "How do we get down?"

"What's the hurry?" He cradled her bottom, trapping him inside her even deeper, if that were possible. "Will you remove our clothing?"

"Now you ask, after you'd ripped my panties?" But she complied. He was magnificent naked, his chest sprinkled with dark hair, his muscles clearly defined.

His response was to lay claim to her revealed breast

with his all too clever mouth. His tongue and teeth against her sensitive peak soon had her writhing against him, the ache building again, the need never ceasing.

By the time he turned his attention to her other breast, he had swelled once more inside her, filling her completely as if made for her.

She gasped in surprise when he lowered them to the bed. She found herself lying flat, Brand over her as he continued his slow, intimate torture, driving her to the brink of explosion.

"Brand . . ."

He lifted his head and grinned. "Now for the slow version."

"I can't." The tension in her gut was already too much.

"Oh, you can." He withdrew from her and she cried out in protest, but he merely grabbed one of the few remaining roses and returned to straddle her hips.

With deliberate slowness he ran the soft petals over her skin, her too sensitive nipples, every inch of her body until she could no longer think, could only want. She bucked against him, begging, pleading for the feel of him inside her.

But he used exquisite slowness to heighten her senses, her desire, until their final joining left her exhausted. She rested within his embrace, her breathing ragged, her pulse still racing.

"You're going to kill me," she murmured.

He nuzzled her ear. "But what a way to go."

She had to smile. What a way to go indeed.

For once Brand was nearly late arriving at the bus the morning after their midway stop. Rose grinned as he suffered good-natured teasing from Carter and Sequoia. After all, it had been his own fault that they'd been delayed.

Not that she'd complained when he'd interrupted their packing with a joyous sharing of their bodies.

As the bus departed for Las Vegas, she sat opposite him in the comfortable chairs, longing to snuggle close.

Yet the heat of his gaze felt every bit as erotic as his touch until she had to avoid looking at him in order to control the sensations invading her body.

Maybe she ought to transport them both ahead of the bus to the new hotel. With the way Sequoia and Ewan cuddled together on the couch, they wouldn't mind.

Explaining it to Carter would be more difficult.

She sighed and Brand grinned. "Think you'll make it?" he asked.

"I doubt it." She drew her feet up under her to keep from jumping onto his lap.

Extending his hand to touch her leg, Brand leaned forward, a wicked gleam in his eyes. "Good." He ran his thumb lightly along her inner thigh and Rose sucked in a deep breath, her desire building.

"You're an evil man," she muttered.

He laughed. "It's going to be a long trip for both of us."

"You're telling me?"

"Hey, Brand." Carter paused beside them and Brand drew away from her. "Got a minute to go over some stuff?"

"Sure." Brand stood, then magically produced a single rose that he handed to her. "Don't go away."

As Rose inhaled the fragrance, memories of the previous night sent heat to her cheeks. She had to get a grip. Use reason instead of emotion.

"So, nothing happening?" Sequoia asked, raising her eyebrows.

Rose gave a casual shrug, belying her tension, and refused to answer.

"Give me a break. You two nearly set the bus on fire."

"Sure that's not coming from you and Ewan?" Rose aimed a telling look at the couple. They sat so close together, she couldn't tell where one started and the other ended.

"No, we only set the bedroom on fire," Ewan said. "But

we were able to extinguish the flames before any real damage occurred."

Sequoia's eyes grew wide and her cheeks stained pink while Rose laughed. That would teach her cousin to tease her.

After Brand spent several hours in conversation with Carter, Rose wandered toward the table where they had papers spread. Spotting her, Carter immediately leaned over the papers, scooting them into one pile.

She bit back a grin. Magic secrets, no doubt. "Gary says if we take a quick lunch break, we can reach Vegas by dinnertime. Okay with you?"

"The sooner the better," Brand said. "I'm getting a little tired of riding on the bus."

Rose raised one eyebrow. She could fix that. Not that she would. "Only a few more hours."

Meeting her gaze, Brand allowed a wicked smile to spread across his face, his meaning clear. Only a few more hours.

She could last that long. If *he* could.

But by the time the bus pulled up in front of the MGM Hotel, Rose could have sworn several days had passed. Thank goodness Brand's tour ended here with the climax of his moon-disappearance illusion—an illusion she still had to discover.

Or should she try?

No doubt the papers Carter had covered pertained to that illusion. Brand hadn't rehearsed it since she'd joined his show, so she had nothing to base any speculation on. Maybe she should let it go and turn in what she already had.

But that meant leaving Brand—something she wasn't yet willing to do.

He caught her hand as they stepped off the bus. "Don't go too far away."

"I don't plan to."

Approaching the entrance, he wrapped his arm tight

around her shoulders. "Want to skip dinner?" he asked, his voice low and rough.

"I don't know." She shot him an impish grin. "I'm pretty hungry." Though not necessarily for food.

"Me, too." The gleam in his eyes reflected exactly what kind of hunger he meant.

A surge of desire sparked through her veins. "Well, we could have room service."

Brand lowered his head to kiss her as they stepped inside the hotel lobby. "My thoughts exactly."

His kiss promised fast, hot coupling and long, lazy seduction. Her heart added an extra beat as she lifted one hand to curve around his neck. *Okay*.

He drew away, his gaze heated. "We—"

"Brand."

They turned and Rose's heart tumbled to her toes at the sight of the approaching couple.

Brand's parents.

Seventeen

Brand dropped his arm from Rose's shoulders. He'd expected his family to be in Vegas, but not early enough to meet him on arrival. "Mom, I didn't know you'd be here this soon."

His mother came to wrap him in a warm hug. "I wanted to have all the time I could with you. We see so little of you anymore. You don't mind, do you?"

"Of course not." He adored his mother. It was his father he dreaded spending more than an hour with. "Are Sequoia's parents here as well?"

"We drove down together. They just went to get a drink. Ah, there they are."

Brand turned with his mother to see Liz and Michael Adams approaching. Glancing back, he caught the hesitant smile Sequoia pasted on her face as she went to greet them. The next few days promised to be very interesting.

"Are you checked in already?" he asked.

"Just finished a little while ago. We were heading out for dinner when we saw you arrive. If you want to find your room, we'll wait for you." His mother, Kate, waved at his father to join them.

Brand looked at Rose. There went the evening he had planned. She returned a tight smile, apparently feeling as awkward as he did.

"Rose is welcome to join us, too, of course," his mother added.

Liz and Michael reached Brand at the same time his father, Robin, did. "Why don't we all go together?" Liz suggested. She had her arm wrapped around Sequoia's waist. Brand never doubted that Sequoia's parents loved her. It was the way they tried to run her life that irritated him. He hoped by now they'd realized she was a grown woman.

"Wonderful," Kate said. She smiled at Brand. "Don't you agree, hon?"

What could he say? "The more, the merrier."

"Can Ewan come, too?" Sequoia asked.

Liz frowned. "Who's Ewan?"

"A friend of mine." Sequoia pointed to the faery while Brand resisted the urge to shake his head. She was actually going to invite that fruitcake along?

"He needs a haircut," Michael said, his tone matter-of-fact.

Sequoia rolled her eyes. "Dad, I like him just the way he is."

"Is it serious?" her father demanded. "Why haven't we heard of him?"

Brand caught the hesitation before Sequoia replied, but he doubted her parents did. "There's nothing serious. He's just a good friend."

"Of course, he's welcome." Kate, always the peacemaker, intervened and went to introduce herself.

Grinning, Brand watched her. His mom had a way of making people feel at ease. Between her friendliness and his dad's charm, no normal person, not even a faery, had a chance.

Turning back, he met his father's gaze and extended his hand in a formal gesture. "Hi, Dad."

Robin clasped it firmly, his smile not quite diminishing

the sadness from his eyes. "Good to see you, son."

Rose had remained silent all this time, but now she saw an escape. "Why don't I go and get us all registered while you talk?"

"Good idea," Robin answered before Brand could. Once she left their group, he continued, his tone conversational, but his disapproval clear. "I'm surprised to see her here."

Unwilling to discuss Rose, Brand shrugged. His father had long ago warned Brand not to get involved with Rose. It was too late now. "It's a long story."

"One I hope to hear. Soon."

Kate returned with Ewan in tow. "Ewan has agreed to accompany us to dinner. We'll have quite a group."

That was an understatement. Brand met Sequoia's gaze and they exchanged wry smiles. The meal should be very interesting.

When Rose returned with the keys, she handed him his with a grin. "You, O exalted one, have the Marquee Suite with a large whirlpool tub."

"Good to know." And Brand could think of several ways to put those items to use—most of which involved getting naked with Rose. How could he want her so much all the time? Was it because she was Fae or because he'd always wanted her?

He turned to his mother. "Shall we set a time to meet somewhere?"

"I've always wanted to try Emeril's," she said.

"Sounds good. Why don't we meet there in about thirty minutes? That will give the rest of us a chance to freshen up first."

"All right." Kate linked her arm through Robin's as she faced Liz and Michael. "I think we can find something to do while we wait."

"If you want me to play the slots again . . . ," Robin said.

Kate only laughed as she led him away. "Well, you do have the most extraordinary luck."

Once they were out of range, Brand led Rose to the elevator. "I hope you didn't get a room of your own." He had plans for keeping her close at hand.

"I did." She shot him a sharp look. "I'm not about to share a room with you while your parents are here."

"You'll be there most of the time anyway."

As the elevator rose, Rose stepped out of his hold. "I'm not sure. We need to talk about this, Brand."

His chest tightened. *We need to talk* had to be the most ominous words in the English language—right along with *I have something to tell you.* "Why ruin it?"

A hot emotion flashed in her eyes, then quickly disappeared. "I don't want to ruin it. I just want to know where we're going. Is this relationship about sex alone? Or being friends? What? Have you all of a sudden accepted that my magic is a part of me?"

He hesitated. He didn't have answers for all those questions. "I want to be with you." That was true enough. The rest could wait.

Rose met his gaze. "I still have an exposé to write. Do you really want me close to you?" Though she kept her voice even, he caught the worry in her eyes.

He'd forgotten about the exposé. Stupid of him. He knew how she felt about it.

But he was careful in regard to his illusions. He'd always been careful.

"I want you with me," he repeated. His desire for her wasn't going away.

"Your parents—"

He held up his hand. "Let me handle my parents. They've always liked you."

"They liked me best when we were apart. Though your father helped me quite a bit when I first gained my powers, he also warned me repeatedly about the risks of getting involved with anyone."

"Like he has room to talk." Brand clenched his fists, suddenly anxious to see his father again. It was bad enough his father had lectured him not to see Rose. Robin had no right to make demands of Rose.

Rose touched his arm. "Don't worry about it. My parents told me the same thing. Why do you think you were my first lover?"

The elevator stopped, but he didn't step out when the doors opened. "Then why get involved with me?" Waiting for her response, he caught his breath at her slight hesitation.

Her slow smile triggered the always-present fire in his blood. "Because I couldn't help myself."

He could breathe again. "Must be the Goodfellow charm."

"And here I thought you'd put a spell on me." She jabbed the Door Open button and stepped out. "My floor. I'll see you later."

The doors closed again, but he didn't push any buttons right away, the urge to go after her warring with his common sense. The sex between them was great—better than great—but she was right, it didn't magically make all their differences go away.

He snorted and hit the button for his floor. Magic. It all came back to that.

And he honestly didn't know how to handle it.

When everyone was finally shown to a table at Emeril's, Rose tried to distance herself from Brand, but he refused to let her, insisting she sit beside him. In actuality, he didn't have to try hard to persuade her, but she couldn't shake the feeling that this family dinner was going to be a lot more than he'd anticipated. She'd seen the inquisitive looks Kate and Robin had given her as they took the seats on Brand's opposite side at the round table.

Kate immediately engaged Brand in conversation and Rose sighed. She could survive this. She didn't have much choice.

As if sensing Rose's unease, Sequoia immediately claimed the chair beside her. Rose smiled at her, then wondered who would comfort whom? Her cousin looked even more uncomfortable than Rose felt.

Ewan seated Sequoia, then sat beside her, glaring defiantly at her parents. Was he providing a buffer? Rose studied him, actually taking time to see him as more than an irritant. He didn't appear to be nearly as bold or brash as when he'd first appeared. Was he mellowing? Unlikely. From what she'd been told of the Fae, Ewan's rude behavior was more the norm than not.

Glancing across the table, she noticed Sequoia's parents watching Ewan as well. "How long have you two been friends?" Aunt Liz asked Sequoia.

"Not long. A couple of weeks," Sequoia said with an oblique glance at Ewan.

Uncle Michael frowned at the faery. "Do you work with Brand?"

"No. I have other business."

Rose grimaced. Yeah, making her life miserable. Though she had to admit since Sequoia had started keeping him out of her hair, he'd grown a lot less irritating.

Hoping to give Sequoia a reprieve, Rose jumped in. "How are Mom and Dad?" She'd talked to them just a week ago, but the question at least switched the subject.

Aunt Liz, sister of Rose's father, rolled her eyes. "He's building a greenhouse for your mother. I don't understand it. Maybe you can explain. Ariel already has the best garden I've ever seen. Why on God's green earth does she need a greenhouse?"

Rose grinned. "Growing plants means a lot to Mom." It was where her mother excelled. "She loves it but can't grow things in Colorado in the winter. Knowing Dad, all she had to do was mention once how she'd love a greenhouse and he was on it."

"That's true. For all his complaining of having so much to do, I think Rand enjoys it," Aunt Liz said.

"I know he does. And how are Tay and Jake?" She hadn't spoken to her brothers in ages, usually because none of them ever stayed in one place very long.

"Jake was just home last week. Your mom was thrilled. Then he's off to some other hotspot—Argentina, I think." Aunt Liz shook her head. "Rand and Ariel are beginning to despair that any of you will ever settle down."

"From what I've heard about Dad, I don't think he has room to talk." Rose grinned. Her father had been a confirmed bachelor . . . until he'd met her mother. "And Tay?"

"Last I heard he was busy with the ski resort. Snow in the mountains is good this year."

That would make Tay happy. The most athletic of the three Thayer children, he'd missed a berth on the Olympics downhill squad only because he'd broken an ankle during finals. Running a ski resort at Breckenridge filled his life now. "I'll have to swing by home soon."

"Do that." Uncle Michael aimed his penetrating stare at Rose, then gave into a broad smile when she quirked her eyebrow. He could never be tough with her.

"How are the twins?" Rose asked. That would keep her aunt and uncle busy for several minutes at least, and it did as they went into detail on Val's and Ginny's accomplishments. The twins were several years younger than Sequoia, just finishing high school, in fact, and Liz and Michael never lacked for stories about their exploits. By the time their meals arrived, everyone at the table was caught up in good-natured laughter.

As they ate, Rose glanced at Brand. She'd deliberately left him to his parents. Though Robin had been a tremendous help when she'd first received her magic, he'd also made it clear at that time that she was not to get involved with Brand. He hadn't wanted to see his son hurt.

And that was inevitable now.

As much as Rose wanted a future with Brand, she wasn't willing to give up everything she was to be with him and he wasn't willing to accept her magic unconditionally. In the long run, they'd end up hating each other.

Brand nudged her side and she jerked around. "Mom asked you a question."

"Oh, sorry. Daydreaming. Do you mind repeating, Kate?"

"I just asked if your parents knew you were here. If I'd known, I would have invited them to accompany us."

Rose shrugged. "That's okay. I'll see them soon."

"Why are you here, Rose?" Robin spoke matter-of-factly, but his gaze held her captive.

She hesitated but couldn't answer with anything other than the truth. "I'm writing a story on Brand."

"One of your exposés?" Kate drew back, her eyes wide. "On Brand? Rose, how could you?"

"It's what I do." She placed her fork beside her plate, her appetite fleeing. "Brand is the next assignment."

"And you allow her access to you and your equipment?" Robin asked Brand.

Brand's hold tightened on his silverware. "We made a deal."

"A deal?" A muscle jumped in Robin's jaw. "I imagine you did," he said dryly.

Rose tensed, her heart dropping into her stomach. Robin's implication was obvious. He believed she was sleeping with Brand in order to obtain his secrets. Was that what everyone thought? Lifting her chin, she met Robin's gaze. "You know me better than that."

She pushed away from the table. "If you'll excuse me, I've lost my appetite."

Brand reached out to stop her, anger churning in his gut, but she eluded him. Before he could follow, she stepped outside the restaurant and vanished. Damn!

He whirled on his father. "You're wrong about her."

"I'm only concerned that—"

"I'm plenty old enough to handle my own life and protect my professional secrets. If I want to be with Rose or any other woman, that's my decision." Did his father want to ensure that Brand never knew any happiness?

"Rose isn't like other women." Robin sent a quick glance at Sequoia's parents, who didn't know about Rose being Fae.

"You're right. She's not." Brand stood, giving his mother a tight smile. "Tell them to put this on my bill."

"Brand—"

His mother called after him, but he ignored her. He was the one with the most to lose here. If he could trust Rose, why couldn't they? She would probably write her exposé. He didn't doubt that. He just had to make sure she never discovered the details to his moon illusion. That was one secret he intended to keep.

He found her room and rapped on the door. "Rose? Answer the door." She was there. He could feel her presence. But she didn't speak.

He knocked harder. "Dammit, Rose. Come on."

Only silence.

He sighed. "Please, Rose."

Still nothing.

"Come to me, Rose. I'll be waiting." He had to talk to her, hold her, kiss her. With a final pound on the door, he turned away and headed for his room. Now what?

Rose sat on the balcony railing, swinging her legs into the night, as she stared at the myriad lights dotting the landscape below. Some flashed, others remained constant. Across the street she could hear the screams from people riding the roller coaster on top of New York, New York. Las Vegas always blazed with life. In the past she'd found it an exciting place to visit.

But not tonight.

She shouldn't have taken this assignment. She'd initially refused when her editor had directed her to get the lowdown on Brand, until he'd dangled the carrot he knew she wanted—the promise that this would be the end of the exposés, that she could tackle more exciting stories, get a promotion that reflected her hard work.

But she should have known better. Brand had been an important part of her life for as long as she could remember. He never—okay, rarely—had annoyed her like her brothers had.

To be honest, she'd been half in love with him since she'd turned ten. And now she was totally, completely, foolishly in love with him.

Her parents had warned her. Even Robin had warned her against this. Though she resented Robin's insinuation, she understood why he'd said it. He wanted to protect his son from the folly of involvement with someone who wouldn't age, someone who would never be normal.

Too late for that.

The problem now was how to handle it. She should leave. Now. Before it became any more difficult to do so. Especially since her editor was nagging her almost daily to turn in her article.

She didn't have all the information she needed, but she had enough to write something. Maybe that would be good enough.

"Is it always like that?" Ewan appeared beside her, startling Rose enough that she almost lost her balance.

Grabbing the railing to right herself, she glared at him. "Is what like what?"

"Family gatherings. One moment everyone is happy and laughing. The next angry and accusing. I fail to see how this is a good thing."

He looked confused and Rose grimaced. "Family dynamics are difficult to explain. There's love involved. Sometimes possessive love, sometimes protective love, sometimes freeing love."

He sighed. "And yet you place such high value on this love."

"It's the best feeling a person can have." And the worst.

"I don't understand."

"From what Mom has told me, the Fae don't experience intense emotions. You've lived forever. To have those highs and lows would tear apart your world. But mortals don't live forever and those highs and lows are part of experiencing life to the fullest. It's what keeps life interesting for us."

"Us? You include yourself with the mortals?"

"I think like a mortal, but I'll never be one." Rose blinked back the sudden surge of tears. "I'm Fae and yet not Fae, human yet not human."

Ewan touched her arm in a gentle gesture. "Then come with me, Rose. You may discover a place where you can belong."

For a moment she was tempted. "No. Not now anyway. Check with me in a hundred years or so." Perhaps when everyone she loved was gone, she'd find no reason to stay here.

"Are you unhappy because of what was said to you?"

"Some. Robin only said what he did because he's trying to protect Brand, but it still hurts that he'd think so little of me." She had always valued Robin's opinion. Surely he knew her better than that.

"Did he not imply the truth? You are having sex with Brand."

Hard to hide that kind of thing from a faery. "Yes, but not so I can steal his secrets."

"Then why?"

She had to grin. "Because I enjoy it."

"Do you want to be with him now?"

More than anything. She ached for the feel of his hands upon her. "Yes."

"And he wants you with him?"

"Yes." She'd almost weakened and let him in when he'd pounded on her door hours earlier.

Ewan frowned. "So you are allowing his father's words to keep you from Brand?"

Put like that, she flinched. Was she running away to avoid Robin's censure? "I guess so."

"Is not the pleasure you share more important?"

She drew back, staring at him in surprise. "You're actually making sense, Ewan. This frightens me."

He produced a broad smile. "I have been learning about mortals, about love."

"From Sequoia." Her cousin was destined to end up as hurt as Brand.

"She is . . . special." Ewan gazed off into the distance. "I have learned far more from her than I thought I would."

"Don't hurt her." Easier said than done, as she well knew.

"I have no intentions of doing so. I will be with her tonight, as that is what we both want." A glimmer of a challenge appeared in his eyes. "Can you say the same?"

Before Rose could respond, he vanished, and she sighed. He had a point. She wanted to be with Brand, ached to touch him. Was that so wrong?

Not giving herself a chance to think about it, she transported herself into his room. Brand had his back to her, working over some papers spread on his table. Or attempting to work. From the way he propped his chin on his hand and tapped his pencil against the papers, his mind was elsewhere.

"Brand?"

He jumped up at once and whirled to face her. "You came."

"I tried to stay away, but I couldn't." He mattered too much.

"Good." He stepped toward her. "My father was wrong. I know that."

One tight band around her heart vanished. A small part of her had feared that he would believe Robin's hints. "I'm here because I want to be with you."

Brand stopped before her and ran his hands over her arms to rest on her shoulders. "And I want you. All I can think about is you."

Her throat tightened. "I guess that works both ways."

He cradled the back of her head. "Make love with me, Rose. I need you."

She was lost before he even kissed her. "Oh, yes."

Hours later he slept exhausted beside her, but the peace of slumber eluded Rose. She lay on her side, her heart full, studying his handsome face—now relaxed and boyish. How could she exist without him?

Yet how could they build a realistic future together?

The sex was awesome, but they needed more than that. One day—not today or tomorrow, but soon—his resentment of her magic would surface again, and she couldn't change what she was.

What then?

Restless, she slid from the bed, wrapped a blanket around herself, and padded to the windows. The city still lived, the lights blazing, people continuing to plug their dollars into machines. Life went on.

With a sigh, she roamed the room, the outside flashing signs providing enough illumination to see clearly. As she passed the table, her blanket caught the edge of one of the papers and sent it flying.

She retrieved the paper, glancing at it as she set it back on the table. Her heart skipped a beat. Was it? She hesitated for only a moment, curiosity driving her to examine the other sheets, absorbing the information. The final piece. Here it was—everything she needed to know about how Brand would make the moon disappear.

Everything she needed to complete her exposé.

Damn.

Now what was she going to do?

Eighteen

~

Sequoia straightened her shoulders, drawing in a deep breath as the charge nurse presented her to the gathered children. She wasn't nervous, just disappointed that Ewan had refused to accompany her to the hospital today.

Especially after the way he'd made her feel last night— not only sexy, but precious and special. She'd awakened in the circle of his arms, marveling at the depth of her feelings. She barely knew him, but she knew enough to love him, to want to be with him.

And she also knew he would leave her.

"And now, the Sensational Sequoia."

Sequoia burst into the room and launched into her act. Though she constantly experimented and added new twists, she could perform her few illusions effortlessly, which allowed her to concentrate on the children. She loved to see them laugh, to see their faces light up, to draw them into her routine, which was more fun than magic.

This group was particularly lively and their enthusiasm fed hers until she forgot about Ewan. This was as close as she could get to her initial ambition—the job goal that had horrified her parents.

What was so wrong with wanting to be a clown? With making people laugh? It was a time-honored profession that required training and aptitude. Why couldn't Mom and Dad understand that?

"I'm now going to pull a rabbit out of my sleeve." As Sequoia first pulled one wrong item after another out of her sleeve, the kids howled with laughter. Last time Ewan had worked with her and produced the rabbit from his sleeve, which helped since she didn't use live animals as a rule.

"Well, I know it's here somewhere." She did have a toy stuffed rabbit that she produced last, but before she could slip it out, a small white bunny hopped across the room.

Sequoia quickly worked the animal into her patter, then glanced over her shoulder with a smile, expecting to see Ewan. Her smile faded as her heart rose to her throat.

Ewan stood by the door as she'd thought, but her parents accompanied him, their expressions revealing nothing. What were they doing here?

She sucked in a deep breath, drawing on all her concentration to continue her performance to the end. The children helped, shouting out answers to her teasing questions, their eyes growing round as she made a piece of paper float between her hands.

When she finally finished, the kids swarmed around her, demanding more tricks, wanting answers to how she'd made the rabbit appear, and best of all, they offered hugs and smiles—the reward that made this all worthwhile.

Fifteen minutes later the charge nurse had managed to steer them away, and Sequoia swallowed as she turned to face her unexpected audience.

Her mother rushed forward to wrap her in a tight hug. "Honey, that was marvelous. Why didn't you tell us you did this kind of thing?"

Sequoia blinked. "Any time I mentioned wanting to be a clown, you refused to listen."

"But this wasn't being a clown."

"You brought these children some hope," her father added as he joined them.

"That's part of what a clown does." Sequoia studied their faces. For the first time they were actually listening. "It's more than putting on a silly costume and doing fake spills. It's making people happy. It's using skills to keep folks entertained."

"I'd never looked at it that way before," Mom said. "I thought being a clown was silly."

"What kind of future is there in this?" Dad asked.

Sequoia didn't mind the questions. At least they were talking about this instead of ignoring her input. "You'd be surprised, Dad. Clowns are in demand everywhere—hospitals, benefits, parties, circuses. There are even special schools that teach how to be a clown, which have classes on psychology and things like that."

"There are colleges for clowns?" Her father's voice rose in surprise.

"Good ones. I have literature on some of them if you'd like to see it." Sequoia held her breath, waiting for her parents' response.

Her mom and dad exchanged glances, then Dad nodded. "Yes, I'd like to see it."

Sequoia smiled. "It's at the hotel."

Her father wrapped his arm around her shoulder. "Then let's head back there. I'm buying lunch." He led her to the door, where Ewan waited. "You're coming, too, right, Ewan?"

He nodded once, his gaze holding Sequoia's. "I would like that."

Dad dropped his arm to hold open the door. "Your friend was the one who insisted we come watch you in action. I'll admit I was dubious, but now I'm glad I came."

"So am I." Sequoia waited for her parents to precede

her through the door, then paused to touch Ewan's arm. "Why did you do it?"

"You have said that love made your parents want you to be happy. I thought if they could see how happy your work made you, how happy you made others, they would understand."

"I think they might, or at least they're beginning to." Sequoia kissed him. He'd done this—made the impossible happen—without using magic. Instead, he'd used his heart. Did he even realize it? "Thank you. You're actually getting this emotion stuff down."

Ewan hesitated. "I still do not understand love."

She kissed him again, lingering until she felt his response, then drew back to smile slowly. "Oh, you understand much more than you think you do."

Confusion mingled with heat in his eyes, but he didn't answer. Instead he linked his fingers through hers and led her to join her parents.

Sequoia resisted the urge to dance through the hallway. Maybe life would turn out all right after all.

Brand frowned at the papers spread on his table. He'd forgotten what he'd been working on when Rose had appeared last night. All his attention had been focused on her.

Attention equally rewarded. He would never tire of making love to her.

But she had left with the dawn and his sanity had returned. What had he done? The plans for his moon illusion covered the tabletop. He'd been trying to review them when Rose appeared last night, and he had quickly dismissed them.

Had she seen them?

Of course. He bit back a groan as his gut twisted. She'd had complete freedom to explore his room. No wonder she fled so quickly this morning. He'd given her everything she needed for her exposé.

Dammit.

With a swipe of his hand, he tossed all the papers on the floor. She wouldn't have gone snooping in his room, but she hadn't had to. He'd stupidly left everything sitting out. How could he expect her to ignore it?

She was probably at this moment composing the article that would reveal all his hard earned secrets to the world. Who would come see him once they knew how he created fire? Made the moon disappear?

With a groan Brand fled his room and rushed to pound on her door. "Rose. I need to talk to you. Now."

No answer.

Only deafening silence.

Damn.

Spotting a maid approaching, he greeted her with a smile. "Hi. I'm Brand Goodfellow, the headliner for this weekend. I'm trying to get something from one of my crew's room, but the key she gave me doesn't work. Can you let me in for just a moment?"

The card swipe keys were notorious for failing, and this saved him flying to her balcony and breaking in.

The middle-aged woman eyed him with a slight squint. "Just for a moment. I'll be watching you."

"That's fine." Either Rose was there or she wasn't.

Opening the door, the maid stepped aside for him to enter. He knew right away Rose wasn't there, though her floral scent lingered, triggering memories he preferred not to recall at that moment.

Her desk was a mess. Her laptop computer was gone, but small sheets of paper littered the top. Lifting one and reading it, he smothered a groan. His secrets. All of them. Jotted on the torn pages of her notepad.

Even his moon illusion.

His gut cramped. She'd already done the story. He knew it.

He'd hoped for one ridiculous moment that she wouldn't do it, that what they'd shared would influence her. He should have known better.

"You done?" the maid asked.

"I'm done." He stepped into the hall and returned to his suite with slow steps. More than done. He was ruined.

Rose had never lied, never said she wouldn't do the exposé. In fact, she'd warned him of this problem, and he'd chosen to ignore it like all the other things that stood between them.

How could he have been so foolish?

Ha, he knew that answer.

Lust, pure and simple. He'd wanted Rose with a passion beyond control. So he'd had her.

And lost everything else.

Brand spent the day with his parents, forcing a smile for his mother's sake, ignoring his father for the most part. Rose remained absent. Though he asked everyone, no one had seen her. Not even Sequoia.

Had Rose written the story and run?

Why not? That had been their original deal. She could stay until she had the information she needed.

Now the hint of sadness in her last kiss made sense. She'd been planning to leave. Her story, her chance for a promotion, meant more than him. Why was he surprised?

His father had told him more than once about the world of the Fae, about their unfaithfulness, about their lack of responsibility. Yet Robin had fallen in love with Kate and married her. Rose's mother had done the same with Rand. There were exceptions.

And Brand had known Rose all her life. She was nothing like the Fae of Robin's stories. Maybe he was blowing this out of proportion. Maybe she hadn't written the exposé. Maybe even now she was telling her editor to take a flying leap.

Or not.

He begged off supper with his folks, claiming he needed to review his plans for his big illusion. But once he reached his room, he couldn't find the energy to do anything, his thoughts in turmoil.

Should he call Rose's magazine? Demand to talk to

her? As if that would do any good. Rose had always been
stubborn. He smiled briefly, recalling how she'd always
called it tenacity.

He sank into a chair with a groan, burying his face in
his hands. What now?

A quiet knock on his door caught his attention and he
lifted his head. His mother?

Opening the door, he froze. Rose stood outside, her
face pale. "Can I come in?"

"I'm surprised you didn't let yourself in," Brand
snapped, unable to control his initial surge of anger.

She didn't respond, but met his gaze without flinching.
Damn. What was he doing? He wanted to talk to her,
didn't he? Brand stepped back and allowed her inside,
then pushed the door closed with more force than he'd
intended so that the slam echoed in the room.

To her credit, Rose didn't jump, but turned to face him.
"You were in my room."

"You stole my secrets."

"You left them lying out."

"Which you assumed meant you were welcome to
them." Brand clenched his fists and stormed across the
room, needing to put distance between them. Part of him
still wanted to hold her, kiss her.

The stupid part.

"Was I supposed to ignore them?" Sparks flashed in
her eyes.

"Yeah, you were."

"So sorry. I didn't get that message." Rose closed her
eyes for a moment and drew in a deep breath. "Look,
Brand, I didn't come here to argue."

"Then why are you here? More secrets? Or just hot
sex?"

She pressed her lips together and shook her head. "Neither." She held out several typed pages. "I wanted to give
you a copy of the exposé."

She'd actually written it. Was she asking his approval

before she turned it in? Brand took the papers. "Have you submitted it already?"

"Yes."

He stared at her. So, this wasn't a copy for approval, it was merely a chance for him to see his career die before the rest of the world. Bands tightened around his chest. "Then it doesn't matter if I read it." He tore the pages into small pieces and let them drift to the floor. "I'd prefer not knowing how you destroyed me."

Her gaze narrowed. "Why not? I was particularly eloquent."

"I'm sure you were." A knife through the heart wouldn't hurt as much as this betrayal. "Was my father right all along? Were you sleeping with me to uncover my secrets?" Even as he said the words, he knew they were untrue, but he meant to hurt her.

From her flinch, he'd succeeded.

Rose lifted her chin. "I guess that's for you to decide."

Brand opened and closed his fists, struggling to keep them by his side. He wanted to shake her. He wanted to kiss her.

"Dammit all," he growled. "I should have known never to trust a faery."

Her cheeks flooded with color, then paled. Angry flames illuminated her eyes. For a moment he wouldn't have been surprised if she'd fried him on the spot.

Instead, she disappeared.

Taking all his dreams for the future with her.

Nineteen

~

Seeing Ewan sitting close to Sequoia in the hotel restaurant didn't improve Brand's spirits the next morning. Though he'd tried to maintain his anger from the night before, he'd failed. Now resignation took its place, along with the inescapable thought that he'd lost something important—even more important than his illusions.

"You look terrible," Sequoia said as he joined them at the table. "Busy night?" Mischief danced in her eyes.

"Didn't sleep much," he muttered, flipping up the menu in front of him to block her view.

"Where's Rose?"

Brand continued to focus on the menu, although the words were incomprehensible. "Don't know. Don't care." Or at least that was what he wanted to believe.

Sequoia slapped the menu onto the table, forcing him to look at her. "What happened? You two have a fight?"

"Worse." He had no trouble working up righteous indignation. "She did the exposé."

His assistant frowned. "Did she ever say she wouldn't?"

"Well, no, but—" He'd assumed . . .

"Wasn't she honest with you? Didn't she come to you from the beginning and tell you what she was doing?"

"Yes, but—"

"But what?"

He grimaced. "She betrayed me. She has the moon illusion."

"How did she get that? I thought you were careful about protecting that."

"She came to my room while I was working on it," he muttered, glancing down at the menu. Sequoia didn't need to know the details.

"Didn't you take the time to put it away?"

He lifted one shoulder. "I was distracted."

"I'll bet." Sequoia shook her head. "How about this? Rose appeared, you went hot and horny and forgot all about your illusion. Close?"

Too close. Damn. "Something like that."

"So you expected her to ignore those papers even though you just left them out there for her?"

"It wasn't like that." Okay, so he'd forgotten they were even there. Making love to Rose tended to do that to him.

"Come on, Brand, get real. That's like asking someone to ignore a hundred-dollar bill lying on the sidewalk."

She had a point, but that didn't make what Rose had done right. Why hadn't she discussed it with him first? Before she'd turned in the story?

When he didn't respond, Sequoia sighed. "What are you going to do now?"

"What I've said I will—give the performances I'm contracted for." He had no other option. The show must go on. "At least the article won't come out until after I perform the moon illusion."

"Not that. What about Rose?"

His gut clenched. "What about her?"

"She'd come back if you asked her to."

"And why would I do that?" Hadn't he wanted to get rid of her from the beginning? She'd been nothing but a distraction from the first day she'd invaded his life again.

Sequoia sent him a dry look, her head tilted, her lips pressed together. "I wonder."

He tried to ignore the sudden tightening around his chest. "We had some fun together and now it's over. We never had a future anyway." Something Rose had constantly told him.

Yet he'd refused to believe it.

Then.

"And whose fault is that?" Sequoia asked.

What fault? He couldn't change what Rose was. "What does that mean?"

"You're a smart man. Figure it out."

Spotting the approaching waitress, Brand pushed back his chair. "I'm not hungry. Excuse me."

He fled the restaurant, avoiding Sequoia's penetrating stare. Figure it out? What if he didn't want to?

He needed to walk off his frustration, and the vast hotel gave him room to roam. He should have known Sequoia would defend Rose. They were best friends as well as cousins. Yet he couldn't deny the truth of her words.

Rose had been honest with him from the start. She'd never hinted that she wouldn't write her exposé. And it wasn't as if he couldn't create new illusions. He had some he'd been working on for years that no one knew about. Any good magician constantly worked on new illusions.

Like levitation. With an exaggerated swish, he motioned for a nearby planter to rise, then gaped when it lifted several inches off the floor.

Glancing around to make sure no one had noticed, he lowered it again, his heart thudding, a warm buzz in his veins. How had that happened? Magic, of course. It had to be a residual effect from his ability to fly. Fantastic. His career was far from over after all.

Yet Rose couldn't know that. She'd still written her article, revealing his secrets. Why should he have expected different? Because they were having great sex?

Hell, awesome sex. Sex that left him tingling for several minutes afterward.

Or because he cared about her and had assumed that maybe she cared about him?

He grimaced. No assuming about it. She cared about him. Her lips, her eyes, her body had told him that in so many ways.

Was that why the betrayal hurt so much? She cared more for her work than for him?

A job that proved to her she was more than her magic. How could she not know that she was so much more than that? She was intelligent, good-natured, lighthearted, fun to be with, sexy, caring. She was Rose and her magic was a part of that, an integral part of who she was, yet it wasn't *all* she was.

Brand froze in midstep and slapped his hand against his forehead. "I have been a total idiot."

"I would agree with that."

He spun around to see Ewan standing behind him. "Will you stop that? I hate when you Fae just appear."

"I didn't. I followed you."

"Oh." He'd been so engrossed in his thoughts, he hadn't noticed. "What do you want?"

"I need to talk to someone. Without Rose here, you are the next best choice."

What an honor. Brand's first reaction called for him to ignore the faery, but a glance at Ewan's serious expression stayed him. "What?"

"Since I have met Sequoia, I am experiencing unusual feelings, things I do not understand."

Welcome to the club. Brand had yet to understand any woman. "Like what?"

"I have lost my desire to return to the magical realm. I find I want to be with Sequoia, to hear her laugh, to share my thoughts with her, to have sex with her."

Brand scowled. The thought of Ewan boinking his assistant made him shiver. "So?"

"I feel . . . confused." Ewan spread his hands. "Uncertain. I am never uncertain. I have never been influenced by any female like this before. What does it mean?"

Brand had to laugh, though he noticed it contained more than a touch of bitterness. "Welcome to the mortal world, Ewan. You're in love."

"Love?" Ewan's face reflected horror. "This is human love?"

" 'Fraid so." Brand narrowed his eyes. "And if I know Sequoia at all, which I do, she's crazy about you." Not a pleasant thought. Was he about to lose his assistant as well as his career?

A thoughtful gleam entered Ewan's eyes. "This is love," he repeated, his tone more reverent now.

The damned faery didn't deserve Sequoia. And he would leave her. Brand knew it. "And if you hurt Sequoia, I will find a way to destroy you," he said, enunciating each word.

Ewan lifted a corner of his lips, as if amused at Brand's threat. "I have no intention of hurting her. She is very special to me."

"Me, too." Sequoia had been a part of his life since childhood.

"Why is that?" Ewan appeared actually curious.

"She's my friend. I've known her forever." Brand glared at him. "I've seen her cry over guys who weren't worthy of her, and you aren't, either."

"She seems to feel I am." The faery sounded smug now.

"Sequoia doesn't always have the best judgment when it comes to men." Brand had tried to shield her in the past and often failed. Just as he had failed now.

"I am not a man."

Brand grimaced. A perfectly good reason why Ewan and Sequoia didn't belong together. "You're telling me?"

Ewan cocked his head, studying Brand. "Do you love her?"

"Of course." She meant as much as his younger sister.

"Is this love confusing? Does it make you feel a burning within?"

"No, it's different from that. It's a family type of love." Brand had never lusted for Sequoia, but he had shared her pain and her joy throughout her life.

"Then how would you describe the love you feel for Rose?"

"Consuming, frustrating, agonizing, and wonderful." Brand answered at once, listing the twisting emotions within him.

"Yes." Ewan nodded. "Just what I experience with Sequoia. She is everything that makes life important to me."

Brand stared at the faery. Ewan really did love Sequoia. Lord help them both.

Worse, he'd forced Brand to be honest with himself. He loved Rose. Loved her beyond reason, beyond desire. "I am so screwed," he muttered. "I love Rose."

"Of course you do." A twinkle appeared in Ewan's eyes as he grinned and vanished.

Brand shoved his fingers through his hair. He really was an idiot. Somehow, somewhere, he'd accepted Rose, accepted her power, and fallen in love with her.

He had to find her, had to tell her.

Grimacing, he turned toward the elevators. After the stupid things he'd said, he really was going to need some magic now.

Sequoia jumped when Ewan appeared beside her in the elevator. Thank goodness she was alone. The way he constantly ignored the people around them was going to get him into trouble.

Not that he cared.

She smiled. He'd tell anyone exactly what he was, and none of them would believe him.

"Did you find Brand?" she asked. Ewan had taken off after her friend with no explanation except that he needed to talk to him.

"I did."

"Did you talk?" She studied him. "About Rose?"

"This was not about Rose." Ewan paused, as if searching for words.

Sequoia frowned. Ewan was never at a loss for words. "What, then?"

He hesitated, then spoke quickly. "I am returning to the magical realm."

Her heart froze, then sank to her stomach. "What?"

The elevator doors opened at her floor, but she didn't move, couldn't move. She could only stare at him, her world shattering around her.

Now? He was leaving *now*? She'd hoped for more time, for a chance to convince him they had something special together.

When the doors closed again, Ewan took her hand in his and transported them into her room.

His touch jarred her from her stupor. "Why?"

"Rose will not come to my world. I am obliged to inform Titania."

"But she'll destroy you." Sequoia had heard enough horror stories about the Queen of the Fae to know her temper ran hot. And mean.

"She won't do that." Ewan spoke with assurance, but Sequoia wasn't sure if it was for her benefit or his.

"Let me come with you." Her words escaped ahead of her brain, but she meant them. Going for broke, she met his gaze. "I love you, Ewan."

"I know." He drew her close, wrapping her in his embrace. "But I cannot take you with me. Titania hates mortals. You, she would destroy."

Sequoia blinked away the threatening tears. She'd failed to teach him about love. Otherwise he'd know how much he meant to her, how much his leaving would hurt. "I don't want you to go."

He drew one finger along her cheek in a tender caress. "I do not want to go, but I must. I must fulfill my obligation to my queen."

"Can't you wait a little longer?" Even another day would be a precious gift.

"The longer I wait, the more difficult it will be." He held her chin in his palm. "You are a special woman, Sequoia."

"Please—"

His kiss cut her off—a soul-searing kiss that flooded her senses and wove her heart with his. She loved him. Would always love him.

And would never see him again.

He pressed his lips against the tears streaming down her cheek. "I will be back."

"Will you?" As much as she wanted to believe him, she knew how fickle the Fae were. She'd been an amusement, nothing more. Once back in the magical realm, he'd find many sensual faeries eager to share their bodies with him.

"I swear it." He drew her away from him, his eyes gleaming. "You have taught me much about mortals and emotions, more than I wanted to know."

She forced a watery smile. "Guess you're a good learner."

His fingers clung to hers, his smile sad. "I will be back," he repeated with a firmness that gave her hope. Maybe he meant it.

"You'd better."

Sliding his hands out from under hers, he met her gaze. "I love you, Sequoia."

Her jaw dropped. "What?"

But she spoke to empty air.

He was gone.

And had taken her heart with him.

Yet he'd left her with the fragile hope that he'd meant his last words. That he would be back. That he loved her.

So, she would wait.

Brand waited until the end of dinner with his parents to invite his father to join him on a walk. He needed to review the outdoor stage setup for his moon illusion the next night and wanted to speak to his father. Though

Robin blinked with surprise, he quickly agreed.

Now walking beside his father, Brand couldn't find the words to begin. What could he say?

"You were quiet at dinner," Robin said. "Bad day?"

"The worst." Brand had been unable to find Rose anywhere. Her magazine said she wasn't there. If she'd returned to her apartment, she'd refused to answer her phone. Her parents, surprised by his phone call, told him she planned to visit soon, but wasn't there yet. Calling out for her in the privacy of his room had brought nothing but a feeling of foolishness.

It was as if she'd disappeared off the face of the Earth.

Had she gone to the magical realm? Had he driven her away forever?

He walked in silence with Robin until they emerged outside. The approaching thunderstorm and its brilliant streaks of lightning illuminating the sky competed with the flashing neon of Vegas. Brand paused and sucked in a fortifying breath. "I'm sorry," he blurted.

Robin shot him a quizzical glance.

"I thought you were stupid. I didn't understand why you'd give up everything for Mom. Magic always seemed far more important to me."

"And now you understand?" Robin asked, his voice quiet.

"Yeah, I do." Brand was willing to do anything to win Rose back, but he had nothing to offer, no magic to sacrifice. All he had was the knowledge that he'd been so damned stubborn and stupid he might have lost the best thing in his life.

Robin rested his hand on Brand's shoulder. "You must love her very much."

Brand grimaced. "You could say that."

"Is Rose willing to give up her magic to be with you?"

Startled, Brand drew back. "I don't want her to do that. Her magic is part of who she is. I love Rose—with her magic." He'd taken long enough to realize that and wasn't about to change his mind now.

"What kind of future can you have together?" The obvious concern in his father's voice kept Brand from bristling.

"Whatever future she'll give me." He stared out toward the darkened stage, briefly revealed by a nearby flash of lightning.

"It'll be a difficult life for both of you. I know." Robin turned to stand beside Brand. "You'll age, she won't. You'll die and she'll be left to go on without you."

"But if we're lucky, we'll share many good years before that." He wanted every moment he could have with Rose.

Of course, he was assuming she'd agree. *If* he could find her. *If* she would ever talk to him again.

Robin wrapped his arm around Brand's shoulders in a fatherly hug. Brand enjoyed the surge of warmth that support gave him. He'd missed this. Years ago they'd been close. Maybe they could find that again.

"Go for it, son. Love is worth it."

"Thanks. I intend to." All he had to do was locate Rose. Somehow.

After several moments of companionable silence, Robin finally spoke. "Still want company?"

"Actually, no. I have some thinking to do." His life had changed. For better or worse, he'd never be the same again.

Once his father returned inside, no doubt eager to talk to his mother, Brand continued to the set and went through the routine of examining every facet necessary for his illusion. He'd make the moon disappear, all right. He would show the world that Brandon Goodfellow was still a great illusionist.

Who cared if Rose revealed his secrets afterward? Once this tour was over, he'd create an entire new repertoire of illusions. Bigger. Better. More impressive.

And he'd find Rose.

He knew her too well. She couldn't avoid him forever. He made his way to the stage and glanced up at the churning clouds. If the storm didn't clear by tomorrow, he'd be in trouble.

But that wasn't important. Not now.

Damn, he missed her.

"Brand."

Whirling around, he found Rose standing behind him, her hands on her hips. Before he could speak, she advanced on him, her eyes sparking.

"You're going to listen to me, Brandon Goodfellow, or I swear I'm going to turn you into a rat."

He smothered his smile. "I guess I'd better listen then."

He'd listen, all right.

And then she was going to listen to him.

Twenty

Rose noticed the mischievous light in Brand's eye and the hint of a smile around his lips. What the hell was going on? This wasn't the reception she'd expected, especially after the way they'd parted.

But no matter what, he was going to hear about her exposé.

"You're going to stay right there and read this article," she ordered.

His expression tightened for a moment, then cleared. To her surprise, he nodded. "Do I have a choice?" A strange note sounded in his voice—not anger, but not acceptance, either.

"No." She jammed her typewritten sheets into his hand. "And don't you dare tear it up again."

He didn't respond, but glanced at the papers. "Before I do I need to tell you something."

"What?" She had to force the single word from her tight throat.

"I'm not giving up—no matter what you've written here. I'll create new illusions. Better ones. I will survive."

"I know." She'd never doubted that, but his certainty gave her hope. Other talented magicians had survived her exposés—they'd grown, become even more spectacular. And Brand was the best of them all.

While he read, the line of his lips grew hard, the muscle in his jaw twitched, and Rose's stomach twisted into an unending knot. Would he understand? Would he forgive her?

She'd done what she'd had to do after wrestling with the most difficult decision of her life. Her job meant a lot to her, but she loved Brand. How could she possibly keep both?

Her exposé revealed exactly how several of his illusions were accomplished—his ability to create fire on his palms, his clothing swap, his mind reading. But these were illusions that had become standard for him. He'd outgrown them.

She knew when he reached the end of her article, for he paused and glanced up at her. "This is what you turned in?" he asked, his voice quiet.

"It'll come out in next month's issue." Her mouth felt as if she'd swallowed an entire sand dune. His expression revealed nothing.

" 'But the illusions revealed above have been in Brandon Goodfellow's repertoire for the past several years and are more easily explained,' " Brand read. " 'However, his newer illusions, especially those of flying and making the moon disappear, defy explanation. Even after several weeks of observation, I was unable to discover the secrets to these incredible feats, giving validation to the claim that he is the world's greatest illusionist. Or else we have to accept that perhaps magic truly does exist.' "

Brand raised his gaze to hers. "You didn't give it all away."

"I couldn't." Though she'd been tempted for a moment, her sense of justice had prevailed. "Just because I found the papers on your moon illusion didn't mean I could use that information. I didn't solve the mystery. You gave it to me. That doesn't count."

"What about your editor, your promotion?"

Brand's tone remained even, his expression shuttered. What was going on behind that expressionless facade?

Rose shrugged. "Larry wasn't happy that I didn't get everything, but he accepted it."

"And the promotion?"

"I didn't get it." She'd expected as much when she didn't reveal all Brand's secrets, but that hadn't hurt as much as she'd expected. Brand's loss of trust had hurt far more. "But I don't have to write any more exposés, so I'm still ahead."

Folding the papers into a precise square, then making it vanish, Brand approached her, his gaze never leaving hers. Rose's heart filled her throat. "But you lied in this article," he said. "I thought you couldn't do that."

A common mistake her parents had made, too. Rose smiled. "I can't tell a lie, but I *can* write one. That's known as fiction."

His lips twitched. "You are most definitely one of a kind, Rose Thayer."

She could barely breathe. "Is that good or bad?"

He rested his hands on her shoulders. "Good," he murmured. "I wouldn't want you any other way."

"I doubt that." He'd made it clear that her magic would always stand between them.

"I mean it, Rose." He tightened his hold. "I've finally grown up."

Her pulse quickened. "What does that mean?"

"It means I've realized that the only reason I was jealous of your magic was because I was insecure in my own talent. Knowing you'd written this exposé opened my eyes to many things. I may never be able to do all that you can, but I am a damned good magician. If you give away one of my illusions, I'll create another."

Her jaw dropped. What could she say to that? She'd known all along he was an incredible magician.

He grinned and tucked her hair behind her ear. "I also realized that I had probably thrown away the best thing to ever happen to me, and that was far worse than revealing all my secrets."

Her eyes widened. Did he mean . . . ?

Sliding his hand behind her head, he drew her closer to him until his lips brushed hers as he spoke. "I love you, Rose."

Not giving her a chance to answer, he kissed her, echoing his words with a passion that soared to every corner of her soul. He loved her.

Rose wrapped her arms around his neck, responding with an equal fervor.

He loved her!

Thunder rumbled overhead, but she wasn't sure if it came from her thudding heart or the threatening storm. Tears stung her eyes. She'd only hoped to gain his forgiveness. This . . . this was beyond comprehension, beyond imagination.

This was magic.

Drawing away, he caught the tear that slid down her cheek on his fingertip and watched it change into a gleaming opal. He placed the gem in the palm of her hand and closed her fingers over it before lifting his gaze to hers. "I'm probably a poor comparison to the Fae, but none of them will ever love you the way I do. You've been a part of me since we were kids, even when I was too stupid to realize it."

"You're all I've ever wanted," she whispered. "Always."

An emotion she recognized lit his eyes—hope . . . and love. With a groan, he pulled her into another kiss, sharing all he was through the mastery of his mouth. Her heart raced, her soul sang. If she'd leaked magic before, she felt certain it exploded from her at this moment.

The wind buffeted them, wild and strong, matching the surge of desire within her. "Are you sure?" she murmured. "About the magic?" Could he really accept that?

He placed a gentle kiss on her forehead. "I'm far from perfect, Rose, but I know this. Your magic is a part of you. If I love you, then I love all of you. The magic, the bad jokes, and the sexy dresses."

"And I—"

An explosion of thunder above interrupted her. They whirled around in time to see a spear of lightning stab the stage's backdrop. The force of it threw her and Brand to the ground as the wiring burst into flame.

By the time she could climb to her feet, the entire stage was engulfed with hungry flames. "Oh, my God."

Brand rushed for a fire extinguisher fastened to the burning wall. "I'll get it," he called to her.

Rose surveyed the fire, already whipped into a frenzy by the spiraling winds. More equipment exploded and she ducked, covering her head as a shower of spark and ash rained over her. This was going to take more than a single fire extinguisher.

She had to do something.

Jumping onto the stage, she faced the blaze and extended her hands, summoning every ounce of magic within her. Fighting nature always took more energy. Unless she acted quickly, this could reach a point where even she couldn't stop it.

Murmuring a spell, she focused on smothering the fire, forcing it to give up its hold on destruction. She felt the power leave her as the flames abated somewhat.

At a sudden loud noise she turned to see Brand dive to the ground as a tank of air exploded. Was he all right?

She stepped toward him, momentarily forgetting to keep her magic focused. "Brand?"

The stage cracked below her, hungry flames shooting up from below. She jumped back, only to have a side wall tumble toward her. She tried to toss up a shield around herself and failed. Too much energy had gone into fighting the power of nature.

Something smashed against the side of her head. Pain.

Dizziness. She staggered to her knees, tried to rise. Fell. And succumbed to the blackness.

As he stood, Brand saw the board hit Rose and his heart filled his chest. She fell to the stage and remained still, a wall of flame only a short distance away. "Rose!"

He reached her in a few long steps and knelt beside her. "Rose?" Her pulse throbbed in her neck, but she remained unconscious, oblivious to the danger. The heat pulsated around him as he gathered her in his arms.

Rising, he felt the first stirrings of fear. In that short amount of time, the fire had surrounded them, devouring the stage and everything in its path. They were trapped.

A single thread of flame licked out, searing his hand, so that he almost dropped Rose. What now? What could he do?

He could see safety only a short distance away, yet the actuality of reaching it made it appear miles off. He tried to picture them standing there.

Shifting as the heat grew oppressive, he hugged Rose closer. Did she still leak magic? He'd never wanted it more in his life. "I wish we were safe," he muttered.

To his surprise, he found himself at the far end of the outdoor theater, chest aching, pulse racing, and a hot tingling prickling through his veins. Rose's magic must have worked.

He lowered her to the ground and concentrated on reviving her. Did she have a concussion? Feeling gently, he located a bump on the side of her head. A bump was a good thing, right?

Did she have any magic left? "I wish you well."

The bump shrank beneath his fingers to disappear entirely, and he jerked back. Now, *that* was spooky.

Her eyes fluttered open, then focused. "Brand?" She blinked several times, then tried to sit up.

He eased her into position, his arm around her shoulders. "You okay?"

"I . . . I think so." She wrinkled her nose as a drop of rain plopped upon it. "What happened?"

"You were knocked unconscious. When I went to get you, the fire surrounded us." Brand kissed her forehead. "Good thing your magic is still leaking."

She frowned. "It's not leaking."

"Of course it is. There's no other way we could have gotten out of there." No illusion could have saved them.

"Trust me, Brand. I have no magic left to leak. All I have at the moment went into trying to stop the fire."

"But . . ." He glanced toward the stage. The rain fell harder now, drowning the fire, clouds of gray smoke drifting skyward, but the damage had been done. His set was destroyed. He wouldn't be doing his illusion tomorrow night. "How else could we have gotten here from there? I didn't do it."

Rose studied him for several long heartbeats. "Are you sure?"

She'd given him the ability to fly, not the total package. "What you're suggesting is impossible."

"I tend to believe in the impossible." Rose pushed to her feet and he followed. They watched the burning stage turn into a sodden mess of charred board and wire as the sound of too late sirens screamed in the distance. "Fix it, Brand."

"Fix it?" He stared at her. "Me?"

She touched his cheek, a gentle pressure of her fingers. "Try."

He couldn't do it, but he'd humor her. He faced the stage. "I wish—"

"No. No wishes. Picture what you want. Reach deep inside yourself and draw on the power. You can feel it. It's like a tingling through your entire body."

A tingling? Like what he'd felt only minutes ago? Brand's gut twisted as he focused on the ruined set. Could she be right? He pictured the restored stage as he mentally reached out for . . . what? . . . magic?

He gasped at the sudden rush of heat and sizzle through his veins, staggering backward a step as it shot out of

him. For a moment he imagined he could see it—a sparkling shimmer in the air.

And the stage changed in an instant.

All trace of the fire disappeared. The stage, the walls,
the curtains all appeared untouched, as pristine as when
he'd first strolled through it. This couldn't be happening.

He blinked, rubbed his eyes, and looked again.

Everything had been restored.

"Dear Lord." His voice came out in a rasp. He couldn't
stop staring until Rose wrapped her arms around his waist.

"You have magic, Brand," she whispered. "The real
thing."

"How?" He'd been happy enough to have Rose by his
side. This . . . this was beyond comprehension.

"I don't know. Have you felt the tingling before?"

"Yes." He hugged her close to him. "A few times. Always when we made love. I thought it was you."

Her smile held more than a trace of sensual appeal.
"Me. And you, I think. Us together."

"You think your magic did this?"

"I think that you have your father's Fae blood, as
you've always said. He gave up his magic, but it was still
there, dormant somehow." Rose's voice held unconfined
excitement. "What if making love triggered it somehow?
What if my magic awakened your magic?"

Her explanation sounded almost plausible. "Can that
happen?"

"I don't know. You and I are odd ones, Brand. We both
had Fae parents outside the magical realm. Why wouldn't
it be possible?"

He examined his palm, searching for some outward
sign that he was different. Aside from the tingling that
even now waned within him, he felt the same. "Am I Fae
now? Am I immortal?"

"Why not?" Rose smiled and pulled his lips to hers.
"Anything is possible where magic is concerned."

Her lips met his with a fierceness that replaced his tingling with an inward passion. He couldn't imagine a life without her, without needing her.

The blare of sirens jerked him back to awareness. "Take us to your room," Rose whispered.

He hesitated. Could he do it? Holding her close, he imagined them in his suite, imagined peeling her clothing off her as he explored her curves.

The heat and tingle tore through him again, stealing his breath. He closed his eyes as he struggled for air. Was it supposed to be like this or was it his lack of experience?

Opening his eyes he discovered they stood in his suite, Rose still within his embrace. Even better, their clothing had vanished en route. Not altogether a bad thing.

Rose produced an impish smile. "I can see where you're going to be very dangerous now."

He bent to nibble on her earlobe. "You have no idea." Her breasts swelled against his chest, triggering an equal swelling in his lower extremities. "You have to marry me, you know."

He wasn't sure what kind of future they had—perhaps forever—but they would be together.

"Oh, I have to, do I?" Rose drew away, but he found her breast, thumbing her peak until she moaned.

Drawing on his new power, he imagined an engagement ring on her finger. It appeared, a gold band containing a brilliant blue topaz that matched her eyes. "You do. I love you, Rose. I'm not letting you get away."

"Good." She smiled at the ring, then slid her arms around his neck. "I love you, too."

"Magic and all?" Would this change in him affect her feelings?

Rose laughed. "Magic and all."

He kissed her, long and slow until the need to bury himself in her had him pressing her down against the bed. How could he be so lucky?

He had true magic. He had established peace with his

father. Most important, he had the woman he loved, who loved him.

For the first time in his life, he no longer needed illusions. He had the real thing.

Dear Reader,

I hope you enjoyed Brand and Rose's story. I had such fun with it. I knew once Rose was born in *Buttercup Baby* that she needed her own story, but I couldn't decide who was the man for her. After discarding several ideas, Robin and Kate's (*Prince of Charming*) son, Brandon, who also made his appearance in *Buttercup Baby*, insisted he was the one. How right he was.

I learned a lot about illusionists while researching this book and even had the opportunity to see David Copperfield in action, which gave me a whole new respect for these talented individuals. For that reason I deliberately didn't reveal any secrets in this book. Let's believe it's magic.

I hope to continue writing stories about the Fae if you're willing to keep reading them. After all, I really want to know if Ewan is going to come back for Sequoia, don't you?

I love to hear from my readers. You can e-mail me at karen@karenafox.com or write me at P.O. Box 31541, Colorado Springs, CO 80931-1541.

Karen Fox